DARK SKY'S ASHES

CASEY GRIMES #3.5

AJ VANDERHORST

Published by Lion & Co. Press

www.ajvanderhorst.com

Dark Sky's Ashes (Casey Grimes #3.5)/AJ Vanderhorst. - 1st ed.

PRAISE FOR CASEY GRIMES

★ **2020 Wishing Shelf Book Awards Silver**
★ **2020 Readers' Favorite International Awards Contest Bronze**

"A steppingstone path of small mysteries and action scenes. Sylvan Woods is a splendid conception...fast moving and exuberant, packed with imagination." – *Kirkus Reviews*

"The Mostly Invisible Boy excels, venturing into unpredictable territory, combining the feel of a fantasy with a treasure hunt." – *Midwest Book Review*

"A true adventure, where the stakes are high, the danger real, and the goal is almost impossible to reach." – **Bookworm for Kids**

"The Mostly Invisible Boy is a gripping book from start to finish...riveting." – **LitPick**

"Brimming with intrigue, danger and humor." – **Book Craic**

"Original and inventive, full of courage and heart." – **Amy Wilson**, author of *A Far Away Magic, Shadows of Winterspell,* and *The Wild Way Home*

"Fun, funny and imaginative, The Mostly Invisible Boy is a rollicking good adventure." – **Andrew Chilton**, author of *The Goblin's Puzzle*

"Perfect for middle grade—not too scary but enough to keep you flipping the pages. Surprises at every turn keep the plot moving at a quick pace." – **Always in the Middle**

"Vanderhorst has created a character in Casey Grimes who is so relatable, and so tangible...a must-read fantasy novel for middle grade readers." – **Frank Morelli**, author of *No Sad Songs* and the *Please Return To* series

"A gripping fantasy adventure." – **Wishing Shelf Book Award**

"Incredibly imaginative and fun."– **Book Pipeline**

"Likable characters, clever plot, and unexpected twists and turns." – **Indie Reader**

"Vanderhorst connects to the deep feelings many middle school children deal with day in and day out." – **Reader's Favorite five-star review**

"Enchanting and unusual...the story entertains from the first page to the last." – **Story Sanctuary**

"A once-in-a-lifetime adventure. The characters are all so witty and eloquent, and yet the dialogue feels so natural and flowing. The story itself is fast-paced and fun, it doesn't ever get stuck on anything or leave you bored." – **The Artsy Reader**

"AJ Vanderhorst has the most beautiful imagination. The way he puts this world in your mind is nothing short of brilliant. The journey to Sylvan Woods had me on the edge of my seat, and I wouldn't have it any other way." – **Bookish Bliss**

"If you love unique and fun middle-grade fantasy stories with great and interesting characters, a cute little sister you can't help but love, a forest setting with a school and 'magical' community, lots of secrets and things just waiting to be revealed, monsters, missions and bravery... this is the book for you." – **Read to Ramble**

"Kind of gives off treetop Percy Jackson vibes, and I am totally here for it. I would love to get lost in the magical treetop world of Sylvan Woods, but I don't think I'd like to face all of those awful creatures! There's a lot of excitement and edge of the seat moments throughout the story, and the ending was no different." – **For Books' Sake**

"This is such a refreshing and delightful depiction of sibling relationships. In a world with magical trees, dangerous beasts, a far-off war and tree-top school for warriors there is such a rich font for the imagination. The over-arching idea of finding where you belong and fighting so that you can stay there is a great one." – **Broken Geek**

"This book had me on the edge of my seat." – **Reading Through the Looking Glass**

"An engaging and charming Middle Grade Fantasy story...and there's danger, too." – **I'm a Voracious Reader**

"The world with magic trees, vicious monsters, a far-off war that needs preparing for and a tree-top school for future warriors just speaks to my imagination and let it run wild." – **Tirilu**

"A bit Harry Potteresque...and what I hope will be a long series of adventures with Casey and his friends. But this is very much an original tale." – **The Strawberry Post**

"You aren't always sure if we are in a world of imagination or magic. The characters are Alice in Wonderlandesque...this would make an amazing cartoon film." – **Books, Occupation...Magic!**

"A new, heightened reality, a world of magic, monsters, honor, adventure, and danger...dynamite worldbuilding and it should be a great world to explore in the volumes to come." – **Irresponsible Reader**

"Fun, bold and whimsical...a compelling, entertaining read packed full of magic, escapades and bravery." – **Amy's Bookish Life**

"The adventure these characters go on is incredible and I wish I was right alongside them, battling the creepy monsters, exploring the new world and getting to know all the secrets of Sylvan forest." – **Ellie Mai Blogs**

"I loved the hints of magic, the terrifying creatures, and I want to learn everything I can about Sylvan Woods." – **Books Are 42**

"Gritty for a children's novel but made in a way that's child-friendly and something that the kids would love!" – **Gazer of Books**

"A fun and imaginative Middle Grade fantasy which has at its heart the need to belong." – **Good Night to Read**

Dedicated to the original Brick House crew and to people who don't flame out and disappear when things get dark.

THE BOOKS...A QUICK INTRO

The Mostly Invisible Boy (Casey Grimes 1)

Need friends? Try fighting monsters. Casey Grimes thinks his invisibility is permanent until he finds a secret forest society in charge of monster control.

Trickery School (Casey Grimes 2)

Classes have begun. Please don't die. Monster-control academy starts for Casey and Gloria, but there's one little problem: A secret enemy who's playing for keeps.

Crooked Castle (Casey Grimes 2.5)

Don't mind the dragon. When Brook is dumped on a deadly island by a beast that shouldn't exist, she's haunted by a past that stays just out of reach.

Twisting Trails (Casey Grimes 3)

Something's moving in the woods. Casey and Gloria finally have a chance to carve out a home in Sylvan Woods. But something is terribly wrong with the forest itself.

The Ghost of CreepCat (A Sylvan Woods Novella)

Track the ghost-cat! When Lila Banks takes a hike, she doesn't expect to be stalked by the ghost of her recently-deceased cat.

HOW 'BOUT?

Want a free Casey Grimes story?

Sign up for *The Sylvan Spy* at **ajvanderhorst.com/invisible.**

LION & CO PRESS

REMEMBER TO STAY
DANGEROUS.

Loneliness, loneliness will run you through.
All the kids are laughing—I'm laughing too.
– "We Can't Be Beat" by The Walkmen

FOREWARNING

The Brick House was the tallest building on the street and I swear the Brick House knew it. On hot days, its windows smelled like burnt barbecue and firecrackers. Red stains spotted its chalky mortar. Old air shafts whistled in the dark. It was three stories tall and I think it knew a thousand of them.

A century of home inspectors had said, "Completely safe and stable," and each time, the house grinned quietly. It had lived through Kansas City's dragon days. It was fireproof and smart and tough as nails but the *best* word to describe it was dangerous.

It had its eyes open, biding its time. Its jazz-blue front door and curling ivy vines said, "Hey kid, get a load of this." The Brick House was strong and good-looking—and the Brick House was kind of a jerk. But that didn't change the things it had seen and the lives it helped begin and end. Didn't change the dark corners it would show the right people. Or the questionable plans it had for my future.

Because long before I figured any of this out, the Brick

House had chosen *me*, twelve-year-old Conley Hoss—which was crazy, because no one else ever did. That partly explains why my whole family was packed in our car, house-hunting, on a scorching July morning at the very same time the house was hunting *us*.

CHAPTER 1
HOUSE HUNT

"Get your feet out of my fa—OW!" I said as we made a sharp turn. We came out of the curve and my brother Wyatt squirmed away, grinning. I rubbed my toe-poked eye, waited—and swatted him with my book, *Dragons in the Mist*. His yelp made me smile. Getting the drop on that kid wasn't easy.

"The house-hunt starts now," Dad said in the rearview mirror.

A jolt of energy shot through me. Downtown Kansas City was fixed up after the Dragon Uprising a hundred years ago, but this was where all the scaly, toothy stuff in my history books had happened. Cranking down the window, I pictured myself sneaking up on a house, holding a harpoon.

"House-hunting," I said. "Let's go."

"Hey Conley, can you believe this?" Mom smiled at me, clutching her real estate notes.

"Not even a little." I couldn't believe we were gonna live in Kansas City, where dragons used to roam.

"Goodbye, Prairie Refuge. Hello, Kansas City." Mom raised one hand in a wave.

"Eat our dust, Prairie Refuge." I thumped the seat.

"Booo! Gaah! Scaredy Refuge!" my three little brothers shouted. Yep, three of them. Our dented minivan was a rolling daycare.

"Let's do this," Wyatt said, acting all cool even though he was only ten—Top Ten, he liked to be called.

Our smaller brothers clapped in the back.

Mom glanced at her notes. "Option one, coming up on our right."

We all held our breath.

It was a modern-looking rectangle that reminded me of biology lab.

"We can't live in a glass habitat," I said. "Are you kidding me?" The idea made my head spin—and no one disagreed with me, not even Wyatt, who treated arguing like a hobby.

"Don't give up, little darling." Mom would've ruffled my hair if she could reach me.

"Mom, I'm twelve," I said. "Big, not little."

For a second, I was afraid she was about to burst into song the way she sometimes did. When you combined her drama with Dad's swagger, it was no wonder us kids had a bad time. Their genes were a terrible fit for Prairie Refuge.

House Option Two had a yard so crammed with statues you couldn't see the ground. Gnomes and animals squared off against pudgy cherubs. There was a moment of confused silence.

"Purple shag carpet," Mom read aloud, choosing to ignore the scenery. "Orange wallpaper, popcorn ceilings. Maybe we could update it?"

By then I'd pulled myself together. "But look at the yard— it's a petting zoo for old people."

Wyatt snickered. Mom sighed. Even six-year-old Keller was quiet, and he *liked* weird, artsy stuff. We turned down a wide boulevard, and an old advertisement caught my eye. Painted on the side of a cafe, a shadowy man in a suit and hat was lighting a pipe—with help from a dragon. INVISA-FADE— TAKE ONE FOR ADVENTURE, said the slogan.

I couldn't believe my eyes. Since when was adventure encouraged? My family slogan would've been the opposite: ADVENTURE—WE'RE BEING KEPT FROM HAVING IT.

So unjust.

I stuck my head out for a better view. Just then a yapping chihuahua dashed in front of our car. Dad hit the brakes and my skull bounced off the window frame.

"Oww." I rubbed my head.

"Brainless rat-dog," Dad muttered as he rolled down his window.

On the sidewalk, a large woman in a security uniform glowered at us.

"Can I have that dog's license, officer?" Dad said.

She made a rude gesture.

And that's when I saw it.

Out my window, a brick house towered so high I couldn't see the top. Its front door was indigo blue. Ivy vines grew on huge pillars, leaves waving like a thousand green hands: *Pick me, pick me, pick me.*

I stopped rubbing my head to tap Dad's shoulder. "How about that one."

Mom glanced over. "Not for sale, honey."

As we rolled forward, I slumped in my seat. You may not believe it, but I'd started to lose hope, and I had a pretty good reason.

Our home in richy Johnson County, Kansas, had a flat lawn and tan siding like every other house in the subdivision. A hundred years back when contractors started building dragon-proof homes in the farmland, they'd used flame-resistant materials. Slate roofs, tungsten-lined walls. People were terrified by the dragon violence in downtown Kansas City, eager to escape—and I understood that part. But the dragons were long gone, outlawed and hunted down in North America. Extinct.

Unfortunately, Prairie Refuge hadn't moved on.

The neighborhood slogan was, Safety first. Safety last. Safety in the middle. You might think that's a joke but it's not. We were always getting fines addressed to Hoss Boy #13, or #10, or #17, like there was a whole army of us crammed into our two-story house.

"Overly Enthusiastic Swimming" was a popular citation. "Excessive Bike and Trike Speeds" and "Unsafe Trampoline Tricks" were a couple others. I'd even been targeted for "Reading in Trees at Deadly Heights." The whole subdivision watched us through binoculars. It was a real drag, being fined whenever you tried to live a little. That's why we felt fed up and a little crazy on that scorching July day.

I'd started to roll my window up when someone yelled at us, which was normal. What wasn't normal was that he sounded friendly.

"HEY, COME BACK!" An old man struggled to rise from a rocking chair on the brick building's shady front porch. He was as dark as a raisin and almost as wrinkled.

"House-hunting, aren't you? I can always tell."

We all stared, even four-year-old James, mouth open in the middle of complaining. The old man's eyes shone, too young for the rest of him.

"Today is your lucky day, mister," he told Dad. "I decided to sell this place about thirty seconds ago."

Huh? It didn't look like a home you made snap decisions

about. The castle-like columns seemed to say, "People plan *around* me, kid."

"This place was just weather-proofed and tuck-pointed," the old guy said as we jumped out. "It has new AC, new heating, new windows, new everything—except it's really, really old." He grinned. "Also, its value is trending up and it's tax-abated, being a historical landmark."

I didn't know what all that meant, but Dad seemed to like it.

The house's roofline dipped and straightened, like a quick smile.

Wait, what? I blinked and glanced at the old guy .

"It's way too big for me." He shrugged. "Too many rooms, too many walk-in closets. I never use the bar or hot tub and the kitchen has too much counter-space."

Mom covered her mouth. "My goodness, that sounds —terrible."

Dad said she'd been an amazing actress in college, but she was really bad at lying.

"Another week of this and I might go belly up, so I'll give you a deal," the old guy said.

It would have to be a really good deal because the place was three times the size of our house in Prairie Refuge.

As the old man pointed at the gutters, talking about high-carbon steel, a blue-tailed skink scampered up a pillar. Okay, that was cool. I had a thing for reptiles, the African Boomslang excluded. That snake waits in a tree for the unwary, falls on them and kills them in seconds. Bladed umbrellas are the obvious answer.

Then the house's blue front door creaked open. A gust of wind swept out and tugged my elbow, making my toes twitch inside my battered sneakers. An old metal plaque gleamed in the wall by the door: *1925, MIDWEST DRAGON HOU...*

The word DRAGON made my heart stand at attention.

Rust had eaten the other words except, *Watson Adagio, Director.* And in smaller letters at the bottom, *Azarel...*

"Well sir, I'm intrigued," Dad was saying. "But this place is older than the Civil War."

The old man chuckled. "Built to last." He patted one of the house's columns. "Of course, you'll want to see its *bones.* Come take a look."

I should've known better, but I stepped inside.

Wood floors creaked just loud enough to make me wonder who'd walked on them before. Vaulted ceilings soared into shadow. Dusty corners and winding stairs pulled me in like a mystery book at bedtime.

"Let's check for secret rooms," Wyatt said.

"Absolutely."

It was pretty rare for us to agree on things.

Stairs groaned under our feet like they agreed too. *Mmhm, mmhm.*

"Wyatt, did you hear that?"

"Hear what?" He put his head on one side.

"I thought I heard—never mind. This house is not normal."

"Maybe you could be friends." He laughed.

Very funny. But he had a point, because in fifth grade I'd tried to start a Dragon History Club. "Put yourself out there," Mom said. "Go in swinging," Dad said. Big mistake. I'd been a social outcast ever since.

Prairie Refuge had created a new fine in my honor: "Discussing Unsafe History" ($100). Dad had shredded dozens of them. As a result, I didn't have any friends—unless you count brothers, and who does that? Basically, I had more in common with people in the past than I did with people in the present.

Down the hall, a heavy door swayed half-open, painted with some kind of family crest. Two roaring dragons—one crimson, one the color of a starless night—grappled against a city skyline. Written in bold script under the painting were the words:

BLUE FOR GRIT, GREEN FOR LUCK, WHITE FOR WITS, RED FOR BLOOD.

It had to be the most intriguing picture I'd ever seen.

"It looks like a dragon battlecry," I said. "The kind of thing they'd roar before they–"

"Wow, someone is great at art-ing." Next to me, six-year-old Keller's mouth hung open. He loved watercolors—definitely more than he loved my dragon knowledge.

I gave in to the door's magnetic force and yanked it open. Behind it, wide stone stairs twisted into darkness. Our parents were exploring the second or third library, so I flicked a light switch and we all tramped down. In a giant basement, golden dust-specks floated over paving stones. We turned in circles, staring.

"This place is built like a fortress," I said.

A hot water heater flared like the house was saying, *You think?* The noise made me think of a flamethrower—or a baby dragon.

"Amazing," I said.

"I have 'dea!" yelled James. He held an orange stuffed fox by one paw. "Let's play game. Let's run 'round and play game!"

"Deal," I said, feeling generous. We started playing tag, and I was trailing Keller's flip-flop prints when I saw strange marks in the dust, like bird feet—but with extra claws.

"Time out! Guys, come take a look." I swatted away eager fingers as my brothers crowded around. "Don't touch the little bird tracks." We got down on our hands and knees and crawled. I thought we were about to solve a mystery, but instead, the tracks wound around a corner of the basement and ended at a stone wall.

"Hey kids, let's go," Dad called.

Darn it. My heart got heavy as we trudged up the stairs. The place was enormous and my family wasn't made of money. We only got new shoes once a year—so I knew what would happen next. We'd get back in the car and keep looking. And whatever we'd find would be a lot cheaper and a lot less cool than this.

Hey, you'll still be in the Dragon District, I told myself.

But when you're going to end up with the basic version, maybe it's not always great to look at the extra-special, limited edition first.

When we stepped into the front hall, Mom gave us a smile, breathed out a crazy little laugh, and wrapped her arms around Dad's neck.

"Look out! Gross!" my brothers screamed.

That kiss was my first clue I had no idea what was happening.

"What's going on?" I peered out from behind my fingers.

"We're going for it." Dad grinned. "Doing it."

A tingly feeling came over me.

"What was it you always used to say?" Mom squeezed his hand. "Anything worth doing–"

"–is worth overdoing? Ha!" Dad put an arm around her. "I did used to say that, didn't I?"

Feeling dizzy, I grabbed the bannister. Could it be true?

The old guy smiled at me. "Congratulations, kid, the keys are yours." He took a breath and glanced around, taking in every corner of the foyer. "It's been a good run, old friend."

Our parents were grinning and dabbing their eyes. Us kids yelled, jumping up and down. James smacked everyone joyously with his stuffed fox. And just like that, it was over.

Chalk up a win for the house and the old man with their one-two punch.

We moved in two weeks later and named it, "The Brick House."

Better names would've involved blistering fire, mind control and slow death.

But at the time, it just fit.

CHAPTER 2
THE NIGHT VISITOR

W e'd been in the Brick House two days, and it had been forty-eight hours of pure, joyous chaos. My brothers and I ran up and down the four-story stairs, playing tag. Eight stories total, since they were front and back. We threw a football in the cavernous great room. We dove for coins in the whale-sized hot tub. Wyatt climbed the ivy vines to a second floor window and dared me to follow. Maybe I still would.

As I lay in my bunk bed, trying to fall asleep, something *clinkety-clinked* through an air shaft in the wall. Probably loose mortar, falling to the basement. Oh yeah, the basement. It was almost like the house was making a suggestion.

"Good idea, I'll try and get down there tomorrow," I said.

The Brick House and I talked to each other.

I mean, sort of. Not in a weird way.

The house didn't use words. Obviously. But it gave you the idea it could if it wanted. In my imagination, it sounded like a raspy old godfather. *Hey, kid, you're part of the family now.* Floors creaked in a familiar way. Lights glowed to life when I entered a room. Doors swayed open for me when my hands were full. The house seemed to really like me.

And that was cool. It felt good to be picked—even if it was just my imagination. If the vibe had been different, say dark and creepy, I might've felt different. But the Brick House had a great personality.

I didn't suspect a thing until it was too late.

But on that third night, I leaned back in bed and punched my pillow a few times to make it comfy. A draft of cool air rustled across my sheets.

Thanks Brick House, I thought.

My brothers and I had voted to sleep in the same bedroom. Not that I needed them close by, of course not. But the house was so huge and ancient. Once we'd mapped all the rooms, got the place explored, we'd branch out and claim our own territory. Just a matter of time.

I was deciding whether a dent in the ceiling looked like an alligator or an amoeba when I noticed the draft. The window had been shut when Dad hugged me goodnight. Now a warm breeze flowed over my top bunk, making my forehead sticky.

Someone had opened a window. And what was that smell, like the zoo?

I sat up. Outside, something scratched against the house.

My fingers knotted the sheets.

Scritch, scritch. The sound got louder, the smell stronger.

I ran my hands through my hair, wishing the Brick House would say something. Maybe it was already asleep. Obviously, I didn't expect the house to actually talk. But a little reminder that it had my back would've been nice.

I slid down the bunk ladder, and stood still, listening. The *scritch, scritch* sound stopped. Probably one of Mom's apple saplings, blowing in the wind.

Except trees don't climb walls.

I rubbed the freckles on my nose. This was getting weird. Wyatt could be a jerk but he would love this. Maybe I should accidentally wake up him up. I reached up to flick him, but his top bunk was empty. Both the bottom bunks were empty too. Something weird was happening. My little brothers were never this coordinated in their trickery.

I frowned, took a deep breath and slid to the window. Pretend you're a spy, darkness is your friend, I told myself. And this is just a drill—a creepy missing-brothers drill. When I leaned out, hot air washed over my face and I wrinkled my nose. It was the gross, fishy aroma you get at a zoo's reptile house.

Two eyes snapped open under the window—yellow head-lights with vertical pupils. I yelled and threw myself back as a huge lizard slithered through and crouched in the bedroom.

Oh wow, much quicker than a crocodile—more snakily-shaped.

My legs wobbled under me.

Its dark claws sank into the hardwood floor.

I took a slow step back, my gut sinking.

The beast was covered in midnight scales, a line of crimson down its spine.

Another step and my back brushed the door.

Its mouth cracked open, tongue flicking out.

My shaking fingers grazed the door knob.

Cobra-quick, the reptile arched its long neck toward me. Its jaws paused a foot from my face. Then its grin became very, very toothy.

"Go ahead and run, I'd love to see you try," the dragon said.

I screamed and turned to escape. But like my brothers, I was too slow.

"DAD! DAD, IT'S GOT ME!"

I woke up yelling, sheets twisted around my legs as the sun

shone through the closed window. Wyatt sprawled belly-down across from me, snoring softly. That kid could sleep through anything. When I checked, there were no claw-marks on the floor. Four-year-old James stood on his bottom bunk, fluffy blond hair grazing the slats.

"Stop crying, I not like that." Holding his stuffed fox by one ear, he threw it at me.

The grinning fox bounced off my head as the door swung open and Keller came in, pulling Dad.

"Why all the yelling?" Dad said. "Conley, how can Wyatt be fighting you if he's asleep? Are you telling me James—"

"Just a bad dream, Dad." I slumped into my pillow. "A really, really bad dream."

"Sorry to hear it," Dad said, and the three of them marched out of the room like a clown parade. I didn't feel like being left alone, so a few minutes later, I followed.

Downstairs, bacon hissed and spat like a cat-fight. Mom helped James drink orange juice through a straw as Dad headed to the chrome eight-burner stove Mom kept going on about. Mostly-unpacked boxes and mixing bowls dotted the huge kitchen. Four beta fish swam in jars by a window. Below them, a gang of leaky water guns lounged in one of four sinks.

This was the water fight reload sink. Us boys had agreed.

I slumped at the long trestle table. It was big enough for a football team, but Keller sat down next to me, his corn-silk hair radiating out like a young Einstein. James' eyes lit up. He snuck down the bench on his plump feet.

"Mom, James is pulling my hair," Keller whimpered.

"NO I NOT!" James pulled harder.

I sighed. "Hey guys, want to hear my very scary dream?" I was trying to act casual, but I needed someone to know. Anytime you can drag a nightmare into the sunlight, it helps.

"Did you dream about a bear?" Keller's eyes got big. "Once

I dreamed about a mean bear with x-ray glasses and wherever I hid, he could see me."

I shook my head. "Oh no, not a bear. Much worse. You won't believe–"

"Pancake tiiiime!" Mom sang, and my brothers started cheering and waving their plates and forks. Wyatt appeared out of nowhere in his Batman pajamas with a cape hanging off one shoulder. Clearly, the time for intelligent conversation was over.

Oh well, I thought. It was just a dream.

Everyone crowded close as Mom set down a platter and raised her coffee mug.

"Here's to a new home and new adventures," she said.

"CHEERS!" we all shouted.

"Here's to climbing trees without fines," Wyatt said.

"To history coming to life," I said.

"HEAR, HEAR!"

"To cooking bacon without causing a house fire," Dad muttered.

"Hey, Wyatt." I nudged him in the ribs. "Let's explore the basement later."

"Huh? Why?"

We didn't usually coordinate our schedules.

"For fun—and danger. C'mon, Top Ten." You have to know how to talk to Wyatt.

"Fine."

"I want to explore too." Keller bounced in his chair.

"Ok," I said. "Just don't tell James."

Sometime later, after several rounds of pancakes and some water gun reloads, Mom took James and his fox away for a read-aloud. As soon as they disappeared, Wyatt, Keller and I stopped pretending to unpack stuff and zig-zagged across the great room, through the corner library and down the front hall. It was the sneakiest route to the basement.

A few boxes took up a fraction of the cellar's space. There were Dad's old boxing trophies, a toolbox, a toy chest, containers of backup plates and glasses. The tiny claw-prints had been scuffed away but I could still picture them clearly.

Here we go, I told the Brick House. I bet this is gonna be good.

Light beamed through the basement windows, lighting up the wall made of river rocks where the mysterious tracks had vanished.

"Hey, Wyatt, if you were a bird, stuck down here, where would you fly?"

He threw a pebble at the wall. "If I was stuck, I'd peck my way out."

"I'm sure you'd try, but birds don't have jackhammers for beaks."

Dust swirled as I ran my fingers over the cracks. The crooked lines of mortar didn't give much away. "If there's a secret door down here, we'd win the lottery before we found it."

Wyatt sniffed. "Are you saying the bird's smarter than us?" He was always on the look-out for an insult. Few things made him happier than a fight.

I was about to make a comment about his IQ when I was interrupted.

"First of all, I'm not a bird," a raspy voice said. "Second, I'm definitely smarter than you."

CHAPTER 3
THE VAULTED CELLAR

"Aeiaaah!" Sometimes you can't help the sounds you make. As I yelled, Keller sloshed me with some root beer he'd been sipping from a plastic cup.

Wyatt tensed up, making fists.

"Where are you?" My eyes darted wildly, searching for I wasn't sure what.

"Up here," the voice rasped. "On the ceiling."

At first we saw nothing. Then, curled between two beams, a tail—not feathered but scaly. *Scritch, scritch.* A lizard stuck its head down and squinted at us.

Keller let out a quavering wail as I sucked in my breath. Don't freak out, I told myself, it's only a talking reptile. This happens now and then—like in your nightmare.

Not a good thought.

"Pick me up, pick me up!" Keller begged.

Wyatt's mouth hung open but his fists were still clenched. I swallowed and stared back at the lizard. Only a foot long, it had a stubby neck, brown scales, and looked oddly familiar. Where had I seen this reptile before?

Wyatt glared. "Come down here where I can reach you."

"Hey, know what this is?" I put a hand on his shoulder. "It's a bearded dragon, like the ones at PetSpectacular." Talking about the lizard in front of it felt rude. "That's what you are, right?" I said. "A beardie?"

The reptile laughed scratchily as it let go of the ceiling, flipped, and landed on its feet.

"Give yourself a gold star, my little man. And don't be scared, I don't bite." It grinned widely. "Couldn't eat a human even if I wanted to."

We didn't laugh.

"How come you talk?" Wyatt asked suspiciously.

"Because I feel like it." The lizard scratched its shoulder blades with a claw.

That wasn't much of an answer.

Keller stuck his head out from behind me. "Can your tail do things? Do you use your feet for crayon-ing? What's your name?"

"Multiple choice, eh." The beardie's dark eyes glittered. "I'll take the last one. You can call me...Nightshade. And *you* must be Keller, brother number three."

Keller smiled. In introductions, he sometimes got overlooked.

"How do you know—" Wyatt started.

"Because I'm good at paying attention, *Wyatt.*" The lizard sounded like a grumpy school teacher. "That's how I know you're number two. And like big brother said, I'm a dragon." His snout cracked in a smile. "A *bearded* dragon who pays attention. Now, weren't you looking for the secret door?"

Nightshade scrambled to the wall, tail swinging. He climbed a large rock, put his front feet on a mortar joint, closed his eyes and pushed with all his strength. There was a popping sound but nothing happened.

"Ouch." He rubbed his spine. "How about a little help here?"

I should've stopped to weigh the pros and cons. But how can you say no to a talking lizard?

Hands on the mortar seam, I took a deep breath and pushed. Nothing happened for me either. The beardie frowned and Wyatt rolled his eyes. Stepping back, I stuck my hands in my pockets. As usual, my fingers touched a variety of objects, because I believe in being prepared.

Let's see—not the penlight. Not the mini-pliers or bottle opener. Aha. I pulled out an arrowhead, leaf-shaped with a point. This was worth a try. I jabbed it into the mortar joint. With a dull thud and a dragging sound, a chunk of wall retreated.

We stared.

I couldn't believe it. All those years of preparedness had finally paid off.

Inside a small arch was...darkness.

Nightshade's eyes shone. "Who wants to go first, explorers?"

"I will." I took a step forward.

"Wow." Top Ten rubbed his hands together happily. "A real adventure."

Watching him agree made me less eager. Maybe this was a stupid mistake—but I couldn't back out now. In fact, I had to move fast, before Mom came looking for us. At least the Brick House was here to keep an eye on things.

Nightshade watched me inch inside. Three steps into darkness, I stubbed my toe. "Oww." Bouncing on one foot, my head clunked the low ceiling. "Augh, I can't see a thing!"

As I searched my pockets for the penlight, the beardie nodded at Keller. "Is that coca-cola you're drinking?"

Keller clutched his cup. "It's *my* root beer."

The lizard licked its lips but didn't ask him for a drink.

"Aha." Wyatt pulled a battered Batman headlamp from a toy chest. He yanked the elastic strap over his head.

My head throbbed as I clicked on my penlight. The dot darted left and right like a bright insect. Then Wyatt's headlamp flooded the whole tunnel with light. I rolled my eyes as we headed down the dusty stairs, Nightshade scuttling ahead.

The lizard glanced back. "Pick up the pace!"

The stairs turned a corner and descended again. We stepped through a high arch into open space. I shone my penlight around and Wyatt pointed his glowing head. The cavern was as big as the Brick House's basement—even bigger. Stone columns held up ten-foot ceilings. Rusty cages lined one wall and metal sconces jutted from the other. At the far end stood another door.

"Wow," Wyatt said. "Like a second basement."

I turned in a slow circle. "Feels older, though."

"It's more darker." Keller stopped sipping his root beer.

"Ugh, what's that smell?" Wyatt wrinkled his nose.

"It smells like—the zoo." Uh oh. I fought the urge to hide behind a pillar.

Nightshade's tail twitched and his eyes shone. "Look at the cages, my little friends."

Wyatt itched one earlobe. "Why are you calling us little? You're a tiny lizard. And they're just big, empty dog cages."

"Dog cages?" Nightshade snorted. "You think men worked at night by lantern light and dug out clay and carted river rock and hid this place underground so they could build *dog cages*?" His eyes became slits.

My head ached. Part of me wanted to yell at Wyatt, grab Keller's hand and run, sealing the passage behind us. But this was an adventure. Things were supposed to get a little scary.

"Follow me." Nightshade danced into the shadows.

"He doesn't seem quite okay," I said.

"Probably fired up," Wyatt said. "This is exciting."

I had to admit he was right.

We caught up with the beardie as he slid inside a cage. Wyatt jerked the door open. As he slipped through, rust fell off the hinges. I sucked in my ribcage and followed as Keller squeezed my hand.

Walls, floor and ceiling formed a cube of metal and stone. Nightshade crouched in a shadowy corner. We beamed our lights on him, but the darkness didn't lift. Gleaming, midnight-blue particles coated the floor. When Wyatt leaned in with his headlamp, I counted five sides on each rice-sized grain.

"Tiny pentagons," I said, "thousands of them. What are they?"

Nightshade grinned. For a second, I thought I saw teeth. "If I told you, you wouldn't believe me. But you're lucky little brats. You're about to find out anyway."

"Huh?"

He clung to the wall in the corner, arched his back and flung himself at us—claws out, hissing—like a head case who had finally snapped.

CHAPTER 4
RISING FROM THE ASHES

Keller screamed. A claw scraped my wrist as I tried to follow the lizard with my flashlight, but it was too quick. Wyatt lunged and missed. Something splashed the floor as Keller screamed again.

"Noo!" I grabbed my little brother. "Where did it cut you?"

"My root beer," he sobbed. "That mean lizard spilled my root beer." He turned his cup upside down and a few drops spilled out. "It's AAAALL GOOOONE."

"Nightshade, where are you?" Wyatt's headlamp swept the cage but the beardie was gone. In the dark corner, a wet bubbling sound plop-plopped to life. We spun around.

The root beer had drenched the dark dust—but it wasn't dust anymore. Tiny beads bounced in a ring around the soda puddle, getting bigger. The wave reached the edges of the dust and rushed back toward the center.

"This can't be good." My stomach felt soupy, my legs jittery.

The particles crawled toward the base of the wall like

legless ants. They piled up, adding width and depth. Much more than a patch of dust.

Wyatt leaned closer. "It's like a LEGO set, building itself into...what?"

"Keller, get out of here." I gave him a little push and the six-year-old disappeared through the gate. "Top Ten, c'mon." The rusty door screeched as I followed Keller. When I glanced back, I froze.

Wyatt was bent over the bubbling shape, his face inches away. He stretched a finger toward the dark, vibrating ooze.

"Wyatt—stop!"

Something hissed and he threw himself back.

A second later, all three of us were sprinting for the exit. We thudded up the stairs, skidded around the turn, flew through the secret door. When we stood in our own dusty basement, I wiped cold sweat off my forehead.

"Keller, go check on Mommy," I said.

He tugged his wild hair. "Should I tell her about the blob?"

"Absolutely not! I mean...how about not quite yet."

As Keller ran off, I glared at Wyatt. "Why'd you try to touch that thing?"

He glared back. "*Someone* had to."

"No," I said. "Someone really didn't."

He crossed his arms. "Then why are we still down here?"

"*Not* so we can get eaten by deadly goo."

He narrowed his eyes. "If you try to sneak down there without me—"

"There's something wrong with you," I said. "But we do need to go back down."

Wyatt's face lit up.

"We left the cage wide open," I said.

He put his head on one side and nodded, like he could see

how this might be an itsy-bitsy problem. "I know where Dad keeps his bike chain," he said.

A minute later, the two of us snuck back down. My legs felt shaky and we took it one step at a time, pausing to look and listen, but whatever waited in the dark was very still. My imagination was going crazy, boiling with scales and teeth and hungry shadows, and I pressed a hand to my head, trying to slow it down. If a pin had dropped in the cave-like, echoey dark, I would've jumped a mile. My nerves were ragged when we finally peered through the bars of the cage.

What had made me step inside?

It was obviously a prison.

The night-colored blob gleamed under Wyatt's headlamp. Now it was the size of a football and about the same shape. Steam rose from its surface. I shoved the rusty door shut and the dark mass hissed. My fingers shook as I wrapped the lock around the gate.

"Aaaashhh." The sound was low and loud and angry.

I struggled to click the lock shut.

"Aaaashhh!" Now the thing was the size of a watermelon.

Gasping, I rattled the chain. It held firm.

We ran for the stairs.

Sunlight seemed safe, so a minute later we were scrambling up our new favorite tree.

"If you use this rope, you won't fall on your head," I said.

"I don't need a rope," Wyatt grunted. "I never fall."

We were doing our best to act all cool, like we hadn't just sprinted out of the basement, screaming like piglets fleeing a butcher.

"Ah, this branch is my favorite," I said.

"Good and sturdy," Wyatt agreed.

"Nice and cool in the shade."

"Hot weather lately."

We spent a few minutes discussing such things.

The tree was a big Southern Catalpa with long, thin seed-pods perfect for sword fights. This was the Dragon District, the land of opportunity, not Prairie Refuge. There were no stupid neighborhood bylaws.

"What do you think it is?" I finally said.

Wyatt was playing with my Swiss Army Knife, which I'd generously let him borrow. He looked me in the eye.

"That egg is bigger than Nightshade and still growing. You know what it is."

"Egg?" I waved my hands in the air. "What do you mean?"

"Don't play dumb."

My heart sank. I guess I'd tried to tell myself the egg was anything but. Maybe the little blob would grow up to be a big blob and sit there in the cage, vibrating quietly.

"It's in your books," Wyatt said, "but it's not a crocodile or Komodo. It's the real thing—a bearded dragon without a beard."

"Darn it," I said helplessly.

Wyatt's face was unreadable. "It's a dragon."

I knew he was right.

"Wake up, dummy." My brother tested the blade of my knife with his thumb. "We just moved to this dragonish place and there's even a sign on our house that says DRAGON. How did you not see this coming?"

I frowned. "Because dragons are extinct, Wyatt. E-X-I-N–"

Crack. A twig snapped under the Catalpa.

When we looked down, the lady frowning up at us looked like a bag of flour stuffed in a uniform with legs tacked on as an afterthought. It was Desmona the mean security guard, walking her chihuahua.

To our surprise, our new neighbors were just as snobby as our old ones, in a more nasty, less nosy way. They loved their dogs and bike paths but treated kids like aliens. Not what I'd expected in the Dragon District, but I guess even the coolest places can forget what they're supposed to be.

"Get outta my tree," Desmona growled. "Or I'll citizen arrest you."

I squared my shoulders. "This tree is right on the property line."

"We don't have to listen to you." Wyatt stuck out his tongue.

Desmona clenched her pudgy fists. "Maybe I'll take a chainsaw to that tree."

"Um..." I didn't have a comeback to that.

"What was that about chainsaws?" Mom appeared on the sidewalk, winding her dark hair in a ponytail. Her blue eyes were icy.

"Just talking about yard work." Des shot her a rubber-band-smile and slouched up the sidewalk, tugging her dog.

"That meanie," Wyatt said. "I can't believe her job is protecting people."

"Neither can I." Mom's hands were on her hips.

I was already back to thinking about dragons.

CHAPTER 5
DARK SKY

"Hey boys, seen my bike lock?" Dad sipped a cappuccino in the second-story espresso bar and creative studio. Light streamed through windows onto his laptop and notes for the *Kansas City Star* that covered half the twenty foot work surface. We should've known better than to slip through, but it was on the way to our room, not to mention the splash room and second library, and he'd been working very quietly. Like a hidden sniper.

"Hmm," Wyatt said.

"Uhhh," I added.

"That's what I thought." Looking at us sternly, Dad grabbed a pencil off the table and stirred his coffee with it. "I'm at home today but I'll need my lock tomorrow, got it?" He licked the eraser, made a face, and set the pencil down next to a spoon.

All of a sudden, the day felt more normal and I felt a little stupid. I mean, who steals a bike lock to imprison a mythical creature? I started wondering what we'd really seen in the basement. Maybe I was overreacting, and who could blame me? Even small reptiles are scary when they lunge at you, and Nightshade had gone crazy. Did lizards get rabies? I'd have to do an internet search later.

Wyatt and I continued around the corner and down the hall. Judging by Top Ten's face, he was experiencing some heightened mental activity too.

By the time we reached our bedroom, stepping over James' stuffed animals, our secret meeting seemed anticlimactic. We looked at each other uncertainly.

"We don't know for sure it's a dragon," I said.

Wyatt nodded sadly. "That's what I was thinking."

"Dragons are extinct in North America."

We sighed.

I found myself missing the terror I'd felt an hour before. Well, not terror. I hadn't been afraid. I'd been excited. Enthusiastic. And why not? The Brick House had set up this adventure for us. Of course nothing would go terribly wrong. Of course it was safe.

"I guess there's just one thing to do," I said. "Let's get a closer look, and decide what we're dealing with. We'll keep an eye out for Nightshade and be super careful and scientific and—"

Wyatt was already running down the hall.

In minutes, we'd dodged Dad, Mom, Keller and James, and snuck back down to the basement. We took another couple minutes getting ready.

Then we went deeper underground.

"Anyone here?" I whispered. The vaulted sub-basement was as silent as the grave. No *scritch-scratch* of claws, no hissing, no bubbling. Nothing.

I was carrying a shovel, raised like a weapon. Wyatt had Mom's meat tenderizer, stolen from the kitchen. We both wore oversized leather work gloves and I was starting to think it was too much. After all, you *can* be too careful.

Wet sniffing came from across the room.

We froze and shone our lights on the cage.

Nightshade perched on the bars, tail drooping, looking pitiful.

I gave him a dirty look. "You gonna jump at us again?"

A tear trickled down the lizard's snout. "Sorry I went crazy back there," he croaked. "I didn't mean to scare you but this place reminded me of my old life and I kind of lost it."

I felt off balance. This wasn't what I'd expected.

Nightshade drew a long, raspy breath. "Anyway," he said. "This isn't about me. It's about *that*."

My heart gave a sideways lurch. I didn't want to look where his claw was pointing. At the same time, I couldn't look away. We shone our lights through the bars onto a

small

inky

DRAGON.

"No..." I breathed. "Oh no."

At the same moment, my heart was saying, Yeah, that's what I'm talking about!

The dragon was about James' size. Its color was between midnight blue and charcoal, the color of a bruised night sky. Crimson scales streaked its back and vertical pupils slashed its yellow eyes. It looked familiar. What really took me off guard, though, was its tears.

The little dragon was crying.

It wiped its face with a claw.

Top Ten tapped a metal slat. "What's wrong, little fella?"

I wondered if that was the best idea. The dragon seemed

truly miserable, but it had glimmering scales. Opposable claws. Smoky, intelligent eyes. It was like watching history come to life.

"Can it talk?" I heard myself say.

Nightshade looked up. "The question is, will he talk to *you*."

This dragon looked so dejected, it didn't seem fair to connect it to the one in my nightmare, even though they shared similar features. This one was tiny. You wanted to reach down and rub its little snout. It wasn't anything like the monsters of the Dragon Uprising—House Creepers, Bone Burners, Heart Eaters. Huge reptiles with awful, twisted appetites—no, this wasn't one of those.

"What's your name, dragon?" Wyatt asked.

The dragon looked at him for a long moment.

I held my breath as it opened its mouth.

"Dark Sky." You wouldn't confuse it with a human voice. Too rumbly, like it was echoing out of a cave. A big, brassy voice for such a small dragon.

My brother nodded. "I like it."

"How'd you choose that name?" I said.

"Always had it." The dragon's front claws twitched on the floor.

"But you were just born."

A thread of smoke or steam curled from the dragon's nose.

I wondered if I'd somehow insulted it. In the silence, my mind buzzed like a broken lightbulb. *You're talking to a dragon, a dragon, a real live dragon, you're talking to a—*

Nightshade coughed.

I blinked and looked at Wyatt. His eyes took up most of his face.

"Your manners need some work," the beardie told the baby dragon. Nightshade turned to us. "You understand, though.

Imagine *you'd* been trapped in a cellar for endless...hmm, no. Imagine you were born in jail. A baby. Locked up before your life even started. You'd be a little grumpy too."

Nightshade was acting strange. Like a tour guide, describing the scenery. A public relations person, speaking for the dragon.

"Is one of you in charge?" I asked.

Four reptile eyes flicked toward me. Dark Sky glared. Nightshade opened his mouth and shut it. Apparently it was an awkward question.

"Can you fly?" Wyatt asked.

I felt relief as the dragon turned away. "Flight is like nothing else," it rumbled. "It would be my pleasure to take you up into the clouds." The corners of its mouth turned upwards.

Wait, what? I couldn't believe it. The dragon was making an alliance with Top Ten. How had I let this happen? This was my adventure. Now if I tried to join, I'd sound like a copycat.

"I know you're little," I said, "but even though I'm bigger than he is, I don't weigh a lot. My legs *look* big, maybe, because I've got a lot of stuff in my pockets, but–"

"Hrrmph," the dragon scoffed.

Wyatt smiled and rubbed his hands together.

No, I thought. You can't be stranded on the ground. Not left out, not this time. That's when I lost what was left of my common sense.

"Wait," I said desperately. "I can open the lock."

The dragon put its head on one side.

Wyatt stepped to the gate. "I know the combination too."

"No." I elbowed him away. "Let me."

The dragon watched as we fought to open the cell door. It didn't seem especially interested. It yawned as we pulled off our too-big gloves, slapping at each other's hands. In a flurry of shoves and insults, the digits of the combination got punched in. Wyatt and I were sweaty and out of breath by the time the tumblers clicked into place. I shoved him aside, knocking him on his rear, and smirked as I slid the bolt open.

I'd won.

The dragon would like me now.

Time stood still as the chain swung free, clinking the bars of the cage. Wyatt scowled at me. The dragon watched from the corner of one eye. I wished the Brick House would say something, because suddenly...I felt alone.

Silence surrounded me.

That's when I knew something awful was about to happen.

Now the Brick House seemed hushed, walls leaning in, holding its breath. *Concerned.* A cold, prickly feeling squirmed up my spine like centipedes. I fumbled with the lock.

The dragon's eyes blazed to life.

Dark Sky became a blur.

The metal gate flew open, knocking me down.

"AT LAST," the dragon roared. "FREEDOM!" He rolled his shoulders and lashed his tail. Sparks flew as he raked his claws across the wall. "Curse you, Brick House," he snarled. Then he was standing over me. My eyes watered under his hot breath. "You tried to lock me in *again,*" he hissed.

I felt something stab my chest but I couldn't look away from his burning eyes.

"Next time we meet..." the dragon growled in my ear, "I'll eat your heart."

I froze like a mouse in a cobra's stare.

Dark Sky turned to Wyatt, red dripping from his claws.

Maybe he said something to my little brother. I couldn't tell because my heartbeat rang out like footsteps in an underpass. In my mind I was running, faster than the wind. Maybe I really went somewhere. When I came back, my hand was pressed to my chest, wet with blood. Wyatt stared at me with glassy eyes. He looked like he might cry.

The door at the far end of the cellar scraped open.

I caught a gleam of yellow eyes in shadow.

Dark Sky gone.

The sconces flamed to life, dancing down the walls of the vaulted cellar. I struggled up, my blood hot on my fingers. Maybe I'm dying, I thought dizzily. But I've got a little time left. I can undo what just happened.

I yanked the bike chain off the cage and staggered after the dragon.

Behind the open door, a tunnel stretched straight and long. At the far end, Dark Sky crouched, stripes of sunlight falling on his hide. I was halfway there, my hands brushing the walls for balance, when the dragon roared and sprang—but not at me.

He threw himself at the light. As he crashed into the upper wall, his neck and tail lengthened. His body thickened. His shoulders bulged with muscle—and something else that caught the air like canvas. With a loud *clang,* a circle of light appeared in the ceiling and Dark Sky squeezed through.

I reached the end of the empty tunnel and stared up, shading my eyes. Wyatt appeared next to me, biting his lip. We looked through a manhole into blazing sunlight. The circle framed clouds and sky. More light fell through a grate in the wall.

High above, a dark shape circled. It gleamed like a metal airplane but the plane had a long neck and a snake-like tail.

I could hardly make sense of what had happened. But this was real.

Dark Sky was flying overhead.

CHAPTER 6
LIBRARIAN OF THE ASHES

We watched the dragon veer into a bank of clouds. Palms to my face, I groaned and sank against the wall. The tunnel floor rose to meet me. Magically, I found my face against the stone. I focused on taking deep breaths, in and out. My lungs still seemed to work. My heart was hammering away. Maybe I wouldn't die. I forgot Top Ten was there until he spoke up.

"Guess dragons aren't extinct."

A splinter of pain stabbed my heart. Why did that sound familiar? Oh, that's right. An hour ago I'd said they *were*. I sat up slowly. The blood on my hands and shirt was getting sticky. I didn't want to think about what had just happened. But I had to.

I hung my head, feeling like my insides had been hollowed out. Eventually, someone would ask, Hey, Conley, what made you sneak into a secret cellar and break a violent dragon out of prison? I wondered what I'd say.

It was Keller's root beer. No, that was not a good look.

The dragon was too smart for me. It wasn't really true.

The dragon *was* smart. And tricky. But I'd known that. That was the horrible part. I'd seen what the dragon was doing, but if I was being honest I'd have to say, Well, I released the dragon because—because I wanted to be chosen. I wanted to be picked. To be in on something secret and special, the kind of thing I always get left out of. So I fought Wyatt for the chance to release a nasty, vicious dragon.

A bad feeling splashed around my stomach.

"I think you need a band-aid," Wyatt said.

I forced myself to look up. Not known for his soft touch, my brother was trying to show he cared. And he did look worried.

"I can't believe you did that," he said.

"Yeah, a band-aid would be—wait, what? You can't believe *I* did that?"

"I wanted to go slow, but you just *had* to open the cage door."

We stared at each other. So this was how it was going to be.

"Give me a hand, huh?" I held my arm out weakly.

"No way, I'm gonna go find Mom."

"You little–!" When I grabbed for him, Wyatt danced aside. I levered myself upright, using the wall for support. Normally, Top Ten would be long gone, but today he was like a small White Shark, smelling weakness.

As he glared at me, I realized he was mad. Scared and angry. Maybe angry because he was scared. He was blaming me, and sure, I blamed myself, but that didn't mean I was ok being blamed by someone else.

"It's your fault too," I said. "Admit it."

I must have looked serious because he took off down the tunnel, laughing in a loud, kind of insane way. I got to my feet —pulling myself up took a lot of energy—and took a shaky step after him.

He screamed.

Chills traced my body because he wasn't screaming at me. I'm not that scary. My brother was dancing back and forth, pointing at something on the floor. Something that moved— that was alive. Nightshade crouching in the tunnel, hissing.

Both of us hugged the walls.

Sometimes you look around for something, like a pencil or a toothbrush, until you realize you're holding it. That's what I was doing with the bike chain. It jangled against my leg as I turned to search for it.

My anger at Dark Sky and Wyatt and myself boiled over.

"GET OUT OF MY WAY!" I yelled.

The lizard gave a sideways lurch and froze.

I stepped forward, whirling the chain.

Instead of running for cover, the bearded dragon narrowed its eyes. The spiky skin at its throat grew darker. I slowed but kept moving.

The beardie stretched its mouth wide with a venomous hiss. Its spiky collar flared, making it look three times bigger. Nightshade had said he didn't have teeth, but he'd been lying. Those rows in the back looked small but sharp.

My knees wobbled as I raised the bike chain.

"Hold on." The lizard raised a front foot. "We've got off to a bad start."

I stumbled to a stop.

"I'm willing to be reasonable," the beardie said. "You seem upset. The problem is, you must be confusing me with someone else. The other problem is, why are we in the sub- basement? And who are you? And how did we get here?"

Wyatt appeared at my shoulder.

"Another thing," the lizard said. "Why aren't you running away or pointing at me and screaming? You can hear me talk- ing, can't you? Is this a practical joke? Did someone dust me with invisa-fade?"

My head felt like a helium balloon. As the beardie kept talking, the balloon floated into the air. It drifted away, twisting in the breeze.

"Don't try to trick us, Nightshade," Wyatt said. "I don't like you anymore."

"You don't make sense," I croaked. "Did Dark Sky smash your head on the way out?"

The lizard's body stiffened. "Dark Sky?" He turned and scurried into the open cellar.

Wyatt and I stood there.

I cleared my throat. "We should probably make a run for—"

I was cut off by a raspy, quavering yell.

The bearded dragon reappeared, eyes flashing.

"Who—did—this?" He snarled.

But I'd had enough. "Look," I said. "We're leaving. Get out of our way."

I meant it. My chest ached. My stomach burned. I really, really meant it.

Maybe the beardie could see that in my face.

"My name is Watson Adagio." He glared at me. "Former Dragon Director, been here since 1920. If you doubt me, I speak English, Italian, Aramaic, some African dialects, and I'd be happy to prove it. Now I'm the Librarian of the Ashes." He waved his claws toward the basement. "But someone raided the library. Someone woke the ashes. I think it was you." He stared at me grimly.

My shoulders slumped.

"You said your name was Nightshade," Wyatt said.

"I never said that," the lizard said.

Dragging the bike chain, I shuffled past. None of it made sense, but I knew one thing.

"Dark Sky is gone," I said, "and I'm getting out of this stupid cellar."

CHAPTER 7
DARK SKY'S LEGEND

Out of earshot by the curb, Mom picked up sidewalk chalk. James and Keller ate apple slices in their portable teepee under the Catalpa. I'd wanted to take a shower and pull myself together, but Watson Adagio, the beardie formerly known as Nightshade, told me that would be incredibly selfish.

He was probably right.

Now I sat on a branch, feeling dusty and tired.

Watson crouched near us, his eyes pinned to our faces.

"Start from the beginning," he said, and we did. For a little guy, he was very pushy. Every minute or so he nodded, digging his claws into the bark.

"This is a disaster," he said when we'd finished.

"Ok," I said. "I think that's pretty obvious. So why did *you* help Dark Sky escape?"

"I didn't." He frowned, the corners of his mouth darkening. "Not intentionally."

What a copout. For a second, I thought that's all he was

going to say. Then he rubbed a claw across his chin. "Can't be an accident," he muttered. "Can't be as dumb as he looks."

"Wyatt, you mean?" I said.

Top Ten looked up. He'd been busily cracking twigs in half, but he had a way of tuning in whenever his name was mentioned.

"No." Watson pointed a claw at me. "The house seems to have taken a liking to *you*."

I jerked sideways on my branch and almost fell. "How do you know?" I said. "Um, actually, we're not that close. We hardly talk—we barely know each other. Oooh." I groaned and covered my eyes. "Ok, we're friends. Sort of."

"Knew it," Watson said smugly.

Wyatt's expression said: *Dork dork dork dork dork.*

I looked away.

"Well, the Brick House is no fool," Watson admitted. "It must have its reasons."

My insides gave a bubbly *fwoosh*. I hoped no one else heard, because it was a fizzy, glittery, sparkly-unicorn kind of sound.

I *knew* the house liked me, I thought. *Knew* it.

"You gotta play the hand you're dealt," Watson muttered. He took a deep, raspy breath. "Of course, we needed buyers. All that waiting, years, *decades*, looking for the right people. Wentley eager to retire on his yacht. The Brick House getting tired, rusty—it needed someone. *That's* why they couldn't wait, why they had to move fast, without getting my advice."

I wasn't sure if he was talking to himself or us.

He studied me with flat eyes. "I really should've been there though."

That felt insulting. But I was probably misreading things.

"I wouldn't have chosen you," he clarified.

When I opened my mouth, he cut me off.

"It's a big deal, being chosen by a dragon house. You're the liaison, the right hand man. If the house needs something, it comes to you first. If you need something, it'll be there. And you'd better believe it'll speak to you. So pay attention to the house's moods. Keep a lookout on your dreams—and let's hope you don't ruin everything."

"Hey!"

"Enough about you, though," the lizard said. "I was born right here in the Brick House, and straight from the egg, I proved to be a quick study. We're an observant species, we bearded dragons, but my photographic memory made me a natural for the business."

Man, was he smug. But I let it go because I was still thinking about what he'd said. *The house picked me.* Man, it felt good, like being handed a medal when you've never won a contest in your life. The Brick House could tell I had potential. Who knew what would happen next? Whatever it was, it would be amazing.

"As you've probably realized," Watson was saying, "the Brick House was the Kansas City branch of the Dragon Agency."

Had I realized that? I hoped so. The plaque by the front door, *MIDWEST DRAGON HOU*...could've been a clue.

By now even Wyatt was paying attention.

"I shot through the ranks," Watson said. "Youngest lizard ever to be named Dragon Director. I negotiated international contracts, made careers. Made the Brick House famous, the biggest and best Dragon Agency franchise in the Midwest. Everyone wanted our dragons."

Ok, so he'd accomplished a few things.

The little lizard sighed. "When the Brick House closed its doors in 1940, I was the natural choice for Librarian of the Ashes..." He trailed off.

Wait a minute. I raised my hand. "But why did the Brick House—"

Watson's beady eyes tore at me.

Fine. Take your time.

"So you worked with *dragons*?" Wyatt said.

"OBVIOUSLY I DID."

I glanced down to see if Mom had heard the lizard's shout.

Watson ran a claw across his snout. "Dark Sky was born in the 1920s."

I wrinkled my forehead as I did the math.

"You need to understand," he said. "Our dragons drove industry. They built railroads, dug mines, forged steel, guarded cattle, powered steamboats, protected bank vaults—I could go on. They weren't *only* muscle for hire." He flicked his tail.

This was obviously important to him, so I nodded.

"Dark Sky *was* muscle, of course. The best muscle there was. He wasn't just fierce, he was tricky. He wasn't just strong, he was sly. Later we would simply say he was evil."

The cut in my chest ached. I ran my hand over the dried blood on my shirt.

"Sky was a once-in-a-generation talent," Watson said. "No one would touch a politician under his protection. He was the best insurance money could buy. Law enforcement wished they could afford him."

His brown eyes took on a reddish hue. "Dark Sky could name his own salary but he wanted autonomy. He robbed banks, killed civilians and murdered his friends one by one, anyone who could stop him. He gained a following. The rest is in your history books."

I stared. Then I gasped. "The Dragon Uprising?"

"He set the city on fire," Watson said. "He caused the dragon ban."

Wyatt's broken twigs fell from his hands.

"The Brick House formed a posse," Watson said. "It wasn't quick and it wasn't bloodless, but we burnt Dark Sky to ash, and he should have stayed that way forever. No light, no heat. Locked underground. Instead..." Watson shredded bark with his claws. "Someone woke those ashes up."

I swallowed.

"A dragon can speak to you inside your mind," he said, "Especially if you're another reptile. That's what happened to me. Dark Sky made me his puppet until he flew away and I snapped out of it. I'll never forgive him, never."

It was a funny thing for a tiny lizard to say.

The beardie twisted his tail into a knot. "The question is, who unsealed the secret door? Why didn't I see this coming?"

"Um." I looked away. "Was it us?"

Below us, my little brothers screamed with laughter as a cicada buzzed inside their teepee.

"I blame myself," Watson said. "In all my years as Director, I heard the dragons' thoughts and felt their words in the air but I never let them influence me. I was good at my job." He stamped a front foot. "Dark Sky tricked me, but I'll make it up. I'll get him back."

His words dropped into my chest with a hollow thud.

"Boys." Mom stood under the Catalpa, chin raised. "You two watch Keller and James. I'm getting an ice water."

I swept up a hand to cover the blood on my shirt and gave her a little salute, pretending life wasn't spiraling out of control.

"To answer your question, no," Watson said.

"What question?" I said.

"The cellar door was melted shut with dragon fire. You're nowhere near strong enough to have opened it."

I felt totally confused. And guilty, despite what he'd said.

Twigs snapped under our tree.

My mind was far off when I looked down to check on my little brothers. What I saw was very strange. Our neighbor Desmona stared up at me. From my angle, her head looked small, like it was stuck on an inflatable body.

But it got weirder.

The chunky security guard was holding a chainsaw.

CHAPTER 8
BEAR WITH CHAINSAW

Desmona spat on the ground as I tried to make sense of what I was seeing. "No little kids in my half of this tree," she said.

Below us, James and Keller came out of the teepee.

"Where is puppy?" James looked around for the chihuahua.

"No puppy," Desmona said. "He doesn't like loud noises." She pulled the chainsaw's cord but it didn't start. She pulled it again. And again. Wyatt laughed. Maybe our horrible day was taking a turn toward comedy.

"Who is this jackanapes?" Watson hissed. "An enemy of your family?"

I didn't have a good answer.

Des set the chainsaw on the sidewalk, put a foot on it, and reached for the starter cord.

"Look, a bear trying to touch its toes." Wyatt snickered.

She grabbed for the cord and missed. I fought a smile. Then she closed her eyes, sucked in her stomach...and snatched the cord. The chainsaw growled to life and she chopped it back and forth, grinning. "GET DOWN NOW."

James started crying as Keller grabbed his hand and backed away.

I couldn't believe what I was seeing. How could someone so ridiculous be so dangerous? Hard to say what might have happened. I pictured myself riding the Catalpa down as it crashed into the street. But we'd forgotten about Watson.

"I'll take care of this," he rasped.

His eyes became hard points of light and he arched his back.

Then he jumped.

Desmona was sneering, holding the chainsaw at waist level, when the lizard launched himself. With a hiss like soda pop, his spiky collar exploded around a scaly smile.

"RAAAA!" he screamed as he crashed into her face.

When Mom walked out the front door, all four of us boys were standing on the sidewalk, staring at whitish chainsaw gouges that looked like claw marks. She walked over, sipping her ice water and smiling.

"What have we got here, an obstacle course for ants?"

We'd done it before—and it's very entertaining.

"Not exactly," I said.

"Mean lady chop at us!" James said.

"She tried to cut us down," Keller added.

"But we handled it," I said.

"Yeah," Wyatt added. "No big deal."

Mom frowned. "I hope you didn't let her push you around. Did you stand your ground like we discussed?"

"Yeah."

"And you told her not to bother you, firmly and politely?"

"Yup."

"And it worked?"

"It did."

"Why..." She put a hand to her mouth. "That's wonderful! I'm so proud of you. We need to celebrate this."

Mom herded us all inside for sparkling lemonade. Luckily she didn't look too closely at the scarred sidewalk—or notice the chainsaw partly hidden in the high grass where Desmona had flung it as she fled shrieking.

When Dad got home a few hours later, we sat down to a family dinner. Keller and James never stopped talking the whole time, describing the epic battle between good and evil, and their stories were so fantastic that when they wove in a flying lizard (with a cape) and multiple chainsaws, Mom and Dad were already laughing.

That was a relief.

As soon as I could, I slunk away from the table. Wyatt caught up with me on the balcony outside our bedroom where we'd agreed to meet Watson. The beardie crouched on the steel railing, staring at the Kansas City skyline. I followed his gaze, expecting to see a dragon soaring over skyscrapers. Instead I saw a glowing sunset layered with cotton-ball clouds. Watson jumped down and crawled inside without a word.

Unexpected.

Wyatt and I looked at each other and followed. The lizard crawled through our room and down the hallway. Past a spare bedroom, past a bathroom. Past the splash room with the hot tub.

"Uh, Watson?" Keller and James would stampede through any second.

He skipped the art gallery and workout room, turning into the second floor library at the end of the hall. I nudged the door shut behind us as the lizard stood up on his hind legs and sighed, scanning the walls.

Other than a stone fireplace and two windows, the room was floor to ceiling books. We'd added a few of our own but most of the leather-bound volumes had come with the house. A round table stood in deep carpet in the middle of the room with armchairs hunkered around.

"Pull *The Voyage of the Dawn Treader* off that shelf," Watson said. "Slim green book, well worn."

When I obeyed, a ten foot section of the wall swung open.

Watson smiled as we jumped. "Welcome to my office. We can talk in here."

He crawled through the opening.

Even more books lined the walls, including the hinged wall that swung shut behind us. Framed photos of hard-eyed beardies hung over another fireplace. A wheeled cart stood in one corner, covered with glasses, beakers and liquids in bottles. There were no windows. Watson climbed into a tiny chair by a foot-high desk. I would've said it was a play desk made for dolls except a slim notebook computer waited on top.

"Have a seat." He gestured to a couple leather armchairs and I sank into worn upholstery. As Watson's claws click-clacked his keyboard, I wondered if any other kids had sat here. None of them could've been in as much trouble as me. The old leather was comfortable, and my eyelids sagged a little.

I imagined I was someone else, far away, soaring through orange and purple clouds. I'd escaped against all odds, and my heart pounded like crazy. *Freedom.* Soon, if I flew closer to the sun, I'd be strong again, and I'd never have to be sorry for what I'd done. The fading sunset brushed my skin, and I filled my lungs with shimmering air–

"Wake up." Wyatt snapped his fingers.

Watson was looking at me strangely.

"So go ahead," my brother said. "What's Dark Sky's weak point? I'm gonna help fight him."

Attack was Top Ten's first option, every day of the week and twice on Sunday. Not a bad strategy, I thought. Get the enemy in your sights and go right at him. Close in fast, rip with your teeth and claws, tear him to shreds. I shook my head to focus. Since when had I adopted this code of crazy aggression?

"Ironically, extreme heat is a weakness and to a lesser degree, water," Watson said. "Best answer, though, is more dragons. Sure you are. Anything else?"

I narrowed my eyes, trying to follow the lizard's answers. Had he just agreed to let Wyatt fight Dark Sky? My brother's smug expression said yes he had. Oh well. I had questions of my own.

"How did Dark Sky know root beer would wake his ashes?" I said. "Do his flames have dangerous toxins? And what do you think he's doing now?"

Watson's talons tap-tapped his hardwood desk. "He knew any carbonated soda full of chemicals and acid would be toxic enough to get him back on his feet. Yes, they sure do—oily and corrosive. Gaining strength for another theft and murder spree."

I sorted the lizard's answers, A, B, C. He seemed to get some kind of twisted joy from rattling them off.

"Great, my turn," Watson said. "The ironic thing about a total ban on dragons is that to stop a known felon, a criminal dragon, you need more dragons. So it goes without saying that everything I'm about to tell you is illegal. Now let's talk agenda."

He ticked items off on his claws. "First thing in the morning, we find a dragon handler. There's only one choice. Second, we locate an ash stash. Third, we wake our dragons. Fourth, we train. Fifth, we fight Dark Sky and burn him"—his claws became spiky fists—"back to ash. We've got three days, maybe four, before Kansas City turns red for the second time. Once he soaks up enough heat and eats enough flesh, he will be almost unstoppable."

I sank deeper into my chair and pressed a hand to my aching chest. All of a sudden, I felt like I was falling, hurtling through space, wind rushing over me. Pinpoints of light danced across my eyelids. Under my feet, the Brick House gave a shudder—or maybe that was part of the dream. Something thumped my shoulder and I peeled my eyes open.

"You ok?" Wyatt slapped me again.

"Stop hitting me. I'm just tired."

"Get some sleep, kid." Watson gave me a look that was almost kind. "We've got a big day ahead of us." He seemed less on edge now that he'd laid out his horrific plans.

"BOYS." Dad's voice came from somewhere below. "LIGHTS OUT."

Wyatt and I jumped up. Watson clawed to my shoulder like a scaly parrot as we pushed into the corner library. The secret portal swung shut behind us and we rushed down the hall. The sudden movement made my head swim.

As my head hit the pillow, I had the impression the beardie was saying something. He got momentarily quiet when Dad came in to hug us goodnight, but he was talking again as I snuggled between the sheets. Still talking as I drifted off.

"We'll show Dark Sky...who's the best...at fighting." I murmured.

I wanted Watson to think I was listening, but I'd barely heard a word he said. It's hard to focus when your whole life is veering out of control, swerving across lanes, crashing through the median onto a road darker than you can even understand.

CHAPTER 9
SEARCHING THE RUINS

A girl lay in a bed by a window, moonlight spilling down her back. The room was warm with July heat, but she was wrapped in blankets, face turned to the wall. Everything was so quiet and strange that I was careful not to get too close. Her whole existence was a mystery. At the same time, seeing her was not a surprise.

I needed to ask her a question. I didn't have much time.

"Who are you?" As soon as I opened my mouth, I knew it was the wrong thing to say.

Slowly, she rolled to face me.

I held my breath, expecting something horrible—but she was just a girl about my age. Her eyes were closed, face bruised and pale. As I watched, her skin went greenish-yellow and she groaned.

"Hey, wake up," I said.

Her lashes flickered but her eyes didn't open.

I tried again. "What's your name?" Maybe if I found the right words, the scene would change.

She whispered and I leaned in.

"I'm no one, no one, no one." A tear ran down her face.

My fingers brushed her elbow and I jerked back, afraid I'd catch whatever sickness she had. The girl gave a little shudder. Her mouth hung slightly open. Her shoulders were still. I didn't need to touch her pale forehead to know she was dead.

Something inside me felt dead too.

When I woke up, shivering, I'd never been happier to realize it was just a dream.

A short time later, Watson stood on his hind legs in a crate tied to the handlebars of my ten-speed bike. "I've explored pyramids and steered a river barge, but this is a first," the lizard said. "Try and pedal faster."

"What'd you tell Mom?" Wyatt cruised next to us on his orange stunt bike with pegs.

"That we're riding to the park," I muttered.

We turned onto a circle drive overlooking the West Bottoms, a maze of railroad tracks and towering buildings by the Missouri River.

"Back in the Pendergast Era," Watson said, "the Kansas City mafia would meet here to talk with the ladies and arrange contract killings. Made it easy for us to find them."

"Sounds fun," I said.

Wyatt rolled his eyes at me. I glared at him.

Making plans and setting them in motion seemed to energize the beardie. He'd become chatty in a teacher kind of way. Usually I'd be interested in history, but I was off my game today.

"We let Azarel deal with the mafia," Watson said. "He could more than hold his own and it helped that he was partly human."

"Whoa," Wyatt said. "The dragon dude is only partly human."

"Yeah, makes sense." I was struggling to focus.

I'd woken with a lump in my throat, my chest aching, and a lizard whispering in my ear. A terrible way to wake up. The Brick House had seemed out of sorts, creaky and quiet in turns as I dragged myself downstairs. I'd had just one piece of toast for breakfast, Wyatt elbowing me and chewing loudly, Watson clawing me under the table. A bad start to the day all around.

But I needed to snap out of it, I knew that.

Far below us, a train rushed down a track and a UPS truck navigated side streets. A large bus pulled up to a building with candy-striped awnings and people poured out. ANTIQUE TOURS was stenciled on the bus in big letters.

"He's not down there," Watson said. "This isn't his kind of place anymore."

"What is his kind of place?" I gripped my handlebars.

"Old, empty, forgotten." Watson frowned. "Like him."

That didn't sound like a very great dragon handler, someone good at training and bossing dragons. What was the guy's name again? I wished I'd paid closer attention. Maybe if I'd been less focused on shaking off my dream, trying to forget the girl's face. Maybe if the Brick House hadn't been so hushed and tense. Then I wouldn't have kept missing clues that could've saved a life.

We stopped our bikes at the foot of a gravel drive that curved up a hill. A mansion sagged at the top, strangled by vines. Windows and doors boarded up.

"We've never come this far east." I scrubbed at my heart with one hand and spun my pedals in reverse, wishing my chest would hurt less.

"If you pedal up that hill right now, maybe we'll get back before your mom misses you," Watson said. "But she'll notice sooner or later."

"Why?" Wyatt prided himself on his sneakiness.

"Unless we stop Dark Sky, the whole city will notice." The

lizard looked sad. "The police and fire department and emergency rooms will notice the most."

Great, I thought. More bad feelings.

But I leaned into the pedals as we rolled up the empty hill. At the top, we leaned our bikes on trees and circled the mansion. Watson crouched on my shoulder, and Wyatt and I took turns tugging on plywood. The openings were nailed shut, but when I kicked a boarded-up window, mortar showered down.

Top Ten grabbed a half-exposed brick with both hands and yanked. He fell over backwards holding it, which made me smile for the first time that day. I pulled another brick free and the whole window leaned in its frame.

"Why do we need Az—Azar—what's the guy's name?" I said.

Watson sniffed. "Azarel Ahazi. I may *seem* invincible, but I'm no match for a full-grown dragon. Azarel, on the other hand—he's made a career showing up at firefights."

Wyatt and I tugged the window out of its square black socket. Stale cellar air flowed out. A dog barked one block over and I glanced around, my heart hammering. The cut in my chest came to life, pricking like a handful of needles.

"Wouldn't this be considered breaking and entering?" I said.

"Absolutely." Watson crawled through the opening. "Follow me."

I peered in, patting my pockets, but they were empty. It was probably the most perilous day of my entire life and I'd rolled out of bed in a daze without packing even a toothpick.

"Good thing I planned ahead." Wyatt pulled on his batman headlamp.

I sighed and followed him.

We found ourselves in a small, filthy room with no door. I

shook mortar out of my hair and Wyatt snorted cobwebs. A cricket chirped in a corner, then went silent. There were tiny crunching sounds and Watson burped.

My brother shone his headlamp around. "Hey, that's not a wall, that's a barricade." He climbed on a broken sawhorse and shoved hard. The wall moved. He shoved again and something crashed on the other side.

Watson snorted. "So much for stealth."

Wyatt's voice came from the far side of the hole. "I smashed an old toilet in half." He laughed. "Luckily, no one was using it."

"Hilarious." I tensed my fingers and started climbing.

On the other side, we stood in a long, dark hallway lined with doors.

"Move fast and check each room," Watson said. "If you see movement, jerk your head back to safety. Azarel has cat-like reflexes—and who knows what kind of mental state he's in? Let's avoid any sad accidents. Wyatt, take the left. Conley, take the right."

"I don't have a light," I pointed out.

"Wyatt, we'll be right behind you," Watson said.

Top Ten didn't look happy.

The basement rooms were empty except for broken chairs and tables. A half-collapsed flight of stairs groaned as we climbed in the headlamp's beam. On the second floor, we stood in another door-lined hall. Wyatt was enjoying himself by now. The power of his lamp had gone to his head. He trotted down the hall ahead of us, ducking in each room.

"Slow down," Watson rasped.

Wyatt pretended not to hear. "Chairs stacked for a bonfire... a collection of paint cans... Hello, a spooky table with candles."

Watson dug his claws into my shoulder. I knocked my

shins on something as I tried to catch up. Wyatt disappeared around a corner, taking the light with him.

"What the heck," I said.

"Beast guts," Watson muttered.

I took a few slow steps in the dark, then my brother's shape reappeared, walking backwards. Now he was showing off.

"Oh man!" he said in a loud, shaky voice. "I didn't see you there."

Watson tensed up on my shoulder. "Is he joking?"

"Probably. He likes to freak people out."

My brother stood in the center of the hall, talking around the corner to someone neither of us could see. Someone who didn't exist.

"We didn't mean to bother you." He pressed his hands together in an apology. "Um, you look partly human. Are you Azarel?"

There was no answer.

This was getting to be a little much.

"Get moving," Watson hissed in my ear.

I crunched closer to Wyatt. Another couple steps and I could steal that headlamp right off his face. I was reaching out to snatch it when he turned and darted past me. He stopped ten feet away, breathing hard.

"Get back here, faker," I said.

The floor creaked behind me. I turned as a big man with bleached-blond hair stepped around the corner and stood in the shadows, sizing me up with flat yellow eyes.

CHAPTER 10
DRAGONKIN

Wyatt's headlamp shone in the tall man's face, where neck tattoos twisted in the shadow of his grizzled jaw.

"Um, how's it going?" I backed away as I tried to keep my voice from shaking.

"Where'd you come from?" The stranger rolled his head around slowly like he expected a portal to open in a wall.

Wyatt's chin shook. His headlamp danced over the man's skull t-shirt and grimy jeans.

"Lemme ask you again, how'd you get in?" The guy sounded like he had marbles in his mouth and switchblades in his fists. "It's nailed down tight. What'd you do, use a crowbar?"

Wyatt looked at me helplessly.

"Uh, we found an open window." I glanced right and left, trying to catch Watson's eye. When I patted my shoulder blades, he was gone.

"Not a chance, impossible." The man bared his teeth. The

front row was filed sharp. "You're lyin' to me, so I'll ask one more time. How'd—you—get—in?"

His words pricked my chest like nails. My face tingled and I realized I was grinning—and not in a nice way.

"Don't push me," I said through my teeth.

"Speak up, runt." The stranger took a step closer.

So did I.

Anger curled my fingers into claws and pushed me up on my toes.

"THIS PLACE IS ROTTING WHERE IT STANDS," I yelled. "We found an open window—it wasn't hard. Get away from me or you'll rot here too!"

Wyatt gasped behind me.

The big man froze. He hadn't expected this.

And if you lay a hand on me, I thought, you'll lose that hand. We'll see if you're expecting that.

He shifted back and forth on the balls of his feet, twitchy-quick for someone so big.

"That's your story, huh," he said, not backing down.

So he wasn't afraid of me. Well, he was about to learn very quickly. I narrowed my eyes, licked my lips and waited.

Behind me, my brother backed away. Light from his head-lamp pooled under my feet.

The stranger rooted through his pockets, his yellow eyes locked on mine.

"Hold that thought," he hissed. "Don't move an inch." His corner of the hall was suddenly empty.

I blinked as a lizard scampered toward me. "No need to go down fighting." The little guy clawed his way to my shoulder. "Now run."

"But why?" I took a slow step backwards.

"I said go!" he snapped.

Shadows swirled at the edges of my eyes. Then Wyatt's horrified face jerked me awake. Just like that, I was afraid. My scalp prickled as we bolted down the rotten steps. We rushed down the hall, climbed the barricade and crawled into the sunlight. Leaning against the house, breathing hard, I noticed Wyatt staring at me.

"Let's be on our way," Watson said.

"Guess that wasn't Azarel," I said.

"Not Azarel, but he was *like* Azarel, so we got lucky."

"Maybe *he* got lucky," I muttered.

Watson gave me a long glance. "When did you get so tough?"

He had a point. What had I been doing—trying to get us all killed?

We headed for the bikes.

"What did you mean, that dude was *like* Azarel?" Wyatt yelled over the wind as we flew down the hill away from the mansion.

Watson hunkered down in his milk crate. "Live around dragons for awhile, you learn some nasty tricks. Being unemployed doesn't help your attitude. Dragon handlers don't tend to get better with age."

Wyatt stood up on his pedals and frowned.

"Azarel is an older guy, like a grandpa?" I said, fighting to stay focused. Little bursts of anger were still surging through my chest.

"All the dragon handlers are old now, do the math." Watson shook his head like he was disappointed. "They age indefinitely, but not like fine wine. Turn left here."

We rolled through a parking lot with potholes big enough for ducks to swim in. An empty school sprawled in front of us, surrounded by armies of dandelions. A faded sign showed what might have been a decapitated person with a broken leg falling down stairs while being electrocuted.

"Cool," Wyatt said.

I had to agree.

"Wait, pedal back to the sidewalk," Watson hissed.

Wyatt pointed at the sign. "Aww, we just got here."

"Just do it."

As we bumped across the parking lot, a black SUV cruised past at turtle speed. SECURITY was stenciled on the side.

"Uh oh." For some reason, the car made me think about Mom and Dad. It made me feel more cautious, less hot-blooded.

"Uh oh is right." Watson snorted. "Your reflexes are like dragons in the arctic." He ducked into the milk crate. "If that officer talks to you, you're on your own."

The car rolled away.

I gave a sigh of relief.

It turned into a driveway, reversed, and came back.

Wyatt leaned low over his handlebars. "Should we run for it?"

"No way." My feet felt like lead. In fact, my whole body was heavy and I wasn't up to a high speed chase.

The security car stopped next to us. The passenger window rolled down and a pudgy face with a swollen eye looked out.

You've gotta be kidding me, I thought, and something twisted in my chest.

"You kids are a little far from home," Desmona sneered.

"We're just riding our bikes," I said. "We know our way around."

"You're a little liar. You want to break into that building, don't you?"

My fingertips tingled as I tapped her door. A hot, hungry

feeling rubbed my ribs. "You know," I said, "if you were roasted just right, you might even taste good."

"What?" Desmona jerked away. "You little creep." She fumbled in the car, coming up with a 48-ounce drink. I smiled and took a moment to glance at the driver. A big, mean-looking man stared back at me.

"Where's your pet lizard?" Desmona was keeping her distance now.

I put an elbow on the top of the door and leaned in.

"He's very close by, looking forward to meeting you again."

Her face kind of wobbled in on itself. Then she fake-laughed, Hahaha, but it was too late. I'd seen the fear in her eyes.

"Go home," she snapped.

I just smiled. A big, toothy grin.

She rolled up her window and the car pulled away.

"Well, that was satisfying," I said.

"What's wrong with you?" Wyatt gave me a look.

"Let's get moving," Watson said from the crate.

We circled the block, left our bikes in a stand of weed trees and snuck back.

"This school has been closed for years," Watson said from my shoulder. "So it shouldn't be hard to get into."

"Right, cool," I said, trying to focus.

Wyatt tiptoed through a patch of shade. "You think Azarel's here?"

"I'm giving it my best shot, kid," Watson said. "Azarel likes the urban scene and he prefers large buildings." The beardie's head jounced up and down as I walked. My feet kept finding things to trip on.

"Which dragons did Azarel handle?" I asked.

Watson's eyes stared into mine, inches away. "Which one do you think?"

We stood in front of a heavy metal door, spray-painted an ugly pink. Wyatt shoved it open, switched on his headlamp, and stepped through.

The lizard dug his claws into my shoulder.

I gritted my teeth and followed.

CHAPTER 11
MANHUNT

The school looked like it had been plundered by vikings and left to rot. Badly-spelled graffiti crawled across walls. Dim light gleamed through boarded up windows and the floor squished under our feet. We walked down a long hallway where every metal locker stood open like a poltergeist had run through. Now and then, Wyatt's lamp lit up a dark patch and we'd circle a hole in the floor.

"Something is the matter with you," he whispered.

Glued to my shoulder, Watson pretended to be deaf.

"Naw," I muttered. "Just not feeling great. Kind of on edge and..." I licked my lips. "I'm hungry."

Top Ten's light hit my face, then he looked away.

At the middle of the main hall, we pushed through splintered double doors and stood in a high, dark room with a floor that ran downhill. I expected to see a sink hole at the bottom until Wyatt's lamp shone on rows of bolted-down chairs. We stopped in front of a stage with metal scaffolding that disappeared above a stained curtain.

At center stage was a row of empty liquor bottles, lined up like they were on display.

Wyatt tugged the scaffolding while Watson clawed his way up a curtain.

I paced the auditorium stage. It was the perfect moment for a little speech, but my words boiled around in my head and came out strange.

"No one gets in my way," I muttered. "I'll eat whatever I want and no one will ever tell me no again."

"What are you mumbling about?" my brother said.

I itched my shoulder blades and decided not to repeat myself.

Watson was sniffing the empty whiskey bottles. "Let's keep moving."

Getting upstairs took longer than it should have. Broken machinery covered the floor like a lazy tornado had twisted through. We finally found a stairway where snapped-off wooden bannisters leaned like giant skis.

The lizard nodded. "Yes, this could be it."

On the second floor, we walked onto a gym balcony and stood on wooden bleachers. Brown-green water pooled in the aisles like oil. On the hardwood court below, thick climbing ropes ran floor to ceiling.

"I was always good at that," Wyatt whispered.

On the third floor, sunlight filtered through holes in the ceiling. We found a ladder bolted to a wall and climbed onto the flat tar roof. Small trees sprouted from the gutters.

Then we froze.

"Those sirens sound far away," Wyatt said hopefully.

"Getting closer," Watson said. "Head to that open attic."

At the far end of the roof, creaky stairs descended to an upside-down V of a room. Columns towered like trees and moss covered the floorboards. Between the slanted roof and the top of the wall, a line of light shone through. The sirens had stopped.

"We're probably safe now." Without planning to, I slumped to the floor, elbows on my knees, head in my hands. Feverish warmth swept over me.

"What's wrong?" Watson's voice tickled my ear.

I didn't bother to answer. Words take energy.

"This isn't good," Wyatt said—but he wasn't talking about me.

I dragged myself upright and peered through the gap as a security car rolled across the parking lot. My heart revved up like an engine and I gulped deep breaths, filling my lungs with hot July air.

Top Ten creaked to the far wall. "Another car on this side. We're trapped."

I glanced at Watson. "Let's ambush them."

"No, we keep our heads down." The beardie frowned at me. "Use your head, kid. Security guards don't come into abandoned buildings. We keep searching and wait them out."

I glanced hungrily at the cars, but Watson's claws pricked my shoulder. He was getting irritating. I had to remind myself he was on my side.

Back on the ground level, the splintered doors of the auditorium appeared in the headlamp's glow. My fingers were on the knob when I realized we weren't alone. The door was moving, swaying on its hinges. Every muscle in my body stiffened.

"Back away," Wyatt whispered. "Someone's in there."

My spine tingled as I bared my teeth. Of course someone was in there, and they were about to regret it. But then something unexpected happened. A powerful light clicked on and shone through the cracks.

"STAY WHERE YOU ARE AND PUT YOUR HANDS IN THE AIR! DON'T MOVE OR WE'LL SHOOT!"

The door began to open.

Come on, I thought. I'm right here waiting...

But at the same time, in a different corner of my mind, someone was screaming. Run! Run! Run!

"Run!" Watson hissed.

Wyatt gave my hand a jerk.

I teetered on a razor-thin line.

Terror took over.

We raced into the dark.

CHAPTER 12
OUT OF THE FRYING PAN, INTO THE BOILER

Fists pumping, we circled a hole and bolted up the ski-stairs. Behind us, someone kept shouting. The voice sounded angry.

"COME BACK NOW. WALK TOWARD ME WITH YOUR HANDS IN THE AIR."

We slowed to a walk and I found myself laughing like a crazy person. At the same time I was so scared I could hardly speak. Hands on my knees, I drew ragged breaths.

"I can't believe we're running from security guards."

Wyatt giggled, sounding as silly as I did. "Guess we're too fast for them."

Watson wasn't laughing though. Not so much as a sniff.

We stopped walking and listened. I wondered if we were going too far. Maybe we should turn ourselves in. I narrowed my eyes. *Or maybe we should crouch in the shadows, wait until they're right next to us, and lunge for their—*

"Something's not right here," Watson muttered. His claws were embedded in my t-shirt. "People don't rush in with guns blazing. It's not like the old days."

For a few seconds, we might have shuffled back down the hallway with our heads down and our hands up. Instead, we strolled in the opposite direction, hidden by the darkness. Each time we passed an office or closet, we checked for movement—because Azarel might still be there.

A powerful beam of light entered the hall behind us.

"WE KNOW YOU'RE IN HERE." It was the angry voice.

"YOU CAN'T HIDE FOREVER." A second voice, calm but nasty.

My heart did a backflip while my feet watched.

Watson's claws dug into my well-worn shoulder. "Get moving!"

We ran again. The voices and light chased us like noisy ghosts. At the end of the hall, the darkness on the stairs was thick and welcoming.

"Let's go down," I said.

In the basement, the darkness was oily and deep. Wyatt's headlight was getting dim, and I thought the cluttered hall would be perfect for what I had in mind. Then my brother pulled open a door and disappeared. What was he doing?

I bent my fingers into claws and followed. We stood in an ugly bathroom. Peeling paint hung from every stall, and smashed latrines dotted the floor like ice chunks. My brother was reading words scrawled across a wall in black marker:

YOU'RE TOO LATE.

His headlamp went out. "Come back on!" He smacked the light but it didn't obey.

No problem, I knew my eyes would adjust to the dark, gathering up the tiny shards of light. Showing me what others couldn't see. Any second now...

Something crunched in a corner. I felt surprised I couldn't see what it was.

"Stay quiet, Wyatt," I breathed.

"That wasn't me."

"And it isn't me," Watson said in my ear.

Something rustled close by and I realized I wasn't as tough as I thought. Something was wrong with me. I definitely couldn't see in the dark. I didn't want to attack anyone. I didn't even want to be here. I just wanted to get away, out of this rotting school, and ride my bike home and take some medicine for the angry throbbing in my chest.

"Follow my voice." Watson thumped to the floor. "Over here. This way."

When I took a step, I tripped and fell with a crash. Tile shards cut my palms. My face brushed grimy tile.

Behind me, something stepped closer.

No, no, no, thumped my heart.

"Over here," Watson hissed.

I crawled toward him as Wyatt pushed the door open. The room changed from black to grey and I staggered to my feet. As I shoved my way out, I glanced over my shoulder.

Two green lights hung in a corner like fireflies. But they weren't fireflies.

Green eyes in the dark.

The door swung shut.

In the hallway, Watson's silhouette wove around empty boxes and metal pipes that hung from the ceiling. We ran after him. My mouth felt stuffed with cotton. Behind us, the bathroom door creaked open. Ahead of us, voices echoed down more stairs.

"We're trapped," I gasped.

"On the bottom level, Des," Angry Voice said. His walkie

talkie crackled. "I can hear 'em. The hellions are close by." His spotlight splashed our floor.

I felt Watson claw his way to my shoulder as I whirled back and forth and—wait, right next to us on the wall—I jerked open a closet-sized door. Instead of hangers, more stairs led deeper underground. Without a word, we dove down. My fingers brushed cold concrete as I groped around a corner. A second later, we stood on a bumpy floor, light filtering from a high barred window.

Nowhere else to run.

In a cave-like space on our right, a pulley hung from the ceiling. On our left, something like a huge rusty can lay on its side, twenty feet long and ten feet high. Pipes ran from the can into the walls and ceiling. In one end a hinged iron door stood half open.

Watson swiveled his head right and left. "The old boiler room. A dead end."

But maybe he was wrong. I looked up—and saw the last exit.

Rickety metal stairs climbed the wall, partly hidden by the boiler. At the top was a steel service door, sunlight threading its edges.

Hope flooded my chest, burning away the shadows.

Wyatt and I rushed up the stairs and yanked but the door didn't move. Words were scrawled on its surface.

ABANDON HOPE, ALL YE WHO ENTER HERE.

Oh no oh no oh no.

As I panicked, I felt my fingers curving into claws and there wasn't anything I could do. Here and now I'd fight them. Oh well, it was for the best. I was hungry.

Outside the boiler room, someone swore.

"Hey Crane, follow me down." A flashlight swept the wall. "Yeah, all the way down, under the beasting, blood-gutsy basement. Hurry up." He coughed and blew his nose.

I took a slow, hungry step toward the unseen man.

"Stop." Watson crouched in the shadows by the wall. He tapped a wooden post that leaned against the huge metal can. I shook my head no, and he tapped it again, collar flaring angrily. What had he found? Gold bars, a suitcase full of cash? I leaned closer.

Not one but two wooden posts leaned on the boiler. Between them stretched slats of wood. The ladder led up into shadows.

Not interesting. I'd turned away when the beardie's weight hit me in the back. A claw pricked my earlobe. Another needled my neck. How was I to know this little lizard was so heavy... and so deadly?

"Up the ladder, bub," Watson snarled.

I snarled back and started climbing.

CHAPTER 13
THE END OF THE LINE

A blanket of dust covered the boiler, dotted with dead beetles and a mouse skeleton. The dirt muffled my footsteps as Wyatt topped the ladder.

Fuming, I glanced right and left.

"Don't even think about jumping down," Watson growled in my ear.

Feet crunched into the boiler room. Wyatt crouched and froze, one of his shoes hanging over the edge. Smells of dead insects and dry-rot filled my nose.

A flashlight shone on the ceiling.

"Nothin' here but storage," Angry Voice said from the cave area.

The boiler boomed and vibrated under me as someone struck it.

"What about that door?" the cool, nasty voice said.

"Locked, like all the gut-hashed others."

"We've wasted enough time. " The flashlight played along the boiler and shone on the ladder a few inches under Wyatt. The beam jerked back to the floor.

"Let's roll, Jake," Nasty Voice said. "The boss can get those kids later." Metal creaked. Out of the corner of my eye, I watched a shape climb the stairs bolted to the wall.

"Crane, I said it was beasting locked."

"You wanna walk all the way back, go ahead."

If Crane had looked over his shoulder, he would have seen Wyatt crouching ten feet away. Instead, he read the writing on the door.

"Abandon hope, all ye who enter here," he muttered. "Guts to that. We're gonna *exit* here." He pulled a short, thick weapon out of his belt and lifted it with both hands. It looked sort of like a gun, but silver and with extra levers—and the barrel was shaped like a hollow star. He pulled the trigger—and a roaring ball of fire blasted the door off its hinges.

Light flooded the room. Metallic crashes echoed outside.

I blinked in the sudden glare.

Crane put the blaster away and laughed. "Skipped three times on the asphalt and crushed a smart car." He disappeared as Jake's big, shadowy shape hauled itself up the rickety stairs. Outside, a car motor roared to life. A hot breeze blew through the doorway and stirred up dust. Watson crawled off my shoulder. I sat up coughing.

They got away, I thought—but I wasn't sure I cared. I brushed dirt from my mouth and eyelashes. Wyatt stretched a foot down to the ladder's top rung, his eyes big. A minute later, we stood on the floor, staring at the sunny rectangle decorated with snapped-off hinges. The glaring sunlight helped me calm down.

"That was a weird gun." Wyatt shuddered.

"More noise, now," Watson said. "Shout. Kick the boiler."

We stared.

"They're already gone," I said. "We missed our chance to get them."

"We'll talk about that later, Conley Hoss." Watson's eyes flashed. "Now let's do what we came here to do." He stretched, cracking tiny knuckles.

I crossed my arms unhappily.

"You think Azarel is here," Wyatt volunteered.

"Aha," the beardie said. "You're catching on. Let's make it clear we're not leaving so he'll come find us. With a little luck..." He blinked.

"With a little luck, what?" Wyatt asked.

"Never mind."

"No, tell us," I said.

"Very well." Watson glared at me. "With a little luck, he'll let us finish talking."

"And if we're unlucky?" Our eyes burned into each other.

The lizard raised a clawed fist. "If we're unlucky, he'll kill us all—and he'll start with you."

CHAPTER 14
AZAREL

Wyatt smashed the boiler with a chain he'd found. The machine-gun rattle set me on edge. I grabbed a metal pipe from a corner and took a few half-hearted swings. My arms felt like papier-mâché. All I wanted was to curl up in the sun and take a nap.

Wyatt stopped hitting the boiler.

Watson cleared his throat. "Azarel, It's Watson Adagio from the Brick House."

Silence.

"We aren't looking for trouble."

Nothing.

The beardie's neck swiveled as he scanned the shadows.

"AZAREL!" His voice echoed in the concrete tunnel. "COME OUT AND TALK."

I hefted my metal pipe like a baseball bat, feeling grouchy. Behind me, the pulley in the storage area clinked. I spun on my heel, clenching the pipe. A foot scraped the floor to my right but when I turned—no one. Then someone snatched the heavy steel from my hands like a soda straw.

I whirled, hands up to shield my face.

The man was well over six feet tall, with close-cut black hair and dark brown skin. He wore black jeans and boots and a black overcoat. If his eyes had been closed, he might have faded in the shadows. Open, no one could miss him. They flashed like green traffic lights—but these lights were saying *Stop*, not *Go*. Resting on one shoulder was the steel pipe he'd taken from me.

I took a step back, fists balled up.

"Finally we catch up with each other, Watson." The man's voice was molasses poured over gravel, smooth with an edge of menace. "Two boys and a talking lizard. What an under-whelming trap." He chuckled and tossed the pipe in the air, catching it with his thumb and forefinger. "Been a while, Adagio. You used to travel with more firepower."

"Needless to say, a lot has changed." Watson raised a claw. "But if you're done, we need to have a word. A serious word— about a serious matter."

This better be good, Azarel's face said.

"Dark Sky."

"That's ancient history," Azarel snarled. "Get to the point. Yeah, you know what happened last century. You took the high road and I got out—friends dead, reputation shot. Congrats on finding me but I'm happy being lost, thanks."

Watson picked at his claws.

I took another slow step away from Azarel. Being near him gave me flashes of itchy heat. I felt ornery but uneasy, snappish but on a leash. I had the feeling that if I opened my mouth, I'd say something I'd regret—and that irritated me even more. No one should be able to make me sorry. I hated the guy's casual strength. The way he made me listen.

"The last few decades have been grand," Azarel said. "No postcards, no job offers, all fine by me. Now all of a sudden you track me down. And you brought mercenaries on your courtesy call."

Less molasses in his voice, more gravel.

Uh oh. I edged further away. Maybe it would be best to slip out while he was focused on the lizard.

Watson's spiky collar flared out. "Done whining yet?"

The bearded dragon and the big man scowled at each other. The lizard seemed to cast a giant shadow. I paused to see what would happen.

"Let me guess," Watson said. "You've lost your nearest and dearest, no stars in the dark night of your soul. You split your time between boredom and bourbon. Your silent protest against an unjust world. Tell me I'm not right."

The man's knuckles tightened on the steel pipe.

I allowed myself a thin smirk.

Then Azarel rubbed the back of his neck. He dropped the weapon. Worse still, he smiled. "I forgot you could be funny, Wats."

"I didn't forget what a drama king you were."

Azarel extended a pinkie finger and they shook.

"So, honestly, what do you want?" the big man asked. "Because drama aside, I don't socialize much." He yawned and sized me up as I leaned in the doorway, trying to act casual. My brother watched with his mouth hanging open.

"Given your love for grandstanding, here's what I offer," Watson said. "A chance to bury Dark Sky for good."

Azarel's sleepy eyes flamed back to life. "Dark Sky *is* buried for good."

"No. Dark Sky is free."

Something smoldered in my chest as the dragon handler stared down at the lizard. Then Azarel roared and punched the boiler. He hit the rusty metal again and again, until a collection of dents became a deep crease, then a gaping hole.

"Who turned him loose? Who did this?"

Watson licked his lips.

I hunched my shoulders, ready to dodge. Wyatt inched toward the door.

"It can wait." Azarel paced, running his hands through his hair. "If Sky is loose, I have things to do. Let's get out of this pit." He slapped his gloved palms together. "Where are we going? And who are these kids?"

"We're going to the Brick House," Watson said. "They live there."

"The Brick House," Azarel muttered.

The outside world had faded as the two strange creatures spoke to each other. Now the trance was broken. I felt very out of place.

"I'd like to think you're kidding," Azarel said. "But you're not, are you? Beast-guts, you know how I feel about the Brick House." He studied us. "And I'm not running a daycare, Adagio."

"You're not allowed to leave us here," Wyatt said. "Mom would get you in sooo much trouble and Dad, yeah, Dad, he used to box people, so–"

"Don't encourage him," Watson snapped. "Just try to ignore him."

Azarel smiled grimly.

I swallowed and bit my tongue.

CHAPTER 15
BLOWN COVER

Watson leaned his elbows on the milk crate and shut his eyes as we flew down a hill. If the bearded dragon actually had a beard, it would have been blowing in the hot wind.

Back on my bike I was feeling more like myself or at least I thought I was. Looking back, it's obvious that couldn't have been further from the truth.

Up ahead, Top Ten was pedaling his stunt bike fast, and I was struggling to keep up, covered in sweat. This shouldn't be so hard, I thought. Traffic was light and I pulled even with Wyatt as we turned down Truman Road. During the Dragon Uprising, President Truman had sent in the National Guard along with truckloads of food and millions in federal aid. His popularity would never be equaled, at least not in Kansas City.

Thinking about stuff like this helped me ignore what was going on.

Azarel marching behind us, dark coat flapping, long legs eating up the ground.

Me, swerving back and forth between rage and terror.

Dark Sky out there somewhere.

Wyatt and I rolled into the driveway, dropped our bikes and hurried inside.

"Don't worry, Mom, we're home," Wyatt yelled.

Lights were on, Bob Dylan was playing, and coffee steamed on the counter. The kitchen sinks were shiny and clean—even the one we'd chosen for our water guns. Mom's work for sure —but where was she? The whole house seemed silent, no screams, no splashing water, no toys crashing to the floor.

A numb, prickly feeling started at the crown of my head and crept over me, scuttling along my arms, squirming over my legs, writhing in my toes and fingertips.

What's going on? I asked the house. No answer.

"Let's check the basement," I said, trying to sound ok.

We ran out the swinging porch doors onto the deck as Dad parked his bike down in the driveway where rows of evergreens and iron fences hid us from our nosy neighbors. He wore a dress shirt and slacks, a messenger bag over one shoulder. It was great to see him looking so normal and unexciting. As he turned to climb the stairs, a tall, dark man with bright green eyes came striding down the alley. Wyatt and I held our breath as the two of them stared at each other.

"Nice coat," Dad said. "Bet it gets hot, though."

"I like the heat," said Azarel.

The silence got tense.

"Can I help you?" Dad said.

Watson squirmed on my shoulder.

"Yeah, you can as a matter of fact." Azarel raised one hand and pointed a couple fingers in our direction. "Maybe your boys could explain."

It sounded really bad. Like we'd done something terrible

and Azarel had escorted us home. I guess I'd known this moment would come.

"Umm, we can't find Mom," I said. "Maybe she's in the basement."

Dad gave me the cold, hard look that meant he wasn't buying it. "Let's check the basement, by all means. Just a minute, sir." He shot a look at Azarel as Wyatt and I clattered down the deck stairs and pushed open the basement door. Sure enough, squeaky voices echoed from inside.

Relief washed over me. The nasty, crawling sensation on my skin disappeared. Then I heard what they were saying.

"...and we throwed color-balls at the wall." It was Keller. "James hitted me in the head and I wrestled him a million seconds and the secret door opened up."

"Oh my goodness, did Daddy show you this?" It was Mom's voice.

"LITTLE DRAGON'S HOUSE, MOMMY," James yelled.

"We unlocked it all by ourselves," Keller said.

I skidded around our furnace, tripped over a roller-blade, and saw the disaster.

The secret tunnel stood open. Mom was on her knees in a yellow sun dress, looking inside as my brothers tugged her forward. A step-stool stood under the hidden button in the mortar. The floor was covered with rock dust and dented croquet balls.

The little devils.

Mom turned, her eyebrows arching.

A heavy hand fell on my shoulder. Wyatt squirmed next to me.

There was no escape.

"You boys have some explaining to do," Dad said.

Mom's look said that was a huge understatement. And she

hadn't even noticed the bearded dragon hanging on the front of my shirt.

Then, she did.

Watson nodded. "Hello, ma'am."

CHAPTER 16
COUNCIL OF WAR

Silence ruled the dining room table. Dad sat at the head, chair leaned back. Mom next to him, arms folded. Us boys hunched in a row like prisoners on trial.

I knew the trial was real.

Azarel slouched at the far end, tapping his knuckles on the table. Watson sat next to him in a booster seat. I knew they were taking the trial seriously too, because Watson was playing it straight, no wisecracks, and Azarel was gruffly polite. Leafy spinach, ice water, and fish crackers were on the table, along with a very damaging story.

Dad cleared his throat. "Dragons...you're telling us, dragons." He held up his hands.

"I'm just trying to figure out how this could be some kind of set-up," Mom said.

"But I really do talk," Watson said.

"I know, honey."

Foolish lizard. The rest of us knew better than to say a word.

Dad propped his chin on one hand. "Let's review. First, you met a talking lizard—that really *does* talk." He nodded to

Watson. "Second, you listened to his insane advice, opened a tunnel, discovered a secret cellar, and turned loose a killer dragon—or so you say.

Keller stared at the table. "It was the root beer's fault."

Azarel stopped twiddling his thumbs to give him a *good job* sign.

"Making things worse, you said nothing to me or your mother," Dad said. "Then you snuck off, ran from security guards, and brought home a stranger who may or may not be a couple centuries old."

Azarel shook his head in disgust.

Dad eyed his prisoners. "Capping it all off, you lured your mom down to the basement and terrified her by introducing Watson."

Mom rolled her eyes. "*Terrified* is a little strong."

"Those screams were a little loud," Dad said.

She sighed. "Their story really hangs together, though. Their lies are never this good."

"At last." Azarel leaned forward. "Now that you've realized your offspring are telling the truth, we can stop telling stories and skip to the part where we hunt Dark Sky."

He gave us a frightening smile.

"But wait," Mom said. "I'm not sure we've actually reached that—"

"The old fire-keg trick, I was thinking," Azarel told Watson.

"Really?" The beardie crinkled his forehead. "You think you've still got it?"

"Hang on a minute," Dad said.

"My powers have only increased with age," Azarel growled.

Watson shrugged.

"Ok, stop," Dad said. "You're wrong."

Azarel froze, one hand reaching for Watson. "Wrong about *what*?"

"The storytelling's not over," Mom said.

The dragon handler's eyes flicked between her and Dad.

"We need to know more," Dad said.

"From *you*," Mom said.

Huddled beside Wyatt, I was starting to feel nervous.

Azarel grabbed the arms of his chair. "You want *my* story?"

Dad and Mom glanced at each other, doing that weird thing where they talk without words.

"Yeah," Dad said.

Uh oh. I braced myself and Top Ten tensed up next to me. Had we pushed the dragon handler too far?

"You may as well know my dirt," Azarel growled.

Watson rolled his eyes. *Here we go,* he mouthed.

The huge man leaned back, dark coat hanging. "For fourteen years, Dark Sky was our best operative and that was saying a lot. The Kansas City Dragon Agency was at the top— and he kept us there. Snappish and headstrong, but I knew how to keep him in check. Then, one night..." Azarel's eyes became slits.

"I was gone on business, Romania or Hungary, it doesn't matter. When I got back, Kansas City was burning." He ran his hands over his cheekbones. "Later I saw the photos, bodies stacked in the streets. Blackened buildings, like gang violence —but these were gangs of dragons. When I arrived, there was no one here to tell me what had happened, not another living soul in the Brick House."

Watson lowered his head.

Azarel gripped the table edge. "The summer was quiet, no insects, no birds, just the house drawing long, slow breaths. I was at my desk when I heard the front door open. Claws scratched down the hall. When I saw Sky's face, I *knew*."

None of us said a word.

"Something different in his eyes. So hungry and wild, he

might as well have been covered in blood. Under the desk, I cocked my weapon." Azarel flicked his wrist. "Dark Sky had shrunk to come inside. Tiger-sized, to kill me. His own handler."

He sat upright, boots hitting the floor, and I squirmed in my seat.

"Sky came over the desk and I fired everything I had, right in his teeth, and threw myself out the window." Azarel passed a hand over his eyes. "I hid in the cellar," he whispered. "For awhile, I could hear him, my old friend, snarling at the door, but he didn't dare shrink any smaller. Not if he was going to face me. Darkness became my true friend that day."

He stared out the window like the story was over.

Keller chewed a fish cracker nervously, covering his mouth.

James hugged his stuffed fox, and Mom put an arm around him.

Watson cleared his throat but didn't speak.

I felt like there were gaps in the story. But as I inched my hand up, I did something unexpected. My raised arm wilted like a stalk of celery. My body became wobbly. I flopped out of my chair and onto the floor.

CHAPTER 17
NO EXCUSES, NO DELAYS

A grinning dragon slid through my window. A pale, dark-haired girl died slowly in a guest room. Over and over, playing tag in my head. Then adrenalin jolted through me and I spread my wings and soared away, flying through clouds, chasing the sun. Cumulous cliffs parted and I swept into a canyon of pure indigo. Scorching rays hit my skin like a shower of gold coins. Far below, rivers twisted like silver worms, reminding me of other worms, the human kind, with paper-thin hide enclosing their blood and guts and hearts—

Something tickled my chest.

The sky faded.

"...take him to the ER right now..." Mom said, far off.

"...not a bit of good, untreatable..." Watson rasped, closer.

"...wake our dragons and cut the anchor." Azarel—angry and close by.

I opened my eyes to see Watson's scaly face peering into mine. I was reclined on one of the couches in the great room, my feet propped on a stack of pillows. Pain explored each corner of my chest, taking its time.

"Honey, how are you?" Mom's cool fingers swept my forehead.

"At first we thought you were just really tired." Dad squeezed my knee.

Azarel leaned against the cave-sized fireplace, scowling. Wyatt perched on the edge of an armchair, kicking his feet. Muffled crashing came from upstairs.

"I should've checked you out sooner," Watson said. "Your cut is more than a scratch."

I pulled up my shirt and frowned. The puncture wound from Dark Sky's claw wasn't healing. The edges were yellowish-black, radiating outward like my whole chest was bruised.

"No wonder I've been feeling sick," I said. "Did you disinfect it, Mom?"

"I did, baby." Her eyes looked sad.

"What bad timing." I swung my legs to the floor and sat up slowly. "Hey, I feel better."

No one seemed convinced.

"Tell us about your dreams." Azarel pushed off the mantel to stand over me.

Confused, I looked over at Dad.

"It's ok, son."

"Um, well." It seemed rude for them to ask. Dreams are kind of private, especially the ones I'd been having. Then I had a weird thought. The Brick House knew about my dreams and it still liked me, so maybe things would be ok. But even so...

"I'm late for school," I said, "and I run into class—but I forgot my clothes."

No one seemed impressed, not even Wyatt, who normally would've laughed his head off. I tried again.

"I'm at the swimming pool–"

"You were talking in your sleep," Watson said.

"Oh."

"Tell us about the one with the dragon," Azarel said.

I didn't want to, but I did. I told how I looked out the window and the toothy reptile came lunging in. The room got very quiet as I reached the awful ending.

Azarel was rubbing his jaw. Watson squinted thoughtfully.

"Is that all?" Mom sounded hopeful.

I wanted to say yes, because reliving your own death is not fun. But the way they were looking at me, I knew I wouldn't get away with it.

"There's one where I'm in the sky...flying." I felt my face turning red.

Watson's eyes hardened to pinpoints.

Mom gave a little sigh and Dad took her hand.

Azarel leaned over me. "What did you see?"

"Clouds, the sun, fields and rivers way below."

"Are you with anyone?" Watson asked.

"I'm alone. Happy in the sun, soaking it in, getting stronger..."

Cold slithered down my spine as I finished the sentence.

"... and I snarled."

Watson's tail twitched. "Well, at least you were alone," he said. "You must have some idea what's happening, don't you?"

I sank back onto the couch. Maybe I understood. But I didn't want to say it out loud.

"Dark Sky is a coward," Watson said. "A thief."

Azarel's hands were fists. "A leech. Stealing your strength."

"It's bad dragon magic," Watson said. "He's using you like a protein drink. When he feels tired, he takes a sip."

Mom winced.

"Here's the thing, though," Watson said. "He wants you quiet and scared, and that's not going to happen, is it?" The beardie gave me a fierce smile. "And he didn't count on you having help from us. His pride and greed have made him vulnerable—we can strike back. Here's what I want you to remember, Conley."

The lizard raised three claws. "One, you'll sometimes see into the dragon's world, so you must pay attention. What you see might help us. Two, you'll sometimes feel what he feels, wild, dragonish urges, especially when you're scared—but you can fight those down. Be strong, be ready. And three, maybe most important—this is not forever."

It all made sense, in a horrible, twisted way.

"How long?" I asked.

No one replied until Dad said, "Not long. We just need to stop Dark Sky, you know, hunt him down, burn him to ash—that sort of thing. No biggie."

Wow. I couldn't imagine what Watson and Azarel must've said to my parents. A weight lifted from my shoulders. Now I wouldn't have to deal with the killer dragon on my own. Everything was out in the open. Everything would be ok.

"Great," I said. "So I'm not in trouble or anything?"

It was a dumb question, the kind a kid should never ask, and Mom showed signs of life.

Luckily, someone knocked on the front door. That broke the moment.

"Keep me posted on the dreams, kid," Watson whispered.

Snatches of conversation reached me from the foyer. Dad didn't sound pleased. Neither did the person he was talking to. I pried myself off the couch. Wait, I knew that voice, bossy, nasal and out of breath.

"...need to talk to your boys," Desmona the security guard was saying. "They were seen near an abandoned building that's—"

"Not a chance." Dad started to close the door.

"Wait, wait, wait," she whined.

I imagined her chubby foot stuck in the crack.

"Did your kids bring anyone home with them?"

I could hear the frown in Dad's voice. "Goodbye, ma'am."

Desmona was crazy if she thought our own parents were gonna turn on us. In the dining room, Mom was setting out a late lunch. I was still trying to get my mind around how well she and Dad were taking all this. They didn't seem happy. But they seemed to have their minds made up. It was surprising.

"So we're going to help Watson and Azarel?" I asked Dad when he reappeared.

He nodded. "We are."

I didn't get it but I liked it. "Good," I said.

A loud thud came from somewhere under us. It made sense, since my little brothers weren't in the room. I joined Wyatt, who was poking at his nachos and staring at Azarel, waiting for him to levitate or start a fire with his mind, probably. Mom plunked a salad, a boiled egg and a glass of green juice down in front of me.

"Mom!"

"Eat it all."

Maybe this was her way of getting even.

"How are we for transportation?" Azarel took an enormous bite of roast beef sandwich.

"Times have changed," Watson said through a mouthful of spinach. "All the steamboats and airships were sold when the Brick House went dark."

Azarel groaned. "Every last boat?"

"Afraid so."

"Every last plane?

"Yup."

"Every last–"

"Stop. You know the Agency wanted us gone without a trace."

"Rotting blood worms." Azarel rolled his big shoulders. "That's gonna make things difficult."

"We have to wake our ashes," Watson said. "No excuses, no delay."

"No excuses, no delay," Azarel agreed. He grabbed another sandwich.

Somewhere below us, a door slammed.

Dad got up to shout into the basement. "Keller, James, come eat."

A grinding crash shook the floor.

"Enough is enough," Dad said.

Keller and James appeared from the direction of the upstairs splash room, looking damp.

"That a bad sound!" James said happily.

For a second, everyone stared at them.

Azarel jumped to his feet. "If the kids are upstairs, who in beast guts is down there?"

CHAPTER 18
STOLEN ASHES

Azarel charged into the stone-walled basement, the rest of us close behind. The back door hung on one hinge, telling us we were too late. Tires squealed as we ran through the broken door and watched a black sedan peel up the alley.

Dad shook a fist. "Get back here!"

Azarel turned and rushed through the basement to the arched tunnel, us kids hot on his heels.

The secret door stood open.

His eyes smoldered. "They're in for a world of pain."

With a snap, light glowed at his feet.

Wyatt elbowed me. "See that? He carries a flashlight too."

We followed Azarel down the stairs. Without a psychotic lizard or caged dragon, the place wasn't nearly as creepy. Then again, now there was Azarel.

He disappeared inside the first cage and reappeared, scowling. "Sure enough." He stuck his head in the second cage as we crowded closer. "Two down."

His eyes swept the third cage. The dragon handler didn't

say a word as he brushed past Dark Sky's prison and headed to the fifth locker. He took a look, then slammed the door.

"Hell's bells! Now we've got nothing, Watson!"

On my shoulder, the lizard was tense.

"Just so I understand," Dad said. "Our herd of dragons was in these cages?"

"Our inferno," Azarel muttered.

"That's right," Watson said. "Our dragon inferno was in those cages. At least their ashes were."

"What about the last one?" Mom pointed but didn't get too close.

I'd been wondering the same thing.

Azarel kicked cage six. "Empty for decades," he muttered. "Held an infamous crystal dragon." He shot Watson a look and the beardie nodded.

"Long gone."

I wished with all my heart that we'd wandered into a different cell and spilled root beer on a different dragon. Any dragon except Dark Sky. We watched Azarel slam the cage door a few more times.

"Mind if I borrow your light for a quick look around?" Dad asked.

"Sure, but this light is hard to loan out." The dragon handler raised his right palm. The cellar brightened with a *whoosh* as he raised a flaming lantern. No, not a lantern.

Flames radiated from his clenched fist.

The dragon handler grinned wickedly as we yelled and gasped.

"Well, at least someone feels a little better," Watson said.

Back upstairs, I slumped on a sofa next to Mom as Azarel paced the great room.

Watson marched along a windowsill. "What I wouldn't give for FBI site access," he muttered.

I didn't feel so hungry and mean, now that my life wasn't being threatened. The dragonish urges had faded. Since I kind of understood what was going on, the pain in my chest was more manageable. But thinking about it was worse.

Dark Sky was trying to use me to get what he wanted—use me up and throw me away—and it made me furious.

It was like Watson had said, and the killer dragon had a long, invisible drinking straw stuck in my chest. He was taking sips whenever he felt like it, sucking my life through his grimy teeth. Maybe his backwash was infecting me. The idea made me want to yank the straw out of my chest and take a bath in bleach and scalding water.

It made me want to fight.

You need to stop thinking about this, I told myself.

"What are we gonna do next?" I said.

Azarel ignored me, focused on wearing a path in our carpet.

"Tough to know where to start," Watson said. "Our files on known felons are out of date by fifty years."

"Shouldn't we start by, um, grabbing the villain?" I hoped that was an appropriate way to describe the capture of a large, obnoxious security guard.

"Always," Azarel said.

"Grab whom?" said Watson.

That took me off-guard. "Desmona, of course."

"You think *Desmona* is behind this?" Dad said.

Everyone stared at me.

"You mean you don't think so?" I said.

Keh-keh-keh.

It took me a second to realize the sound was Watson cracking up.

"But she's gotta be," I said. "She hates us and she showed

up at the school and tried to stop us—and she wasn't alone, there was a big scary guy in the car with her."

"Hmm," Watson said.

Azarel nodded at me grudgingly.

"I've got an idea," I said. All the sitting around and fuming was making me a little crazy.

"All I need is some help from Watson."

The beardie narrowed his eyes. "This better be good."

CHAPTER 19
BEARDIE BEATDOWN

I stood on one leg, tugging a loose shoelace on Desmona's front porch. A backpack hung over my right shoulder. When I knocked, the screen door banged in its frame. It was after three o'clock but I had a hunch Desmona took very long lunch breaks.

She opened the door, mayonnaise streaking her chin, and stared at me.

"Hello, ma'am," I said. "My dad said you wanted to talk to me about what happened earlier." In reality, Dad was listening from the corner of the house. Wyatt spied on us from the Catalpa tree. Those were the conditions.

Desmona studied me. The skin under one of her eyes had turned greenish black. "Yeah, I did have some questions..." She kept the door between us, one hand on the latch.

I hadn't expected this.

"Um, yeah," I said. "Happy to help."

I took a step back and gazed up the block to show I didn't care either way.

Desmona hesitated. Finally she said, "Well, I guess so."

It was silly that I was sweet-talking a security guard into doing her job.

"Let's see." She glanced around the small front porch, which held a couple flowerpots with dead plants. "I guess we can step inside."

The door creaked open and I followed her down a long hallway. She stole glances at me over her shoulder. We passed a cluttered stairway and a room with an unmade bed and entered a living room with two beat-up recliners. A shiny widescreen television was the only thing that looked clean. It made me feel a little sad.

Desmona looked at me uncertainly. I looked at the recliners in the same way. Then her eyes changed. It happened slowly. She sidled away until she blocked the doorway and pulled out her cell phone.

Finally.

Time to enter phase two of the plan.

"Here's the deal," I said. "Give us full rights to the climbing tree and I'll tell you about the super important thing we found in the school."

Desmona shook her head no. "You're gonna get what's coming to you."

Aha, there she was. The real Desmona. And to think, I'd been almost feeling sorry for her.

She smiled as she punched in a number. "Yeah hello—it's me. Got one of 'em here, right in my living room. Naw, he's going nowhere."

She wasn't scared of me anymore, I realized. She was large, in charge, and eager for payback. I pulled the backpack off my shoulder. My hands scrabbled at the zipper.

"This is worth something extra, right," Desmona said into the phone. "This kid should be able to tell you all about—

eeeee!"—a little screech of pure terror as Watson crawled out of my pack.

Whew. I let out a long breath.

"Drop the phone," the lizard snarled. "Sit down NOW!"

She froze, her eyes widening. "It talks," she whispered. "It talks..."

This could go either way, I thought. If she took a step into the room and flopped on top of Watson, she'd flatten him like a pancake.

Desmona took a step into the room.

Watson's tail twisted nervously.

Her hand rose to her bruised eye...and started to tremble.

Thank goodness.

The phone fell from her shaking fingers. She staggered in a small circle and fell to her knees. "Don't hurt me," she sobbed. "I want to live." Tears splattered the carpet.

"Stop sniveling," snapped the beardie. "Answer my questions and you won't be hurt. Now take a seat."

Dust whooshed as she collapsed in a recliner.

Watson gave a raspy sigh as her enormous bulk plunked down. He casually tore at the carpet and Desmona watched, her face pale.

"Tell me everything, sweetheart," the beardie hissed.

If it had been me, I knew I'd tell him anything he wanted.

A few minutes after that, we walked out Desmona's front door.

Dad stood on the sidewalk trying to act casual, which was hard since he was holding a sledgehammer and shifting his weight back and forth.

"I didn't hear any alarm signal," he said. "Did you give the alarm signal?"

The signal was me screaming at the top of my lungs. I realized we were lucky Desmona hadn't let out a wail, because Dad might've become confused and smashed her front door. Of course, our screams would've sounded nothing alike.

"Everything went great," I said.

He gave a quick smile and tucked the sledge under one arm.

"I'm coming down," Wyatt yelled from the Catalpa.

Perched on my shoulder, Watson looked smug.

We found Azarel in the first floor library, thumbing through *The Art of War*. As we entered he tossed it aside. Mom appeared, carrying a stack of board books. When she saw me, she shoveled them into an armchair. We gathered at the round oak table.

"Mission accomplished," I said.

"Hey, great," Azarel said. "It actually worked."

"What?" Mom stared. "In the future"—she raised a finger like she was lecturing me or Wyatt—"you'd better not treat my kids like guinea pigs. I expect professionalism from someone your age."

"Fine," the dragon handler grunted.

I got the idea he liked Mom even though he didn't like being lectured.

"Shall we continue?" Watson said.

"Please do," Dad said. "And for the record, I concur with my wife."

"I conn-curr also," I said, rolling the word around on my tongue. "And Desmona's not in charge. Those armed guards from the school hired her."

"Unfortunately, she doesn't know much," Watson said.

Azarel groaned. "So what was the point of this inter-rogation?"

"The point is," Watson said, "now we know the Hosses were targeted and are *being* targeted. That someone's gone to considerable trouble—"

"And they didn't want us to find you," I told Azarel.

"–to steal those ashes," Watson continued. "And here's the most important piece of information." He raised a talon dramatically. "They plan to meet Desmona later–"

"At Chubby's," I said. "It's a place called Chubby's."

Watson glared at me.

"Finally, something actionable." Azarel pushed away from the table, straightening his coat sleeves. "What are we waiting for?"

"One more thing." Watson's dark eyes drilled into mine, and I knew better than to interrupt again. "The other agents— the serious ones—told Desmona their boss will be in town on Friday. Said he was looking forward to meeting her."

Azarel snorted. "Desmona is barbecue."

"Headed for the big crunch," Watson agreed.

"What d'ya mean?" said a voice under the table.

"What's this, a ghost?" Azarel pretended to be surprised. "When was the last time you had this place treated, Watson?" His whole mood had taken a turn for the better.

Dad and Mom exchanged a look as Wyatt stuck his head out.

"I'm not a gho–"

"BOOO!" Azarel yelled.

Everyone jumped or lurched or jerked. Watson's tail lashed the air and Wyatt knocked his head against a chair as the dragon handler roared with laughter.

"I apologize for him," Watson said.

"Let's head over to Chubby's," Azarel said. "And order up some ashes."

"I'm coming." The way Dad said it, you could tell he wasn't asking. He was dead set on meeting a couple dangerous criminals with a scary guy he barely knew. Well, that was Dad for you. But at the same time, I wondered what I was missing.

I watched him and Azarel slide into the cab of Dad's old truck. The blue Ford had a rounded hood, seats that leaked stuffing, and a windshield with a hairline crack. Dad had changed into jeans and a black t-shirt, sunglasses pulled over his eyes. Now that he was alone with Azarel, he looked kind of ticked off. Just the same, he stuck out a hand.

"Miles Hoss."

"Azarel, nice to meet ya—and you have a right to be angry. I'm angry too. Not a big fan of the Brick House, and if it was up to me, you never would've been put in this—"

The truck's old engine turned over, drowning out the words.

Darn, I thought. There's some kind of law, like gravity, that keeps you from ever overhearing a whole conversation.

The truck pulled away from the curb.

Wyatt and I sprawled under a canvas tarp, feeling sorry for ourselves.

"I'm too old to be left behind," I said. "So are you. We're the experts on those guys. We deserve to be there."

"And we found Azarel."

"True." He sounded happier about that than I did.

My mind was all over the place, skipping from Dark Sky to Desmona to Dad and Mom to the dirty drinking straw stuck in my heart. With so much to sort out, it had been really hard to decide how to spend the evening.

"I'm happy you woke up," Wyatt said. "If you hadn't woken up, you know, if you'd been dead, I would've missed you."

He looked away.

Wind rushed overhead.

If you knew Wyatt, you knew this was the same as one of those long, emotional squeezes where people whisper *I love you, I love you* over and over.

"Thanks, Top Ten," I told him. "I'm—I'm glad you're my brother."

He grunted and shoved the tarp off his face. I took a deep breath of cooler air. We lay on our backs with our arms behind our heads and watched stoplights and buildings flicker by over the bed of the pickup.

A few minutes later, Dad pulled up in front of Chubby's. We pulled the tarp back over ourselves as they climbed out and I glanced through a coin-sized rust hole. Even from the curb, the diner's plate glass windows had a greasy look.

"Probably not a mafia joint anymore, but you never know." Azarel pointed to the pavement by the door. "See that? Bloodstains."

"Nope," Dad said. "Ketchup."

We lifted the tarp and snuck glances as they stepped inside.

"What do we do?" Wyatt whispered.

I thought about it. The entire front of the place was glass. But what about the back?

Ten minutes later, we stood in a dim, sticky hall that led to bathrooms and an alley service door. It didn't smell great, but it had a good view of the restaurant as long as we didn't get noticed. A half dozen people ate at tables scattered across a black and white tile floor. Fat, disoriented flies bumped against the windows.

Dad and Azarel stood at a chrome counter. As we watched, a tall waitress came over.

"Do you still serve chicken and waffles?" Azarel asked.

"Does the sign still say Chubby's?" She raised her eyebrows.

"That's what I'll have then, and my friend here..."

"I'll take the same." Dad sat on one of the vinyl stools and gave it a twist. The seat spun slowly, giving him a three-sixty view of the restaurant, and Wyatt and I yanked our heads back.

"I love these old stools," Dad said. "They're getting hard to find."

"Reason being, you keep spinning, the seat falls off." The waitress finished scribbling their orders, ripped them off a pad and slapped them down in the kitchen.

"I'll limit my rotations," Dad said.

She rolled her eyes but smiled.

Azarel drummed his fingers on a napkin holder.

"We're meeting a couple friends here," Dad said.

"Your friends have names?"

"Jake and Crane."

"Hmm, haven't met 'em. Eat something, I bet they'll show up." She walked away.

Azarel crossed and uncrossed his long legs. "You should let me do this my way."

"What's your way?" Dad asked. "Grab her neck and shake?"

"Obviously not." Azarel snorted.

The waitress sauntered back and he cleared his throat. "Can I have a coffee?"

"On the way."

"So, these friends we're meeting..." Azarel leaned forward. "One's real big, reddish eyes, got a mouth on him. The other's taller, black hair, black eyes, has a mean streak. You sure they haven't come in today?"

Wyatt and I had done our best to describe Jake and Crane.

The waitress studied him. "You sure these are friends you're lookin' for?"

"Maybe they're friends, maybe they're America's Most Wanted," Azarel growled. "What's it to you?"

The waitress slammed a mug down in front of him and poured coffee in. She stared at the dragon handler while she poured. She didn't spill a drop and didn't stop pouring until the coffee pooled at the very brim.

"You've got nice eyes." She put down the coffee pot, crossed her arms and leaned against the back counter. "So why be such a jerk?"

Azarel frowned and Dad glanced at the coffee cup, too full to move.

"Here's the situation," he said. "These two are dangerous. You're right, us calling them friends is a stretch. But calling them good customers is a stretch too. You don't want them around."

The waitress curled a dark strand of hair around a finger.

"You cops?"

"No, we just need to talk."

"Heard that one before. Well, those two came through earlier. Paid me to store a cooler in the walk-in freezer. Said they'd come back and get it before close."

"What time is close?"

"Midnight."

Dad sighed and twisted his stool toward Azarel. "How long do you want to wait?"

Azarel grunted.

"We'll wait until they get here," Dad said.

"Suit yourselves." The waitress moved off.

Azarel watched her walk away.

"Maybe you've lost your touch," Dad said.

Wyatt and I shifted back and forth in the hallway, shoes squelching. A couple ladies walked by on the way to the restroom and gave us weird looks.

"Look, Dad is eating waffles," Wyatt said.

My stomach rumbled as the toasty, golden smell reached my nose. I wished I'd finished the green juice Mom had given me for lunch. Or even the kale salad, sprinkled with nuts. I was daydreaming about hamburgers when I felt Wyatt grab my arm.

Two car doors slammed outside. When I looked up, a black sedan was parked behind Dad's pickup. Two familiar figures moved down the sidewalk. In broad daylight, Jake looked even bigger. Linebacker sized. And Crane looked meaner. His flat black eyes and the lines on his face said, *Do not mess with me.*

We stared, and I realized I hadn't expected it to feel this scary.

The two criminals disappeared down the sidewalk.

"Wait, where are they going?" I said. Had Desmona lied? But her terror hadn't been fake. She'd expected to meet those two right here.

"I don't get it," I said. "Tell you what, Wyatt, if they don't show up in five minutes, let's go ask Dad for some–"

The back door creaked open.

Oh no.

Shivery energy rushed over me as I spun around and pulled Wyatt into the empty bathroom. As footsteps squeaked down the hall, I pulled the old door mostly shut. I sucked in a quick breath as the back of a head showed through the crack. Greasy black hair brushed a flannel collar. The man lifted his hands to his face and there was a click and a sucking sound. Bitter smoke drifted through the door and Wyatt made a face.

I put a finger to my lips.

"Where's the fattie?"

The voice had a mean, serrated edge, and my heart knocked my ribs.

"Maybe she got cold feet," said a snuffly voice.

Crane took another puff on his cigarette. "If she shows, we stuff her in the freezer, give her cold feet for real. Or if she doesn't show, no biggie, we grab the cooler and save her for later, turn her in to the boss whenever. Not like she's going anywhere."

"Going nowhere fast," Jake said. "What's she equal to food-wise, ya think? A stack of Oreos? A bag of french fries?"

Crane chuckled. "That's easy—deep-fried twinkie. Y'know the boss gets snacky sometimes. Let's go."

As Crane moved away, my heart fell into my stomach with a sickly *sploosh*. At that moment—in the dirty bathroom in the sticky hall—I understood why people lived in places like Prairie Refuge. Maybe I'd been wrong about dragons. Maybe they weren't fascinating. Maybe they were gross. And cruel. And nasty.

"They shouldn't put Desmona in a freezer," Wyatt said. "She's mean, but what if she got frostbite?"

Top Ten suddenly seemed super young. He was too small to be part of this. He didn't even understand what was going on. I felt angry with myself. And with Dark Sky and with Jake and Crane and the whole situation. I felt angry enough to make a vow, even though I also felt sick.

I'll keep my family safe. Whatever it takes.

You might think this took awhile, but it happened in half a second. Unhooking the lock, I slid into the hallway and looked around the corner. What I saw stopped me in my tracks. My vow was about to be tested.

Jake and Crane stood at the counter like a couple junkyard dogs, growling at Dad and Azarel. Dad and Azarel sat bolt upright, caught in the middle of a waffle dinner.

CHAPTER 21
THE DEAL GOES DOWN

"Why hello," Azarel said. "I feel we sort of know each other, but I've only seen you from a distance, chasing little kids. Strange thing, that."

Crane's hands tightened into fists.

I noticed he didn't ask Azarel who he was.

"Why are you here?" Crane said through his teeth.

Dad spun in a half-circle to face him. "Waiting for you."

"And eager to ask a few questions." Azarel wiped his mouth with a napkin.

"Heard plenty about you," Crane said. "Hoped to meet you earlier but I guess you didn't want to be found."

"Got a real knack for hiding," Jake said.

Azarel frowned.

From my corner, I watched Crane's left hand slide behind his back.

"You're not calling the shots this time," he said.

Azarel raised one palm to say, *Let's slow down*. Crane didn't move, at least not so Azarel could see. But his fingers snaked under his flannel shirt, closing on something at the small of his back.

I had a bad feeling I knew what it was.

"Say what you have to say," Crane growled.

I expected Azarel to snarl back, but instead he sounded polite. "I'm prepared to give you boys a deal," he said. "Promise it'll be worth your while."

Crane put his head on one side and Jake leaned in. It was like watching a couple of predators, maybe a hyena and a panther, focus on their prey.

Dad gave his seat another twist. His eyes were hard.

Crane's teeth looked yellow as he smiled. "Doubt it but go ahead." Behind his back, his hand didn't move.

My heart pounded in my ears. I was stuck in one of those awful moments when you know you have to do something scary—like jump off a high dive or throw yourself from a runaway bike—and timing is vital but at the same time you're frozen, thinking Do it now...do it now...as seconds tick away.

At the same time, another part of me was *snarling*. What was I waiting for? I could take them both.

"Tell us about your connection to Dark Sky." Azarel leaned back against the counter, his black coat dangling. "We already know about the girl next door, so you can leave that out."

"Is that all?" Crane sneered.

"Not quite." Azarel held up an index finger. "We'll also take the cooler."

Jake's arms bulged and his nostrils flared. I couldn't see Crane's face, but his body stiffened. I couldn't wait a second longer.

"He's got a gun!" I yelled as I came around the corner.

Jake was already lunging at Dad. Crane was sweeping his arm out and around, flannel shirt flapping as the waitress screamed. When I yelled, there was a tiny pause. Jake's eyes snapped from Dad to me and back. Crane's shoulders twitched in my direction. Then everything continued—but that freeze-frame moment was enough.

Jake threw a punch at Dad's head, but Dad had moved.

Azarel was in motion too as Crane brought his weapon around.

Red flame blasted Crane backwards—all the way across the room.

Jake doubled over as Dad jabbed him in the gut. Dad swung his barstool high and brought it down like a chrome-and-vinyl mushroom.

Then things slowed down again.

Jake slumped to the the tile. Glass shards fell like icicles from the broken storefront. Customers threw themselves to the floor, not knowing the fight was already over. Azarel flicked dust off his sleeve and stood as Dad gave us a strange look, then hugged us.

Wyatt drew a breath and fought back tears.

I hugged Dad back, hard.

"No one hurts my boneheaded boys," he said. "No one."

I wondered if he'd noticed the split second when I'd yelled and the bad guys had frozen. Dad was good at noticing things. But even if he hadn't, even if he was mad at me for being here, I was glad I'd come. Even though I didn't like dragons anymore and wanted to go home. Because otherwise, who knew what might've happened?

Azarel picked up Crane's strange weapon, studying the wide, star-shaped muzzle. "Black market magical blaster, silver edition—loaded with Campfire Infernos, I'll bet. Not bad." He stuffed the weapon in his belt as the waitress inched her head up from behind the counter.

"I ain't payin' for that window," she said.

"You did ok there," Azarel told Dad.

"You were adequate too," Dad said.

The dragon handler smiled.

"You listening? I'm serious." The waitress tiptoed from behind the counter and looked around. Her hands dropped to her hips. "Your friends, your mess."

"This is a management problem," Azarel said. "Tell your boss you just work here. He ought to cater to a better class of customer."

"Served *you*, didn't I?" the waitress muttered.

"Let's get out of here." Azarel grabbed Jake under the armpits and dragged him toward the door. "We'll take care of the trash," he told the waitress.

She rolled her brown eyes, mouth tight.

Dad frowned but he had his hands full, herding us outside.

On the sidewalk, Crane lay in a pile of broken glass. An elderly lady in sweatpants and a sweater was peering down at him. "You can't sleep here, young man. Disrespectful." She rapped him with her cane and hobbled off.

Crane groaned as Azarel propped him against a parking meter. He struggled to speak. "Taking...your place. Do what... you couldn't."

"That's funny." Azarel gripped Crane's shoulder. "I did what I needed to and now I'm doing it again. Gotta say though..." His face hardened. "It makes me angry, real angry, to have to do it twice. So let's make this quick. Tell me about the meet-up."

Crane's eyes glittered. He sneered at Azarel. Then he pitched sideways onto his face. Sirens wailed in the distance.

"Rotting blood worms." Azarel turned to look at Jake, slumped against the storefront. Jake's eyes snapped shut and his body slumped lower.

Azarel smiled.

Dad jangled the truck keys. "We'd better go."

Whush, whush. Red flames came to life in Azarel's hands like a gas grill firing up.

"Hey big boy," the dragon handler said. "I have the feeling you're one hundred percent human...your hair might actually melt."

I couldn't take my eyes away.

The man's eyelids shot open as the fire crept closer to his face.

"When and where?" Azarel snarled. "Before I test your heat rating."

Jake's eyes looked glassy as sweat poured down his face. "Friday at nine, the Rieger," he muttered. "I'm not one of your kind, I swear..."

"Obviously not," Azarel said. "Have a good life."

As the dragon handler got up, Wyatt was already running for the pickup. I dove into the bed after him as Dad yanked the driver's side open. The truck rocked on its wheels as Azarel lunged into the passenger seat. The motor roared to life.

"Wait," Azarel said. "We need to get our—yow!"

A tall, thin figure leaned through his window.

"Excuse me, baby," the waitress said icily. "We need to clarify something. I own this diner. You smashed *my* window. And the cooler is still in *my* freezer." She ground a high heel against the pavement.

Azarel stared at her. "Fine, you win," he said. "I'll pay for the window. Now get outta the way, so we can pull around back."

She darted her eyebrows and stepped away.

Dad hit the accelerator, and the pickup left rubber on the road. As we rounded the block and shot down the alley, we heard sirens coming up Broadway. The waitress slash restaurant owner leaned against the back door, looking smug. Azarel leapt out of the truck and handed her a business card.

"What's this?" She folded her arms. "I want cash."

"You'll get it." He shoved past her into the diner.

I watched her read his card, shake her head, and punch numbers into a cellphone.

Moments later, the dragon handler reappeared, an aluminum cooler over one shoulder. He shot past the waitress and slammed the cooler next to me and Wyatt. Then he started buzzing. *Bzz, bzz, bzz.* Like a hive of bees had flown inside his coat.

Wyatt and I watched in confusion as he patted his chest, eyes widening.

Was he going to explode?

"What's going on out there?" Dad shouted from the cab.

Azarel pulled a boxy old flip-phone from his coat and stared at it in disbelief.

"Gotcha, you jerk," the waitress said. "I'm LouAnne Jordan and that's my number. Call me. Otherwise..." She held up her phone and snapped his picture.

"You!" Azarel jabbed a finger at her. "You..."

LouAnne Jordan smiled wickedly. Footsteps squelched down the hallway behind her.

"DRIVE!" Azarel roared. He threw himself into the truck bed, crashing down beside us as Dad punched the gas. I bounced off a wheel well and grabbed one of Azarel's knees. When I looked back, LouAnne had one hand raised, fingers gently bent.

Buh-bye.

Azarel leaned on his elbows as uniformed officers appeared. They shrunk as we sped away.

"Hellish rotting blood worms," he whispered. "Your dad was right. I've lost my touch."

CHAPTER 22
DRAGON WARFARE &
CONTAINMENT 101

The sun had dropped below the West Side bluffs when we pulled up in front of the Brick House. Mom sat at a table in the garden bistro with her arms crossed. String lights glimmered overhead as James and Keller drove cars on the brick pavers, avoiding a stuffed fox and a marmalade-colored cat that lay on his side, batting at jeeps and roadsters.

Mom saw us and stood, hands on her hips.

Dad opened his door. "Time to face the music, boys."

"Rotting blood worms," I muttered. I'd been so busy spying and running, I'd forgotten we'd stowed away.

Azarel vaulted over the truck wall, dragging the cooler behind him. Wyatt and I moved more slowly. The dragon handler's face was hard to read as he hugged the cooler.

"You two are in So. Much. Trouble," Mom said.

"Wait until you hear about how they picked a fight." Azarel strolled past her, cooler under his arm.

Five minutes later, we hunched over the swirling marble countertop in what Mom called the Brick House's "juice bar."

Rows of mirrored shelves lined the wall behind the bar. Thomas Edison bulbs haloed our heads as Mom poured orange juice into a couple of glasses. She pushed the glasses toward us to show us she might still be nice—maybe.

"Spill it," she said.

Normally, Wyatt and I would've been all over that.

But not tonight. I pictured Crane's face as he raised his blaster. And the way Jake had looked at Dad, like he'd wanted to break every bone in his body. And these guys *worked* for Dark Sky.

"It's hard to know where to start," I said.

Watson cleared his throat. He was on the bar, using his tail and hind legs to pour a drink from an amber bottle.

Dad looked at Mom and grabbed a couple more glasses. "How 'bout I tell you all about it later," he said.

"That bad?" Mom said as Azarel strolled in.

"Bad?" Azarel reached for a glass of his own. "Not at all. Don't worry. Everything went the way we planned. Ashes back. Thugs in jail. Cops couldn't have read the plates. And bonus, your man's a natural getaway driver." He spread his hands wide. *What more can you ask?*

"What about that waitress?" I said.

His triumphant expression faded. "What a horrible woman."

"I thought she was great," I said to see if his eyes would smolder again.

Sure enough, they did.

"Well, I have this to say." Mom held up an index finger. "You might think we're all in this together. And you're right. But..."

Here it came.

"Wyatt Hoss, I don't care if you call yourself Fantastic, Invincible Top Ten, you will never sneak out of this house again, do you hear me? Conley Hoss, you may think you're some kind of brainiac young Indiana Jones without the fear of snakes, but that makes no difference, do you understand?"

We hung our heads.

"Beast-guts," Wyatt mumbled.

"What?"

"Yes, Mom," we said.

"Good." She drained her orange juice and clunked her glass down.

"I would like to say something as well." Azarel glowered at us and my heart sank. Then he raised his glass. "Here's to saving all our lives. Thanks, boys. Cheers."

Mom glared at him.

Noticing her glass was empty, the dragon handler poured her a drink.

"Not helpful," she breathed.

Wyatt and I sat up straighter.

Dad stepped to the window overlooking downtown. He seemed eager to take in the city lights. Shaking her head, Mom picked up her glass, sniffed it, and set it down.

Azarel stuck out a large hand. "Azarel Ahazi."

"Oh!" Mom said. "Right, Flannery Hoss. Thanks for keeping my boys safe."

"Of course," Azarel said. "That's what really matters. Thanks for having such fierce little blighters. "

The huge man winked at us as Mom sighed.

Everyone else had already eaten, so Wyatt and I had reheated tacos down in the gleaming kitchen. Mine were dosed with salsa verde and guacamole—and were those ground nuts?—but I was so hungry I ate them anyway. Watson joined us for some greens and pico de gallo.

"There's something I don't understand," I said.

He looked at me warily, cilantro hanging from his mouth. For a lizard with a high IQ, he was sure a messy eater.

"What's so important about those dragon ashes?" Wyatt asked.

"Hey." I stared at him. "That's right." Maybe he deserved more credit than I was giving him.

"Simple," Watson said. "We need our own dragons to stop Dark Sky. Without our own inferno, we don't stand a chance. "

I swallowed some barbacoa. "I guess it makes sense they stole the ashes, but why didn't they destroy them when they could?" As much as I knew, there were obviously some gaps in my dragon knowledge.

"Aha." Watson's eyes gleamed as he held up a claw. "Now we're getting into Dragon Warfare and Containment 101. Why do you think we didn't destroy Dark Sky's ashes?"

Hmm. I couldn't think of a single good reason.

"You were saving them for a museum?" Wyatt asked.

"Because we can't," the bearded dragon said. "An atomic bomb would do it—maybe. Lesser explosives are accelerants. Dropping them in molten lava is asking for disaster. The best you can do is hide them safe and cold and deep. Anything less, you're taking horrible chances."

Guilt coiled in my stomach. This had all been done, taken care of decades ago. Dark Sky had been cremated and locked away. He never would've escaped, except for me.

"In addition," Watson said, "Dark Sky wants our ashes for himself. Young dragons are impressionable. Suggestible. Like most babies, they trust the first faces they see. If Dark Sky had woken them, it would've been the final nail in our coffin."

"Oh..." I said.

No wonder he and Azarel had just about lost it.

"Chess," Watson said. "The death version."

"What?" Wyatt and I stared.

"The match began the moment we met." The beardie pushed away his pico de gallo. "Attacks, feints and counter-attacks. We searched for Azarel, Dark Sky's thugs tried to stop us. They stole the ashes, we took them back. A deadly game, and we're barely keeping up."

"I hate losing," Wyatt said.

For some reason, I'd thought we were winning. But that was because I'd been focused on the little stuff, like Dad smashing Jake with the stool. Now I realized we were just trying to avoid disaster. Dodging bullets. Like Watson said, Dark Sky had been a step ahead the whole time.

"What will we do next?" I put a hand to my heart.

"It's time for us to make a move. A big one. Give him something to think about, push him back on his hind claws. Tomorrow we wake up our ashes."

Wyatt perked up. "Whoa, cool."

Great, I thought. More dirty, nasty dragons. Maybe they can all snuff each other out.

As I dragged myself upstairs and down the hall to bed, I heard James and Keller screaming and gurgling in the splash room around the corner. Wyatt had gone off somewhere, probably to look for Azarel. It wasn't my bedtime yet, but I couldn't stay on my feet a minute longer. The ladder to my top bunk seemed like Mount Everest, and when I'd pulled myself up, I collapsed on my mattress. I raked my fingers across the wall, feeling snappish.

It would serve you right, I told the house, *if my fingers were talons and I could just claw you apart.* Because I remembered how the house had lured me in. How we used to talk just days ago when everything seemed exciting and cool.

My chest rose and fell and my heartbeat pounded behind my eyes. "Why'd you bring me here?" I said through my teeth.

"Was this your plan all along—to ruin everything, and—and hurt me?"

The house leaned over me, walls closing in. I could tell it was watching. I knew it heard me. Before it could speak, sleep rose up and snatched me.

CHAPTER 23
TRANSPORT LOGISTICS

You don't have to be a genius to figure out what happened next.

Gator-sized Dark Sky slithered through my window. A pale girl turned toward me, tears sliding down her face. The dreams ended badly, horribly, like they always did.

Then with a jolt, I was high in the night sky. Moonlight brushed my back and shoulders like sequins. Night wind hit my face. Below and far away I could hear screams, getting weaker. The screams brought a smile to my face. I ran my tongue over my teeth and tasted copper. With a twist of my tail and a sweep of my wings, I soared nearer to the stars.

Ahead, still a long way off, city lights glowed. It was almost time to leave the farmland. Almost time to get to work. My leathery tail lashed the sky and I blew a thin stream of smoke over one shoulder. Then I ground my teeth. "I know you're there, Conley Hoss—but not for long."

When I woke up, my fingers were clawing the mattress. Mom must've draped a blanket over me, and I'd thrashed it into a chain around my ankles. I held a shaky hand in front of my face. Fingernails, pink skin, human knuckles. I almost cried, I was so relieved.

And I had stuff to do. We all did. That was a relief, because I needed to get my mind off what was happening to me. It will be over soon, I told myself.

When I arrived downstairs, I found everyone else already working.

"Hey laz-buns," Wyatt said. "I guess you think you're special and can just sleep the whole day. Dad made me pack your stuff. I hope you like turtlenecks in summer."

I squinted at him, my head on one side.

"And jeans. And flannel boxers."

"Ok," I said. "Whatever." I left the stairs and crossed the great room, bumping into a couple chairs. What had gotten into him?

"Oh good, you're up," Mom said in the kitchen. "How are you feeling?"

I put a hand to my chest. "Umm, ok."

Something glided through her eyes as she swung open the double-wide fridge and handed me a bowl of granola and blueberries. And what was this, poured over it—yogurt?

"Mom, why do you keep–"

"Eat it all," she said. "And fast. We're leaving in a few minutes."

"Wait," I said. "What are we–"

"Head to the back drive," she said, "*After* you eat it all."

She wasn't kidding about things happening fast. After I forced down the granola, I pushed through the doors onto the gleaming steel deck. Below, our minivan idled in the driveway, looking old and shabby next to the house. Everyone was down there, even Keller and James. Dad and Azarel were shoving the metal cooler in back, glancing up and down the alley.

"Let's go, slowpoke," Wyatt yelled. Standing in the

driveway with his hands on his hips, he seemed to think he was in charge. Something extra jerky had gotten into him today.

Dad jogged up the stairs and across the metal deck.

"Go," he said. "I'm locking up."

So I did.

"What's going on?" I said as we rolled down the alley.

"You're squishing me," someone croaked.

It was Watson, clawing his way up onto the front dash.

"We need room to train." Azarel looked cramped, legs bent at ninety degrees in the passenger seat. Mom must have insisted he sit there, because if he'd climbed into the back seat he would've broken it.

"We used to train over the Missouri River." Watson stretched out on the fake leather. "People would pack picnics and come from miles around. Vendors would set up their stands, donuts, lemonade, cold beer, and folks would make a weekend of it. We'd cap off the air show with a barbecue dinner, whole pigs and cows slow-roasted by the dragons. Those were the Agency's golden days, back when this town swaggered."

Before the Dragon Uprising. Before Dark Sky.

Watson made it sound wonderful. But I knew the truth about dragons now.

As the van turned onto the highway, I felt like I'd left things in a bad way back at the Brick House. Falling asleep, I'd known there was something the house wanted to say. Leaning in as I tumbled into my dark dreams. Maybe I'd pushed the house too far. *We're done, kid. You're out of the family.*

Or maybe I had it wrong, and the house felt sorry for me. Maybe it wanted to help. But now we were speeding down I-35, headed who knows where, and I'd missed my chance. The yogurt bubbled in my stomach, because this wasn't a day for missed chances. This was a day for getting every little thing right.

"What's our exit?" Dad asked.

"It'll be a while," Watson said.

Mom sat one row back with the little boys. That left me in the rear with Wyatt. Backpacks and camping gear towered behind us, stacked on the metal cooler stuffed with dragon ashes. Now and then, as the van hit a curve, something would topple off the pile and land on me. At least that's what I thought, until I noticed Wyatt sliding his arm along the seat back. A second later, a sleeping bag bounced off my head.

"What's your problem?" I said.

He stared at me. "You are. You're not tough enough."

That wasn't fair. Top Ten didn't know how bad I felt about all this. Not just about the loose dragon. Not just about my aching heart. About all of us being involved, and him in particular. Just yesterday, looking at his confused, scared face in the hallway at Chubby's, I'd vowed to keep him safe.

"I'm going to keep you safe," I said. "Don't worry."

He scoffed. "Hah. I can keep *myself* safe. Look at you, going to bed before James, sleeping late, stumbling into things. You can't take care of yourself even—and I'm *not* worried."

He crossed his arms and made a face.

Scooting away to the far edge of the seat, I looked out the window. That's what you get when you try to be helpful. I put a hand to my chest and snatched it back down. My face felt flushed, my eyes hot and heavy.

"Hey Watson, where are we going?" I half-shouted.

Mom turned to look at me.

I hadn't meant to sound so angry.

The bearded dragon chose to overlook my tone. "Some-place big and empty," he said, peering at me from the dash.

"Open fields, open sky, lots of trees. I ran a vacant property search this morning."

"Why?" I said, rubbing my eyes.

Azarel guffawed.

Dad raised his brows in the rearview mirror.

Wyatt snorted. "Ha, you don't even know *that*."

"We're going dragon-ing." Keller waved a handful of crayons. "I've started drawing them."

"Wake up babies!" squealed James.

"Right, yeah, of course," I said. "I knew that."

Or at least I *had* known. We were waking up our ashes. We'd talked about it last night, right before Mom had rubbed ointment all over my chest. But my dreams were messing with me. And the idea of bringing more dragons into the world did not make me feel better. Hungry, dirty-mouthed dragons who'd sip your life like a milkshake.

"Take this exit," Watson said.

As Dad turned the wheel, a backpack bounced off my shoulder. I kept my eyes straight ahead.

"Not long now," Watson said.

"Not long" turned out to be twenty more minutes. We rolled down a street with a sagging chain link fence on one side. The fence ran on and on for at least a mile, holding back a weedy forest, but the lizard kept his beady eyes fixed on the houses across the street. When he was convinced no one was spying on us, he said, "Ok, we're going in."

Dad twisted the wheel and we surged over the curb, careening down a narrow driveway where the fence line parted. The broken asphalt twisted through high grass and overgrown trees, until a thick chain barred our way. Dad pumped the brakes and Azarel slid out. I watched him lean over the chain, shrug his shoulders—and then he was tossing two sections aside.

Good thing he was on our team.

Twigs crunched under our tires as we rolled down the snaky drive. At the end of the asphalt, an old stone house stood under towering oaks. A rock wall surrounded the home, split by a dirt path that ran up to the front door. It reminded me of something out of a story, maybe something dark by the Brothers Grimm.

We parked under a huge oak and everyone got out and stood in the shade. The sounds of the street had faded and you couldn't tell there was a row of nice old homes just a quarter mile away. The place was as secret as Watson could've hoped.

"Give me a hand up, kid."

I crouched to let the beardie leap to my shoulder. His talons pricked through my shirtsleeve, giving me goosebumps.

"Figured you could use some company," he said.

I nodded. It was nice to not be alone.

"Suppose we should do a security sweep." Azarel yanked the metal cooler out of the van.

"Considering this place's history," Watson said. "Let's run the protocols."

"Take a look at the house?" Dad asked.

The squat stone home wasn't nice to look at. It would probably withstand a tornado or a half-hearted dragon attack but had a kind of heavy, claustrophobic quality—even from outside. I didn't want to go in.

No one else seemed eager either.

"May as well get this over with," Watson muttered.

CHAPTER 24
THE DARK HOUSE

I reached the front porch first. I hadn't meant to, but Watson kept digging his claws into my shoulder like a tiny jockey spurring on his horse. Reluctantly, I turned the knob, and the door swung open. The lizard's tail tickled my neck as we stepped into the dim interior. Someone shoved past us and Wyatt gave me a smug look as he pulled on his headlamp.

Whatever, I thought.

I felt Dad and Azarel at my back and followed Top Ten through the foyer over red-splotched carpet.

"What do you think, ketchup?" Azarel said.

Dad didn't answer.

Wyatt's light shone into a kitchen full of empty cans and bottles. Drawers stood open, and the sink was stacked with plates and trash. The headlamp traced figure-eights on the wall, making it hard to focus, and I was about to snap at Wyatt when a scratching, shuffling sound came from overhead. Something being dragged across a floor.

"We're not alone," Watson said in my ear.

"Good thing we did the security sweep, eh." Azarel ran his fingers over the low ceiling. "Those sound like claws. Let's find the attic."

Light glowed in the dragon handler's palm as he and Dad left. Wyatt ran after them and that left me no choice but to follow. As we moved down a hall, I wondered what we were looking for.

When we caught up with Dad and Azarel, they were circling a corner room with a large stone fireplace. It was the biggest room we'd found, but I still felt like the walls would inch closer if I looked away. The carpet was charred black and stained rusty-red, like something juicy had exploded and then burned.

Something creaked behind us. Azarel was unfolding a stepladder from the ceiling. A sound came from the open hatch.

Scritch-scratch, shuffle.

"Come out, we won't hurt you," Azarel called. "*Too* much," he added under his breath. The dragon handler held up his right fist, blazing like a torch. "Last chance," he called. "If I come up, don't expect a cozy chat."

No one answered.

"What does he think is up there?" I whispered to Watson.

"Hard to say." The beardie's tongue tickled my ear. "If the monster control is lax around here, it could be an Ice Mantis. Or a Razor-Wing or a Butcher Beast—or even a rogue dragon. Best to keep an open mind."

Whoa. I'm not sure my mind had ever been more open.

"Ready or not, here I come," Azarel muttered. The ladder groaned and the flames in his fist cast a long shadow behind him as he disappeared through the ceiling.

"Keep a safe distance," Dad said.

Then he followed Azarel.

We waited about five seconds.

Wyatt and I scrambled for the ladder, shouldering each other aside in our mad rush to see whatever Azarel was about to incinerate. Watson's claws dug into my shoulder as I lunged into the open, dusty attic.

Surprisingly, nothing was on fire. Light streamed from a hole in the roof. Dad and Azarel stood watching something crouched and black. *Scritch-scratch-shuffle.* The creature wobbled crookedly, shuddering toward us and away, like it couldn't make up its mind.

I waited for Azarel to blast it to smithereens.

The thing darted a dark, wrinkled head at us and hissed.

What the heck was it—one of Watson's monsters?

Dad chuckled and I realized what we were looking at.

Hunched in the opening, the vulture parted its hooked beak.

"On your way, black-coat," Azarel said. "There's nothing for you here."

With a hiss and a croak, the vulture spread its wings and plunged into the daylight. Keller and James yelled outside, and I sighed out a long breath and followed Azarel down the ladder. When we stepped into the sunlight, I was happy.

Mom sat on the low stone wall, keeping an eye on my little brothers. When we filed out, she got to her feet and pointed. "Look."

A bone lay half-buried under the oak tree, white and picked clean.

Could be anything, I told myself. Not a big deal.

Azarel shrugged. He agreed with me.

I relaxed a little.

Mom pointed up into the huge tree spreading above us.

We all looked up. And kept looking.

"I've never seen a treehouse made of bones before," she

said. "Something has been here. Maybe it's here right now." The bones were all shapes and sizes, some a few feet long. Jumbled together, they formed a kind of platform, forty feet above the ground.

My shoulders stiffened up. No wonder vultures liked it here.

"What built that?" Wyatt asked.

"Could be dragons." Azarel stared up at the jumbled skeletons. "Wild, shiftless dragons. Sometimes they claim a place for themselves and never leave."

"They do?" Mom said.

Dad put an arm around her. "I've had it up to here," he said, "with undisclosed dragons."

Grasshoppers whirred nearby and a breeze stirred the wilted grass.

I glanced up at the tree's bone necklace. And away.

"Give it a rest, Ahazi," Watson said. "The only dragons here now are *ours*."

"Fine," Azarel said. "And boring. It's no wonder you never got invited to parties. Well, if there are no other comments, let's get this ash party started."

CHAPTER 25
RED & WHITE, GREEN & BLUE

I stood on the second story of a barn, checking the rafters for vultures. Watson was still riding shotgun, and I'd slid a couple paper napkins under my shirt to keep his tiny claws from pricking holes in my skin. The barn was hot. Light streamed through holes in the metal roof and nothing moved.

The loft had no windows but a door opened into thin air, ten feet off the ground. Azarel walked the room, chewing a roast beef sandwich. Wyatt straddled a beam ten feet off the ground. Dad and Mom stood side by side at the top of the stairs, not speaking. In the middle of the floor, water beaded the metal cooler. The barn smelled like old wood, dirt and hay, and made me tired.

Keller and James sat on the plank floor, drawing pictures in the dust.

"AZ-ell, look!" James yelled.

The dragon handler knelt beside them. "Hey, it looks just like us." The little boys slapped his open palm and I looked at their artwork. Three ugly stick figures, two short and one tall, stood by a shaky criss-crossed rectangle—the Brick House.

Overhead was a bird-like shape twice as big as everything else. It had enormous, spiky teeth.

Brushing off his knees, the dragon handler stood. "Let's get started."

"Wish it wasn't wood," Watson said.

Azarel tapped the floor with a boot. "Built with two by tens, it should hold."

"Full speed ahead."

Azarel's eyes flashed as he tore the lid off the cooler. Ice steamed in the July air, and everyone crowded around except Wyatt, who watched from overhead. Mom took out a ziplock bag of sandwiches and some milk. Then Azarel lifted out a stack of packages wrapped in layers of foil.

Excitement twisted across my chest—but at the same time, it hurt. I winced as Top Ten swung from the beam and thudded to the floor.

"Wait," he said. "Let me."

Azarel nodded. Despite myself, I leaned in.

Wyatt took a deep breath and pulled back a corner of foil. "Blue," he whispered.

"Blue prefers the northeast compass point," Watson said. "Near the frozen north, the rising sun. When he wakes, he'll know he's among friends."

Azarel stalked away, cradling the foil package.

"They can tell the difference?" Wyatt asked.

"Dragons have an innate sense of time and space," I said.

Watson gave me an approving look.

"My turn," Keller said.

"Easy does it." Dad held a package out and Keller tore back a corner, bouncing on his toes. "Green, my favorite." The ashes shone like microscopic emeralds.

"Southeast," Watson said. "Green loves forests, open spaces and spring sunlight."

Dad stepped away and Azarel lifted the next package, dripping ice water.

"Who wants this one?" he asked.

Best keep a safe distance, I thought.

"I look, I look!" James ripped off a strip of foil and Azarel cupped one hand to catch a stream of bright red ashes. The tiny pentagons flickered with inner fire.

"Red is happy in the southwest," Watson said. "Loves heat, the fiery sunset. However, red also likes the center."

Azarel rubbed his chin. "You know I've always felt a kinship with the red bloodline. Fierce. Tough. Just what this inferno needs."

"Headstrong," Watson said. "Rash."

"Tenacious," Azarel said. "Brave."

Watson snorted. "So be it," he said like some ancient wizard lizard. "Put red in the middle and let's hope the supporting cast can balance his—"

"Overall excellence," Azarel said.

"Various shortcomings," Watson finished.

Azarel smiled and set the glowing red ashes in the center of the barn.

Dad looked at me as he held out the final package. "Guess it's your turn, Conley."

"Oh. Right." I brushed my fingertips over the foil and snatched them back. Nothing happened, and everyone was staring, especially Wyatt, so I made myself fold back a corner.

"Umm, looks kinda pearly," I said.

"Excellent," Watson said. "Things are looking up. Frost likes the northwest, near icecaps and night. Frost is the dragon of winter sunset, and would've made an excellent leader instead of—"

"Shhh." Azarel put a finger to his lips. "They might hear you."

Dad set the final package down. Now ashes waited in three corners of the barn with the red in the center.

"Would've been nice to have a fifth," the dragon handler said.

"Beggars can't be choosers," Watson said. "We transported nameless ashes—to a barn—in tin foil. Let's count our blessings."

"Will this be a—a good dragon team?" Mom asked.

"THE GREATEST WE HAVE EVER SEEN," Watson yelled, making us jump. "THIS INFERNO WILL NEVER KNOW DEATH, NEVER TASTE DEFEAT. THEY WILL WING TO EVER GREATER GLORY."

Azarel nodded his approval as he pulled a can of root beer from the cooler. "Sorry for breaking protocol," he said. "But we don't have any basilisk blood and we need you now."

For a second I thought he was really thirsty. Then I realized what he was doing.

Root beer sloshed each pile of ashes as the dragon handler moved from corner to corner. He dumped the rest of the can over the red particles and it fizzed on the old plank floor.

"See you soon, my friends," Azarel said loudly. He turned on his heel and marched out of the barn.

The rest of us looked at each other.

"Follow him," Watson whispered in my ear. "Give them some privacy."

So we did.

Outside, the scorching sun had a soothing effect as it hit my skin, but I still felt tense and stressed. *More spilled root beer,* I thought. *More dragons on the way. How are we ever going to get them all back in the cellar?*

Mom and Dad sat in the shade, watching my little brothers build towers with rocks. Wyatt disappeared inside an empty machine shop, carrying a rusty hammer.

"I packed a special lunch for you," Mom called.

"In a minute." I was tired of her feeling sorry for me, especially since she'd forgotten what I liked to eat. When she wasn't looking, I helped myself to a sandwich and found a sunny spot by the rock wall.

Watson crawled off my shoulder and onto a flat stone. "Ahh," he said. "Nothing beats a good bask."

Huh. I leaned back and closed my eyes and it turned out he was right. As I soaked in every ray I could, I got the feeling my parents were watching me. Whenever I looked over, their eyes would drift away.

"So," I said. "Is this close to over?"

"How do you mean?" Watson said without opening his eyes.

"Getting our own dragons was the big thing, right? As soon as they hatch—or materialize, we sic them on Dark Sky and..." I looked over.

Watson sighed. He probably heard the eagerness in my voice.

"Not that simple," he said.

I passed a hand over my forehead. "But dragons are super intelligent. We can send them on a seek and destroy mission, right?"

"Not exactly." He opened one eye. "Dragons are hands-on, Conley."

I slid off my pile of scorching rocks. Why had I thought this was comfortable?

"Hang in there, kid," Watson said. "I know what you're going through, but you're tougher than you look. You'll get past this."

I crawled over the sizzling hot wall and hunched in the shade on the far side, wondering how long I had before my skin started peeling off in strips. You don't know what I'm going through, I thought. No one does.

"Any more dreams?" Watson said.

"Huh? What? Well...yeah." He'd caught me off guard.

I tried to read his face, see if he was mad I hadn't told him, but he didn't give much away.

"Dark Sky knows I'm there now," I said. "He knows I'm watching."

"Ah, yes. I suppose he would, now and then."

He didn't sound surprised and I realized he was trying to calm me down. But it wasn't working. I'd wanted him to say, "Beast blood, this is crazy, we'll fix it right away." I didn't want him to act like I could handle it. I didn't want him to tell me, "Don't give up." Because I wanted this to be over. I wanted my own thoughts and dreams back.

Grabbing the wall, I pulled myself to my feet. My face burned and my legs felt heavy as I turned and ran across the parched grass.

"Wait," Watson called from his rock.

"Conley, come back," Mom yelled.

But I kept running.

Once I'd put some distance between us, I sat in a patch of tall brown weeds and threw pebbles against a metal shed. My heart ached and I scrubbed at my chest with my knuckles.

Watson said we weren't close to done yet. He'd made it sound like the next part would be tricky. Well, I'd promised to make things right.

"You can do this," I said. "You can and you will—Dark Sky goes back in jail and no one gets hurt." But I felt lightheaded, like someone else was saying those words.

A twig snapped behind me. Wyatt stepped around the corner. He had his rusty hammer over one shoulder and a tarnished golf club over the other. Cobwebs clung to his hair and he looked triumphant.

"Hi loser," he said. "Hey, what's the matter?"

I turned away from him. "Nothing."

His steps crunched up behind me.

"Go away," I said.

Instead, he sat down beside me. "Look at this old golf club," he said. "I thought it would make a great regular club—you know, for hitting enemies." He slid it into my lap. "Anyway, what's wrong?"

Up until that point in my life, I'd made it a point not to tell Top Ten about my problems. Half the time, he caused them. He could be quite a jerk for someone his size and it had been a good policy.

But now, looking at his worried face, my resolve crumbled.

I told him everything.

CHAPTER 26
PROPERTIES OF DRAGONS

Wyatt listened to my story about Dark Sky invading my dreams and slurping down my energy like a protein drink.

"I don't just feel bad," I said. "I feel weird, and it's the dragon messing with me, hot and hungry and mean, crawling around inside my skin. After he backs off, I can tell he's been there. But when I'm right in the middle, feeling strange and seeing things, I—I get lost."

My brother looked at my face. Then he did something very strange. He hugged me. His cobwebby head bumped my chin.

"I didn't know it was that bad," he said. "I was mad at you because you were lying around acting like a wimp, and you're supposed to be strong because you're my big brother. But you're not a wimp—you're fighting a dragon. You are very, very tough and I won't let Dark Sky get you."

His blue eyes looked stormy, even though they were bugging out of his face. "The only one who is allowed to fight you is me, and that's because we're brothers."

When I hugged him back, I felt a little better. Wyatt got

scared like anyone else, but he hardly ever backed down. So I wouldn't either.

We sneaked into the barn loft for the umpteenth time as the sun faded. Azarel sat cross-legged in the shadows. When we came in, he put a finger to his lips.

The ashes were on the move. They hummed as they grew into gleaming eggs, slowly gaining size and shape. Now and then, they hissed.

Not like Dark Sky, I thought. We're in charge this time.

"It won't be long now," Azarel said.

As darkness fell, we made a campfire. Mom caught up with me and made me eat some kind of organic wrap stuffed with salad.

"Mom, why?"

"You need to get better."

I was pretty sure it wasn't helping as I watched everyone else eat sandwiches. Dad and Azarel had two apiece. Then, after everyone else was finished, Azarel ate the last three.

"That's not quite normal," Mom said.

He grunted. "Who wants to be normal?"

I sat next to Wyatt, who was prodding the fire with the golf club.

"I wonder which dragon will have the best moves," he said.

"Maybe the red one." I remembered Azarel's bragging, and it checked out with what I'd read in my dragonology books.

"Maybe he can do tricks with flame." Wyatt waved the glowing club around.

"Reds are known for their brute strength and lung capacity," I said. "They blow a crazy volume of fire."

"Huh. That's really cool."

"The cream-colored one is a frost dragon. That comes in pretty useful, counter-attacking other dragons. Plus they tend to be strategic thinkers."

"Didn't know dragons could be so interesting."

"Oh, for sure. At least I used to think so. I always imagined meeting a real dragon, but now..." *Now I know what they're really like.* I took the hot golf club from him before he branded me. Surprisingly he didn't try to grab it back.

Across the fire, Watson was stretched on a flat rock with his eyes shut. Azarel was leaning back on his elbows with our little brothers sitting on him. Dad said something funny. We could tell because Mom rolled her eyes as Azarel guffawed.

"The green dragon should have unusual abilities," I said. "We'll have to wait and see. They're the wild cards of the dragon world."

"You know a lot, Conley." Wyatt rubbed his chin. "What about the blue one?"

"Maybe a water dragon. But who knows if any of it's true? It's just what I read in books."

"Oh no, I'm sure you're right." He smiled. "The blue one can cause thunderstorms and I bet it's a good swimmer, too. Riding on that one would be like whitewater rafting."

"Ha, you're just making stuff up. If you think Mom will let you ride a dragon, you're crazy."

Keller and James dozed off on sleeping bags near the fire. Mom and Dad sat on their log, holding hands. Once or twice I caught them watching me and I pretended not to notice. After awhile, I unrolled my own sleeping bag, just to sit on. My plan was to stay awake. I figured being exhausted was better than being hunted by Dark Sky in my dreams. Top Ten dozed off but I sat upright as Watson started telling a joke about selling life insurance to phoenixes.

Ha, that's funny, I thought. I wonder if phoenixes are really–

And that's as far as I got.

The night was dark but not quiet.

The carcass crunched and popped as I tore it. Strip the flesh, snap the bones, suck the marrow. Yesss. My furnace was roaring now. Ribs bulging with beef, I rolled my shoulders, feeling the weight of irresistible force.

I was ready. The dark star at my center hung in balance. I was back. Back at the top of the food chain—the ultimate alpha, the apex predator. The whole world was my meat market. Soon I'd fly to the city, mine before, mine again. All its blood, all its heat, all its gold. Mine, mine, all mine. And then—wait. I narrowed my eyes.

Hello, Conley Hoss. Guess what? I don't need you anymore.

"Kill another?" Someone said from the shadows.

"The night's still young." Blood dripped down my snout as I snapped up a chunk of meat.

The world turned red.

All mine...

Then I woke up—me, Conley—covered in sweat. The campfire was dead in the grey morning light. My legs wobbled when I stood, so I dropped to my knees and rummaged through my pack, looking for a clean shirt. All I found were turtlenecks and jeans. Wyatt hadn't been joking.

I shuddered, wondering who to wake.

So much hunger. So much blood. That was what was after us.

Then I noticed Watson was missing. So was Azarel.

There was only one place they could be.

As I hurried inside the dark ground floor of the barn, Azarel's voice rang overhead. Something crashed and dust fell from the ceiling. Numbly, I climbed the stairs. When my head cleared the floor, I froze. My first thought was, They're too small.

Four creatures the size of great danes circled the dragon handler. Their heads swayed on thin necks. Wings branched from their shoulder blades, folded against their ribs, and light reflected off their hides. Red and pearl, green and blue.

They looked nothing like Dark Sky, so I caught my breath. Where he was a starless night, they were a box of crayons. But that wasn't the main difference. Watching them, the reality of Sky's age sank in. Even as a reborn baby, he'd had swagger, hunger, and scary timing. The beasts in front of me had none of that. They looked more interested in chasing their tails.

It was hard to even think of them as dragons.

Azarel lifted his right hand and the creatures stopped running. Flame appeared in his palm and they opened their jaws—fire glowed in their throats. Azarel snapped his fingers and their fires went out.

"Very good," Watson said from the big man's shoulder. "You pass your physicals."

The dragons jostled each other, rumbling happily. The pearly one sniffed the air. Without warning, four scaly heads swiveled toward me.

"Intruder alert," the blue said.

"I'll take care of it," the red dragon snarled.

I didn't even have time to scream as he lunged at me.

CHAPTER 27
DRAGON SUNRISE

"Stop!" Watson shrieked. "That's our friend."

The dragon skidded past me, clawing at the floor. Its tail knocked my shins, then it sprang to its feet and sidled away.

"Hate to say I told you so," Watson muttered.

"Conley, come on over," Azarel said warmly.

I pulled my mouth shut, thinking his cheerfulness was overkill.

Overkill. Poor word choice.

Reluctantly, I inched forward. This was close enough.

The pearl dragon closed the distance. The way its face telescoped toward me on the end of its long neck was chilling. I forced myself to hold still, but it wasn't easy. The beast peered into my face, then drew away.

"I think he's scared." Its whisper was like snow rustling over glass.

"What?" I frowned. "No, I'm not."

"Prove it." The pearl dragon was in my face again. Its scales shone like opals and its sea-green eyes were—hmm. The word that came to mind was *pretty*. It was unnerving, like meeting a cuddly vampire. I wondered if a dragon with cute eyes would still kill you.

"Come over here." The glowing face glided away.

I really didn't want to do that. But I also had to prove I wasn't scared. My heart thudded in my throat as I stepped up to the dragon.

"Don't worry—I won't hurt you," I croaked.

"Ha ha ha." The dragon's bell-like laugh surprised me. It had to be a girl. Her triangular head was level with my chest when she arched her neck and looked me in the eye.

"Listen, I don't know my name yet," she said. "When I get it figured out, I'll tell you."

The dragon tried and failed to hide a brilliant, toothy smile.

Obviously this was a pretty big deal to her. So I did my best to put some feeling into my voice as I said, "That's great!"

The dragon's eyes narrowed. She glanced at Azarel.

"Cut him some slack," the big man said. "He's banged up and tired and shy. Once he gets over his fear, he'll be less sarcastic."

"He's smarter than he looks," Watson added.

"Umm, ok." The dragon didn't seem convinced.

"Wait," I said, but the beardie cut me off.

"Make an effort," he said. "Don't let her run laps around you."

"She's not—"

"Let's get everyone else in here," Azarel said.

They just loved interrupting me. Whatever. I shrugged and saw the frost dragon watching me, brows raised in a very superior way.

Feet clattered on the stairs.

"Hi dragons!" James called. He stood next to Keller, Dad

and Mom right behind him. Except for James, they all looked slightly paralyzed.

"C'mon in," Azarel said like a tour guide. "Couldn't have timed it better. Don't be shy."

The red dragon dug its talons in and growled. The blue and green dragons tensed up, rumbling in their throats. Only the pearl dragon seemed relaxed. Maybe even amused.

Azarel's right hand flew up. "Actually, let's slow things down a bit, keep everyone comfortable." My family had frozen at the first note of the red dragon's snarl.

The dragon handler bent his head to whisper with Watson. "Right, ok then." He crooked a finger at James. "Want to meet a dragon?"

It didn't make sense to me.

But it made sense to James. He toddled forward, beaming.

"My baby," Mom gasped. "James, no!" She jumped after him but she was too late.

"What you doin,' dragons?" Without warning, the four-year-old grabbed the red dragon by the nose.

It was a terrible moment.

Mom and Dad lunged forward and Azarel's arm flew up like he was about to blast a hole in the side of the barn—as the red dragon started laughing. It was a low, kind of awful grating sound. James patted its snout, his eyes alight, and the dragon lay down and crossed its front feet like a dog as everyone stared.

"What's your name, little fella?"

"I James."

"Watch this." The dragon cupped its front feet and blew. When it held out its claws, a fiery star blazed for a moment and went out.

"Ha," James said. "I like little fire, do again." He poked the dragon's jaw.

"Fearless, aren't ya," the red dragon said. "I like that."

Azarel and Watson exchanged a nod. It was obvious some kind of experimental, highly-dangerous team-building was going on. But why did we have to be involved at all?

I glanced at the other dragons. Their expressions were hard to read, but the blue one seemed sulky. No, not sulky. Cranky. He caught me looking at him and showed his teeth. I stole a look at the green dragon, but she was holding her claws over her eyes, like this whole thing was just too terrifying.

All of a sudden I felt lucky. The frost dragon might be the only normal one in the bunch. She was smart, had good manners, and eyes that made you think she wouldn't rip your throat out. I darted a glance at her.

"Thanks," she said.

"Huh?"

"What?" She smiled, revealing rows of fangs.

Don't get comfortable, I told myself.

Keller's curiosity had become too much for him and he'd stepped forward to stand by James. The green dragon peered out at him from behind her claws. It hadn't been hiding after all. It had been playing peekaboo. Gracefully, it extended a front foot.

"Hello, young man, I'm Dandelion."

Keller hesitated. He inched his hand forward, touched the dragon's paw—or was it a palm?—and snatched his hand away. A smile spread across his face.

"Your skin is like a sandbox."

"Sandboxes must be amaaazing," Dandelion said.

"Wait a minute," I said, forgetting my plan to play it cool. "How come you have a name? My dragon doesn't know hers."

Maybe I'd been matched with a weird dragon after all.

"Easy now," my dragon said.

Dandelion shrugged. "Born lucky I guess."

"Some dragons arrive with a strong sense of identity," Watson said. "Dragonologists suggest this comes from a previous life that ended in being burnt to ash."

"Or not so lucky," Dandelion said.

"Other beasts take a while to figure things out," Watson said. "Their names are significant. Portentous. Full of meaning. You don't find dragons named Tiffany or Candy."

"Gross." The pearl dragon stuck her snout in the air.

"Once in awhile, a dragon will accept a name she's given," Azarel said.

"I can't imagine doing that unless it's a really good one," the frost dragon said.

I was starting to realize she was kind of a snot.

Dad and Mom joined the strange party.

"Good morning, sir," the red dragon said. "I'm impressed by your offspring here." He stretched a talon toward James, who batted it away.

"I think you should join our team," Dandelion told Mom. The green dragon held out a front foot and Keller gave her a high five.

"Why of course," Mom said. "But what are we doing exactly?" She ruffled Keller's blond hair and shook Dandelion's paw, careful of the claws.

"We are getting acquainted," Azarel said. "Our organization needs to be a well-oiled machine."

We looked at him blankly.

"We all need to get along if this is going to work," Watson said.

That made sense. If we were going to fight Dark Sky, we had to cooperate.

"You have a high IQ, right?" The pearl dragon murmured from the corner of her mouth.

I'd been standing near her, in her general area. Acknowledging we were on friendly terms but not grabbing her nose or giving her high fives or rubbing her scales or anything.

"Um, yeah." I swallowed. "As and Bs, you know. I'm pretty smart, my mom says. I read a lot."

My dragon—I'd started thinking of her that way because we were supposed to be team building—made a humming sound in her throat.

"I hope this works out," she muttered.

"What?" I forced myself to look right in her face.

She rolled her eyes.

I was about to say something cool and smart, you know, a really great put-down, when a voice wailed from the stairs.

"Where's *my* dragon?" Wyatt stood there, rubbing sleep from his eyes. "Why didn't anyone TELL ME the dragons were alive?" He stamped a foot.

"Honey," Mom said. "We *all* knew the dragons were hatching this morning."

"I DIDN'T KNOW!" Wyatt yelled. "BECAUSE I WAS ASLEEP!"

Mom put a hand to her mouth. *I can't believe we forgot him,* she was thinking.

Dad shrugged. *He'll be ok.*

Wyatt stuck his hands in his pockets and glowered at the floor.

"ABOUT TIME!" the blue dragon bellowed. It took a flying leap, skidded to a halt and blew steamy air in my brother's ear. Wyatt and Mom screamed at the same time.

I shuddered and lurched toward Wyatt. Why hadn't Watson and Azarel seen this coming? What was my brother going to do, now that his brains were melted?

He clung to the railing, looking blank.

We'd been friends for about five minutes and now he was a zombie.

"Stop sulking," the blue dragon hissed. "It makes you uglier than humans normally look."

Top Ten seemed to shake himself out of a trance. He balled up his fists and glared.

"You're the ugly one!"

The lake-colored dragon grinned. "Now that's what I'm talkin' about. Put it here, bud." The dragon held out a foot and Wyatt fist-bumped it with all his strength. If the dragon noticed it had been punched, it didn't show it.

"The name's Breaker," the dragon said. "On account of... because...hmm." It scratched its snout.

"Because you're a fierce destructive force," Azarel suggested.

"Well, let's hope it's that," Breaker said. "And not fragile bones or somethin.'"

"Attention everyone." On Azarel's leather-clad shoulder, Watson raised his front legs, claws outspread. "That went well —no blow-ups, no bloodshed."

Mom and Dad's eyes widened.

"Now it's on to phase two. Training day. Of course, you dragons are wondering who we are, what we're all about, and I'll fill you in as we go. We can't stop for barbecue and chit-chat. Right now it's flight lessons."

The dragons rumbled happily. Wyatt began clapping, and the rest of us joined in. We were in this together. It made sense to show support.

"This will be better than an air show." Mom put an arm around my shoulders. "Excited to see our dragons in the sky?"

I smiled at her because I *was* excited. Now we were getting somewhere. Now we had a chance. If these dragons can grow fast, I thought, and if they turn out to be any good at fighting...

The pearl dragon caught my eye. Her look was a dart that popped my helium balloon of hope. *You really don't have a clue, do you?* her expression said. I felt like an idiot but I wasn't sure why.

Give me a break, princess, I wanted to say.

Dandelion coughed. "I sense some confusion in the air."

Tearing my eyes away from the pearl dragon, I noticed Breaker tearing grooves in the floor with his front talons. The red dragon was looking at Dad with a furrowed brow. There was definitely something going on.

"What's the problem now?" Dad said.

The dragons swept their necks around.

Azarel and Watson exchanged looks.

"We have to tell them," Watson whispered.

The barn was so quiet, we could all hear.

Wyatt filled the awkward silence. "It's obvious, Dad. We're gonna fly the dragons. Everybody gets one, except a few people will have to team up."

My mouth dropped open.

The floor creaked under us.

A rooster crowed in the distance.

Nothing I'd read about the Dragon Days had suggested humans had flown them. Not a paragraph. Not a sidebar. Not a footnote. This couldn't be happening.

"Hey, Watson," said a pouty voice. "You told me I'd get a smart, brave human."

It was the pearl dragon. *My* dragon. Her bottom lip was sticking out.

CHAPTER 28
INTO THE SKY

"Oh dear," Dandelion murmured. "I hope none of you are afraid of heights."

"Heights are *not* the problem." Mom's eyes were huge.

"Let's move outside," Azarel said quickly.

The dragons bolted for the stairs and my brothers and I followed a second later.

"Breaker, wait for me," Wyatt yelled. "Or I'll—I'll break you in half—hahaha!"

"Not if I pulverize you first," Breaker roared.

They spoke the same language.

Little James caught up with the red dragon and grabbed its tail.

Keller was pacing next to Dandelion, chattering away, probably about art.

The frost dragon shot me a look over her shoulder and I actually shivered. How had I managed to mess things up so quickly? One thing was obvious. I had to try and fix our relationship *before* we got off the ground.

The grown-ups came out of the barn, talking in low voices. Dad and Azarel both looked fierce. I watched them walk to the rock wall and sit. Watson chimed in now and then from the dragon handler's shoulder. Mom kept waving her hands as she talked.

I glanced back at the dragons and did a double-take.

They were bigger. If you looked at them directly, they kind of shimmered. But if you looked away and back, or watched from the corner of your eye, you realized what was happening. Their frames were filling out as they soaked in the July heat. They already looked less like babies.

My dragon lounged against the rock wall. If she'd been human, her arms and legs would've been crossed. Her expression was haughty and her jade eyes caught mine like a hook. *I can see you watching me.*

I had no idea what to do.

Taking a deep breath, I stepped toward her. It felt like the slow, endless walk across a cafeteria to a table where you won't be welcome. I knew the feeling well.

The dragon didn't give me any help. She just watched.

After about five years, I took a final crunching step and stood in front of her.

"Hi," I said.

"Hi," said the pearl dragon.

"Look, I'm sorry we got off to a bad start. I like dragons." *At least I used to.* "I was just—caught off guard."

She sniffed. "Well, now you can forget about liking, you know, *dragons*"—she waved a claw—"and focus on liking the one important dragon in your life. Me. You've gotta be more on top of things if we're gonna work together."

I wasn't sure I cared for her tone.

Just then Mom stood up, smoothing her shorts. Dad stood behind her, arms folded. Azarel came striding over. "Follow me to the flight field," he called. "Humans, grab a granola bar on the way. Dragons, you'll eat later. Let's go."

"Yay!" The frost dragon said. "This is so exciting."

I didn't trust my voice so I pumped a fist.

Ten minutes later, our ragtag crew stood in a field somewhere near the center of the property. We'd followed an overgrown trail through the woods, munching our snacks, and now the trees fenced us in. Prairie grass grew higher than James, full of buzzing grasshoppers. No houses or roads, not a trace of civilization. Bright blue sky rolled overhead like we were in a forgotten wilderness. With monsters.

"Form a line," Azarel yelled.

I stepped over to my dragon, keeping a safe distance.

"You're gonna have to touch me in a minute," she said over her shoulder. Now she was as long as our minivan, longer if you counted her tail. Her armored back rose higher than my shoulders. She was growing so fast it was alarming. Up and down the line, my little brothers were laughing, their dragons rumbling and fooling around. It made me and the pearl dragon look like a couple of stiff, formal acquaintances.

"Climb up," Azarel shouted.

I'd known this moment was coming, but I still couldn't keep my hand from flying to my heart. My chest tightened and I felt dizzy when I felt rough, silver-dollar scales under my fingers. My dragon's ribcage rose and fell. She curved her neck to look at me, and her sharp eyes softened.

"Go ahead, you don't need a secret password."

I glanced around, catching my breath. Further down the line, Wyatt got a running start and jumped for Breaker's back, but he bounced off and disappeared in the high grass.

"Grab my wing, step on my elbow," the frost dragon said. "I won't break." I nudged her forearm with my foot. It could've been made of marble, so I stepped up. Her wing was cool and smooth under my fingers—just like my old dragonology books had said.

"Wow," I said. "The mineral coating on your exoskeleton is so cool. If I didn't know better, I'd never guess your bones were hollow."

"Huh." She looked at me. "What does it feel like to be a total nerd?"

But I could tell she was impressed, so I grabbed hold and swung up onto her spine behind her shoulder blades.

"That's the idea," she said.

Please don't let me fall, I thought.

"I've never lost a rider," the dragon said like she could read my mind.

"Really? That's great."

Her laugh rang out. "And I've never *had* a rider."

Oh. Well, at least I'd lightened the mood. Her wings unfurled and swayed on either side as I leaned into the hollow at the base of her neck.

"But seriously," she said, "I won't let you fall."

Oh thank you, thank you, I thought.

Azarel stomped through the high grass. "Good work, Conley. She's a bit full of herself. Don't let her give you any grief."

"Thanks for that," the dragon said.

"Listen up." I tried to take Azarel's advice. "Stop giving me grief."

"Yes, master."

I frowned.

"And finally," Azarel shouted. "We're all on our dragons. Ah, I take that back. Come on, Keller, come on. Flick that grasshopper off and—there you go. Now, once you're seated on these glorious beasts, you'll find it's very hard to slide off.

Internal gravity and all that, let Watson bore you with the details later."

Watson's gravelly voice rang out. "More people die from parasailing accidents each year than from all the dragon flights in history. The internal gravity at the heart of a dragon's—"

"Yeah," Azarel said. "Very safe and so on."

I leaned forward, clearing my dragon's wings.

Wyatt was walking on Breaker's spine like a balance beam as the blue dragon chuckled. Dad was seated behind James on the red dragon, who was snapping his jaws with excitement. Keller had successfully joined Mom on Dandelion's back. Mom's lips were tight, her eyes straight ahead. Maybe she felt like I did. All the dragons were keyed up, though, and the frost dragon was no exception. I could feel her joints tensing like a catapult, ready to launch us into the sky.

She looked back at me and smiled. "We've got this."

I nodded weakly. She's different, I told myself. Not out to get you. Not dirty, not nasty. Just a little stuck up.

"Two points of contact at all times," Azarel shouted. "Two feet or two hands or a hand and a foot, you get the idea. Your butt counts as two points of contact."

"Sit down, Wyatt," Dad yelled.

Everything was happening so fast.

"Grab hold, everyone." Azarel raised one arm.

I wrapped both arms around my dragon's neck.

"You're strangling me," she croaked.

"Dragons, stretch your wings."

Her wings unfolded above me like sails, swaying in the breeze.

Up and down the line, my brothers shouted with excitement. Something rose in my gut but I fought it back down. Maybe Azarel caught the look on my face.

"Close your eyes if you want," he yelled. "Pretend you're on a roller coaster and try to enjoy yourselves. Dragons, take it easy on your riders. Any questions?"

Mom started to raise her hand.

"Excellent," he said. "Fly when ready."

I ducked into the hollow of my dragon's wings as strong winds flattened the prairie grass. It felt like a squad of helicopters was lifting off.

"Go Breaker, go!" Wyatt yelled. There was a rush of shimmering blue as they shot into the air. A reddish blur launched skyward at the same time. They kept rising, taking on shape as they got smaller and smaller.

I flattened myself across my dragon's back. Azarel had said two points of contact, but I was aiming for at least six. More if you counted my face. After a few seconds I realized we were still on the ground. I raised my head.

"Are you, um, waiting for me to say 'go' or something?"

"Not a chance, silly." She had her eyes trained on the dragons overhead. "I just want to see how fast they are."

"Why?"

"So I know what we're up against."

"Why does it matter? We're on the same team. It's not like it's a race or—aaah!"

We shot into the sky. About forty feet up, when it seemed we'd drop back to earth, we kept rising, her wings making huge gusts of air. Rising and sinking on the breeze, always gaining speed, we soared along the tree line. Sighting down my dragon's slender neck, I saw the red dragon ahead.

"Here—we—gooo!" The wind caught her words and threw them back. She sounded wild, fierce, and kind of girlish, like she'd strapped on a brand new pair of ice skates. But no one on a skating rink, not even an olympic one, had ever moved this fast.

"Look out!" I screamed as the red dragon's hind end zoomed closer.

We swerved and shot past, the pearl dragon laughing.

She was really, really fast.

Maybe she actually knows what she's doing.

Slowly, carefully, I pried myself off her spine so I had a better view. The wind shoved my hair back from my face, flooding my lungs with air that smelled like sun and wildflowers. The view was incredible, better than any ferris wheel. Trees looked like miniatures in a model. The open field was a wheat-colored rectangle. Cumulous clouds sailed past like ocean liners. The rest of my family was airborne too, and in the golden sunlit sky, we and our dragons seemed bigger and more real than anything else in the world.

I raised one hand, then two, and whooped, pumping my fists in the air.

I did it! I did it!

We did it. The frost dragon twisted to shoot me a look. *I'm sure that's what you meant.*

Man, she could sure say a lot with her eyes.

Dandelion sailed toward us, whistling a tune and breathing out curlicue flames that drifted through the sky like glowing clover.

"Do a loop, Dandy!" Keller squealed.

"Upside-down figure eight coming up, young sir."

"Noooo!" Mom screamed and grabbed Dandelion's neck as the dragon swerved upside down and began looping right and left.

The red dragon had tried and failed to catch up with us. We'd lapped Breaker too, and he hadn't even bothered to compete, too busy with his acrobatics. Now the red flew along the field's edge, brushing the treetops with his wings. Now and then, he'd breathe out a blast of flame that would shimmer and separate into crimson arrows.

It was unbelievably cool.

"Want to see a trick?" he roared over the wind.

"Do a tricky trick!" James shrieked.

The dragon flew straight toward the forest and swerved at the last second. His tail swung around like a spiky hammer. Behind him, a treetop swayed and fell, leaving a splintered trunk.

"Wow," I said. "Can you do anything like that?"

"My tricks are better than that," my dragon sniffed.

Seriously, she sniffed. What she really needs, I thought, is one of those glittery tiaras—and maybe some servants to boss around.

Out loud I said, "So how fast can you go?" The wind was whistling so much, I could hardly hear myself.

Ever heard of a Peregrine Falcon?

Her voice was crystal clear.

"Of course I have." I knew a lot of animal facts and was kind of proud of it. "Everyone knows they're the world's fastest animal. How come I can hear you so well?"

Figure it out, since you're so smart. And by the way, I'm not stuck up and I don't need a tiara—or servants. If I need anything, I'll just ask you to get it for me. And of course I know what I'm doing.

Huh?

There you go, thinking in my direction. You might want to be more careful with your thoughts.

Oh... Oh no.

That's right. I heard all those mean things you thought about me. But you know what? I'll forgive you—because I've been thinking mean things about you too.

She huffed a long breath into the wind. A flurry of snow

flakes streamed over her shoulders, melting instantly on my hot face.

I didn't say anything, just hunched on her back while she swirled around the field, outflying anyone who showed signs of resistance. My brain was hyperventilating, because how do you deal with a dragon who can read your mind? I wasn't sure which ideas I was keeping to myself and which she could see. How do you know if you are thinking secretly?

My books had not prepared me for this.

Making it worse, the harder I tried to avoid unkind thoughts, the more they popped into my head. *She's such a snob, the most stuck-up dragon in the—no, you don't mean that. But it would be funny, really funny, if she was flying over a swamp, and all of a sudden her wings froze up and she fell into—no, think of something else. Breakfast, those huge clouds—anything.*

The pearl dragon smiled sweetly over her shoulder.

You're a jerk, I thought.

Finally, a little backbone, she shot back. *Look, as fun as it is to watch you struggle, I only hear what you think toward me. At me, in my direction. You'll catch on fast now.* She sighed. *My gift to you. We're supposed to be partners after all.*

Fine. Thanks, I guess. Your frost stuff is cool.

Thanks. I guess.

We flew in silence for awhile.

In my opinion, she's a real piece of work, I thought quietly.

If the pearl dragon heard me, she didn't show it.

CHAPTER 29
ONE STEP AHEAD

"Dragon hide is tougher than metal," Azarel bellowed. "If you're in danger, use your dragon as a shield." The big man leaned into the red dragon's neck and stretched his legs along the reptile's spine. "Dragons, never fly through enemy fire. Deflect it with your own. When possible, attack from above. Earth's gravity is your friend."

We stood in the field, getting our ground legs back as Azarel lectured us. The sun was directly overhead, blazing down without an ounce of shade, and while the dragons were focused on the lesson, my legs were rubbery, face hot from sunburn.

Not sure how much more of this I can take, I thought.

The frost dragon examined me. *You look shaky.*

Maybe if you weren't so bony, I shot back.

She stuck her nose in the air.

I wasn't the only one who'd had enough. Keller and James were grouching about being hungry. Wyatt slumped in Breaker's shade, eyes shut. Dad was rubbing his neck and Mom's nose looked pink. I wiped my brow, wishing I had a shorter haircut.

Your hair looks fine the way it is.

Really? Thanks.

When she was nice it made things weird.

"Ok, wrap it up." Azarel decided we'd had enough. "Back to camp, humans. Dragons, hang back for a minute."

My family straggled across the field and down the forest trail. The shade had never felt so good. Everyone looked worn out, but Wyatt had extra bounce in his step.

"Hanging in there, boys?" Dad appeared behind us.

"Oh yeah," Wyatt said. "That was amazing."

"Conley?"

"I'm good." Under the circumstances, it was true. The sickness was wearing me out, but the fatigue was getting familiar, like a backpack settled on my shoulders. When I was calm, I knew I'd keep going, keep pushing ahead until this was over. And now we had help. We weren't alone anymore.

I could sure use a shower though. And a nap.

"Well done, Hosses." Azarel came crashing up the trail behind us. "You're a tough crowd."

Yeah, I told myself. You're tough so don't forget it.

Twenty minutes later, we'd collected our things and stuffed them back into the minivan. My chest throbbed as we crossed the state line into Missouri and I began to worry as we sped closer to downtown. When Wyatt started blabbing, I was glad for the distraction.

"Are there really other monsters besides dragons?" he yelled at the front.

"Of course," Azarel grunted.

He didn't seem to be in a hurry to continue.

"A legitimate question," Watson said from the dash.

The big man pulled his knees a little higher and his seat

creaked ominously. In a fit of generosity, he'd given Mom the passenger seat and now, wedged between James and Keller, he was paying for it. "Are there other kinds of monsters? Yeah, there are. But dragons are where it's at, don't worry. No need to go beating the woods, looking for the next big thing. You're in on the most elite species." He massaged his neck, half-closing his eyes.

It was crazy the way his mind worked.

James leaned against him, snoring.

Wyatt and I waited as Dad accelerated into the left lane, zooming past a semi.

Azarel hugged his log-sized arms to his chest.

"What are some of the, um, less elite species?" I said.

Azarel sighed. "Take the ice mantis. It's a parasite—the kind of thing that lives in your gut and makes you sick, except a million times bigger. They feed on heat and blood, so they like to prey on small dragons."

"How...uncool." The words drifted back from the passenger seat, where Mom was half-reclined, sunglasses pulled over her eyes. Ever since her flight lessons, she'd been very laid back.

"How come I've never heard of 'em?" Wyatt asked.

"Ha ha ha," Azarel said. "There are lots of things you haven't heard of. Me, for example. And lesser legends like Adagio." He avoided the lizard's sharp gaze. "Let's see." He stroked his chin. "Bet you haven't heard of Tree Shrieks."

We shook our heads.

"Bog Creeps, Shin Snips, Murklurkers?"

Nope.

"Jayhawks?"

"I thought they were sports mascots," I said.

"Let's hope you never meet one in the wild. Your ignorance is staggering."

Wyatt leaned half over the seat. "How can all these things exist and no one knows about them?"

"You've led very sheltered lives."

We hung our heads.

"But on the bright side," Azarel said, "that's changing very rapidly. If you survive, remind me to tell you about the UWA."

"Very funny," I said. "Tell us now."

"Oh, very well. It means Unified Wilderness Alliance. They take care of the lower-grade monsters." He smiled and closed his eyes.

"What? Hey, not fair," Wyatt and I said.

In front, Watson's claws skittered on the dash as he turned to face us. "Change of topic. Let's talk strategy. Tonight, Dark Sky expects to meet two men on top of the Rieger. Azarel and your dad won't disappoint him—but they'll bring some extra backup." His mouth became a thin line. "Then we can all get on with our lives."

Mom's left hand gave a little jerk and tightened into a fist on her armrest.

I hoped Watson was right. That brought me right back to the present, and it made me think about our dragons.

"Hey, where's our inferno?" I asked.

"Resting up," Watson said.

"Eating some cows," Azarel said.

"Don't worry, we'll pay for them," Watson added.

"They'll be in position by nightfall," Azarel said. "Ready to do some damage."

"Four on one," I said. "That should be enough to..." I trailed off as I remembered something I'd forgotten from my dream. "Watson." Chills ran down my spine. "I meant to tell you."

The beardie's eyes locked onto mine. "Tell me what?"

"Dark Sky isn't alone. Someone, something, is with him."

CHAPTER 30
BUSINESS MEETING

Watson asked me for details, and when he realized I didn't know anything else, he crouched on the dashboard, staring out over the highway. When the lizard's claws bit into the fake leather, Dad didn't say a word.

Azarel wasn't so easily fazed. "Can't be anything lethal," he muttered, knees grazing his chin. "What can he have recruited on such short notice? Couple of Razor Wings?" He scoffed. "Naw, we'll have the edge." But his eyes kept flicking to Watson.

The van was quiet as we pulled up in front of the Brick House. My parents woke my sleeping little brothers as Wyatt and I staggered inside, dragging pillows and sleeping bags. The Brick House watched in silence as I crossed the garden bistro. Then light flashed down from its gutters like beams from a sphinx's eyes. *Die, Conley, die.* I threw a hand up to shield my face and dove under the shaded columns.

We hadn't parted on the best of terms.

I dumped my pack in my room and headed to the locker

room by the second floor gym. There was a bathroom with a walk-in shower by my bedroom, but I decided it was time for the buddy system.

"Hey, Wyatt," I said, "I'm hitting the locker room. Mom wants you to take a shower too."

He made a face. "Beast-guts."

She hadn't actually said that, but I knew it was true. It was always true. Being clean was not one of Top Ten's priorities.

"C'mon," I said, and he followed, muttering.

Now I wouldn't be alone if the house turned on me. But in the poured concrete locker room, the lights glowed warm and bright. The heated floor didn't scorch me. The water pressure remained constant, the temperature just right. *Ahhh.* I relaxed a little under a gleaming shower head. Maybe the Brick House wasn't out to get me after all.

When we made our way to the great room, I was feeling much better. Even my sunbaked skin felt all right, thanks to a generous slathering of aloe vera. Things will be ok, I thought. Just a few more hours and Dark Sky will be gone for good. You'll stop feeling shivery and weird.

Then I saw Azarel.

Pacing the edges of the room, he looked like a caged tiger, stalking from the hearth to to the arched doorways to the bank of windows and back.

"What's the matter?" I tried to stay relaxed.

He leaned on the mantle, overcoat sweeping the hearth. "It's only four o'clock."

"At his age, you'd think he'd be better at waiting." Watson was back on his favorite windowsill, stretched out in the sun. "But no, centuries of opportunity and he still hasn't learned patience."

Azarel scowled.

"How old are you?" I asked cautiously.

"Eh." He crossed his arms. "Medium old."

"So, like two hundred?"

He shrugged as Watson snorted.

"Not even close," the lizard said.

"Oldest known handler was Pericles," Azarel offered. "Around two thousand last time he was sighted, and he might still be hanging on."

"So..." I glanced between the two of them.

Watson yawned. "He's sensitive about his age, but I know his secret and there's nothing to stop me from telling you that Azarel Ahazi was born in Tanzania in the year—"

"LA-LA-LA!" The dragon handler sang. "Shut up, Adagio—I have dirt on you too."

Watson gave a raspy laugh and I sank into an armchair.

Mom walked into the great room pulling tangles out of her damp hair. "What else can we do to get ready?" She had on workout clothes and sneakers, planning ahead the way she did. I looked down at my frayed shorts and flip-flops and realized I needed to get my head back in the game.

"A few final decisions." Azarel rubbed his palms together, getting looser and happier by the minute. "War plans."

Mom made a face as Dad appeared in jeans, boots and a black t-shirt. They'd both prepared for battle in their own way.

"Now that most of us are here, let's talk flight plans." Azarel pushed off from the mantel and got back to pacing. "Given the events of the last twenty-four hours, I think we can say we've locked in victory." Watson gave a hiss, which Azarel ignored. "Still, I'll understand if you don't want your boys anywhere near the battle zone. In a firefight, there's always gonna be second-hand smoke. Who stays and who goes?"

Mom's eyes got big and so did mine, for different reasons.

Then her eyes got narrow. "I wondered," she said, "if you might try and make plans without me."

"We'd never do that," Dad said.

"So what?" Azarel said at the same time.

Mom's hands tightened on the back of my chair. "You're going?" She jabbed a finger at Dad. "And you"—she pointed to Azarel—"think *some* of the kids are going?"

Dad rubbed his sunburnt neck.

Azarel shrugged.

After our training session, I'd figured I'd be flying the frost dragon into battle. Well, maybe not battle, exactly. My main goal had been not to fall off her back as she froze Dark Sky. But now, was Azarel really saying I could stay home?

"Explain again why these dragons need riders?" Mom said.

Watson stopped basking and looked up. "People don't think of dragons as having soft hearts," he said. "But the advanced data doesn't lie. Dragons with human partners are less reckless and fight smarter. It's a real edge. Despite some unfortunate moments in our history, our species have a connection. Alliances help everyone."

"You make it sound like a game of Risk or global domination," Dad said.

"Exactly." Azarel nodded. "You're catching on."

"Nothing that ambitious," Watson said. "We want to end this tonight. So think of it as a significant tactical advantage leading to a good outcome."

There was a moment of silence.

"But they're just kids," Mom said.

"Hey, I'm twelve." My voice cracked.

"Who better to get the unreserved protection of the most fearsome security force in the world?" Azarel said.

"But do you really think they should all be flying around Kansas City on dragons—after dark?"

Yikes. When she put it that way, it sounded horrible and illegal—but at the same moment, I realized I couldn't stay home. Not a chance. For a second I'd pictured myself babysitting my brothers in the splash room and the grownups rushing in, yelling, "Dark Sky is gone!"

But no way, I needed to face the monster myself. I needed to stop him from hurting the people I loved, and end our awful connection once and for all. And I wanted to fly again. Soaring through the clouds with my dragon—what an amazing feeling. I needed to get back in the sky. Plus, she needed me.

"I'm going." I had to say it several times before anyone paid attention. "And I think we should all go." What I meant was *especially* me. "The dragons will keep us safe and everything will be over fast—and we're a team, right? Team Hoss. You say that all the time."

Mom tilted her head back and stared at the ceiling.

Dad scrubbed his shoulder blades through his shirt.

Slowly, magnetically, their eyes met. I'd made the speech, but there may as well have been no one else in the room.

Dad nodded.

"Ok," Mom said.

And just like that, I'd done it. Right away, I felt sick.

Wyatt walked in half-naked with a towel around his waist, dripping on the hardwood floor. "Time to go yet?"

"Not yet," I said.

But it was coming fast. Maybe too fast. Hurtling right at us, and I'd be there in the middle.

CHAPTER 31
DRAGON ON THE ROOF

The Rieger Hotel was within walking distance from the Brick House, but on this particular Friday night, walking wasn't easy. Thousands of people filled the Dragon District, flowing into bars and bistros, posing for dumb photos. I'd begged Dad to let me walk with him and Azarel, and the dragon handler had shocked me when he said, "Hey, why not?"

Probably they wanted to keep an eye on me, and that was all right. I was remembering my last dream and how Dark Sky said he was done with me. A chill went through me like claws scraping my bones. A few people looking out for me was just fine.

"It's called First Friday," Dad told Azarel. "All the art galleries open and this happens."

"Fun, if you like wearing skin-tight pants and stupid hats." Azarel traced his throat with a thumb and index finger. "First Friday could become Last Friday for these people."

"Way to keep it light," Dad said.

We made our way through a chattering group of girls with

rainbow-colored hair. The Rieger Hotel loomed ahead, surrounded by crowds. A retro advertisement for Rieger Whiskey—O So Good!—was painted on a wall.

"Is it really that good?" Azarel said.

"Business first," Dad said, sounding like Watson.

People filled tables on the sidewalk, flowing in and out of the Rieger. A fire-eater pranced in the street, and people gave him a few extra inches of elbow room.

"The kids and Flannery should be in position." Dad watched the darkening Kansas City skyline.

"Let's move." Azarel shouldered forward and people seemed eager to get out of his way. We waded through the crowded restaurant until we found the stairs—and conveniently, a fire alarm. A minute later, people spurted from the exits as the alarm wailed. By then, we were on the roof. It was set up like an event space with gravel paths, grass and garden beds.

"Let's take a seat." Azarel's fingers tightened on my shoulder.

It wasn't until we'd pulled out chairs at a bistro table that I noticed what he'd seen.

A black speck getting bigger in the glowing sky.

Something twisted inside me like hot wire.

"Here we go." Azarel's fingers drummed the metal table.

Dad put a hand on my arm. "Ready, Conley?"

"Yes," I lied.

The speck became bird-sized, then plane-sized, hurtling through the sunset. For a minute you could believe it was a crow or a jet. But soon we could see sweeping wings and a twisting tail. Dark Sky was flying fast. Shouts rose from the streets. The huge reptile opened his jaws, smoke streaming on the wind, and the screams went up an octave.

"Gone for a hundred years," Azarel muttered. "Now he's

gotta make an entrance. Like it or not, Kansas City's dragon days are back."

Dark Sky landed on the Rieger.

The building shuddered.

Last time I'd seen him in real life, Dark Sky had been three feet long. I knew from my dreams he'd been getting bigger, but I wasn't ready for how big. Locomotive big. Bigger than several elephants. Bigger by far than our biggest dragon.

The apex predator, the top of the food chain.

I hugged myself, wondering how we'd pull this off. Dark Sky crouched on the roof's edge like a forty-foot cat, tail dangling. His hide grated the gravel like a rockslide. Crimson scales gleamed on his spine, and his yellow eyes found me and held on.

Been too long, Conley Hoss.

My hand went to my heart. He was in my head, talking just to me.

No, I thought. I've got nothing to say to you.

Dark Sky winked and I gasped for breath.

"Good evening, Jake and Crane," he said. "You don't look like yourselves." His tail lashed a metal railing off the edge and screams came from below. Moonlight made shadows under his bulging muscles. Then the building vibrated, concrete groaning, metal creaking as he sidled forward.

Your heart is mine, little Hoss.

It's not! I clenched my fists, trying to be brave, but my heart was hammering, my lungs trying to fly away. Dad's arms, wrapped around me, were all that kept me from breaking free and jumping off the roof.

"Azarel." The laughter bled out of the dragon's voice. "You should've kept on hiding in the dark."

"I was just resting," Azarel growled.

Dark Sky relaxed into a crouch. I remembered the accuracy

of his fangs and talons—the way he loved blood the way some people love confetti.

"Your life was different after we fought," the dragon said. "Sure, you won, with your hired bone crushers, but after I was gone—silence. Emptiness. Decades of nothing. How's that for a prize? Fighting me was like fighting yourself."

Azarel didn't reply, which for him was weird.

The dragon's eyes flicked to Dad. "And who are you?"

"Don't answer," Azarel snapped.

"I'm his friend."

The dragon snorted smoke.

"Azarel's friends have a way of dying, Miles Hoss. That's right, I know who you are."

Dad shrugged, still holding me close.

Think you're safe? the reptile asked me. *How cute.*

I squirmed as his snake eyes nailed me in place.

In his chair, Azarel uncrossed his legs. I didn't get how he could still be seated. I was crouching beside Dad, every muscle tense like a sprinter waiting to take off.

"There will be no offers." The dragon handler shoved back his coattails.

"Do you ever remember the good old days?" Dark Sky said.

Azarel finally stood. "For me there are no good old days. You saw to that."

The dragon ignored him. "Kansas City rolling in gold and silver, thanks to us and Mayor Pendergast. Gold under floorboards, gold in the speakeasies, gold in the vaults. It was perfect." He tore at the roof and inspected his claws. "I'll never forget the corpses, guns by their sides in their suits and fedoras."

Azarel's overcoat flapped in the wind. "Enough talk."

Dad and I took our places.

Dark Sky leaned away from us, out over the broken railing, and roared. Screams rose and cameras flashed.

"Would you look at that," the dragon said. "I'll break the internet." He fastened his gaze on us and snapped his jaws. "Azarel, aren't you going to try and kill me?"

Oily fire blasted from Dark Sky's throat, but our protector was ready. Gold fire flared from his raised hands, and the two walls of heat slammed into each other, hissing and sparking. Smoke swirled as the flames ate each other into nothing.

"That all you got?" Dark Sky snarled.

We moved away but he came after us, crushing the garden beds, smashing tables into mangled steel. Dad's fingers dug into my shoulders as he dragged me backwards. More fire flashed from the dragon's mouth and I screamed as oily tendrils snaked through Azarel's shield to singe our clothes. This wasn't supposed to happen. We stumbled away and swayed on the roof edge as Azarel held his flaming fists high.

The dragon opened his jaws again.

"Jump!" Azarel shouted.

CHAPTER 32
EXPLOSIONS IN THE SKY

We jumped, and it was such a relief. I felt like a rabbit throwing itself down a deep, dark burrow. The sky was a gold-streaked blur. The next moment, I crashed into a gritty surface and skidded, scraping my knees and palms. Upside-down, I stared at a sea of faces.

"You've *gotta* improve your aim," the frost dragon said as I dragged myself up her rib cage. Wind whipped my hair as I rolled onto her back and lay there gasping. With a sweep of her wings, she rose over the rooftop. Suddenly we were face to face with Dark Sky.

"Boo!" my dragon said.

Dark Sky jumped back, roaring, as silver fire drenched him. A second later, waves of blue flames pounded over him as Breaker soared in behind us.

"What's the matter?" Breaker snarled. "Are we crashing the party?"

"Take that!" Wyatt yelled from the blue dragon's back

Dark Sky coughed and wheezed.

"Surrender anytime," Azarel bellowed, crouched behind Wyatt.

I ducked behind my dragon's neck, taking shelter the way Azarel had taught us. Storm-strength winds gusted as we held our position in the sky. The air shimmered and heat waves swept past on either side.

Don't breathe that air, my dragon told me.

Don't worry, I said. *Are you going to freeze him again?*

Here goes.

Fwoosh! Wintry haze swirled over Sky's face and the sweltering temperature sank a few degrees. The killer dragon sneezed, clearing the mist.

"What's your plan?" he sneered. "Trying to put me to sleep?" But he kept on snorting and blinking. Then Breaker's fire splashed his scales, making them smoke like a bed of charcoal.

He didn't like that, I said as we dove away from a gush of sulfurous flame.

You're right. Let's do it some more.

On your marks, get set—

Hey, Dark Sky!

Fwoosh!

His vertical pupils caught us like hooks as the cloud engulfed his face.

Oh yeah, he hates us! my dragon said.

He sure does.

"Oh good, he's still here," snarled another voice. The red dragon landed on the roof behind Dark Sky, carrying Dad and a tiny passenger.

There was only one four-year-old in the world crazy enough to fly a combat mission—and only two parents desperate enough to let him come. James hugged the dragon's neck, his fox under one arm, as the reptile lunged forward, blasting crimson flames that flew at our enemy like daggers.

"Go, red dragon!" James squealed.

Dark Sky whirled to face the new threat, moving to the center of the roof. My dragon and Breaker landed in the space he'd abandoned. Glowing gravel crunched under their claws as we fanned out.

I noticed lights blinking in the sky, moving closer—a news copter.

"STAND DOWN," Azarel shouted. "OR WE'LL BURN YOU ON LIVE TV!"

Red, blue and silver fire washed over Dark Sky but he didn't say a word.

The building shook as Dandelion landed on the fourth side of the roof with Mom and Keller on her back. Now Dark Sky was surrounded—we'd sprung our trap. Dandelion on my left, Breaker on the right, and the red dragon straight across. Multi-colored fire pounded Sky no matter where he turned. He twisted and snapped, roaring like a furnace, but he couldn't keep up with our attacks.

He'd underestimated us.

Spotlights hit the roof edges and an amplified voice shouted from below: "WE ARE ARMED, COME DOWN WITH YOUR HANDS UP."

Giddy from all the smoke, I almost laughed.

Guess you're not worried? the white dragon said.

It's almost over, I told her. *And we're gonna win.*

Then something changed.

Dark Sky twisted his neck to look at Wyatt and Azarel. When Breaker bared his teeth, the night-colored dragon smiled. The smile was like an icy claw, sinking through my skin.

What's the matter? my dragon asked.

Explosions lit up the night like July fourth. Sky couldn't stop the bright fire crawling over him, licking at his scales. So why did I feel paralyzed, clinging to my dragon like she was driftwood in a smoky sea?

"WE WON'T STOP," Azarel yelled. "STAND DOWN OR I'LL TURN MY DRAGONS LOOSE."

This is it, the pearl dragon said. *When Azarel says go, we'll strike like lightning.*

Don't you think this is a little too easy?

What if we're just that good?

"TIME IS UP," Azarel yelled.

Dark Sky rose to his full height, front legs swinging like meat hooks. His scales hissed and smoked like a wet campfire, but something was different, I was right. Before he'd been retreating. Now his swagger and his cruelty were back.

"This will be like killing snakes," he sneered.

I felt the frost dragon tighten like a spring.

Hang on—I started to say.

"GET 'IM!" Azarel bellowed.

Our dragons surged forward on all sides.

The building shook as something fell from the sky and struck the roof like a thunderbolt.

CHAPTER 33
THE ROOF ATTACK

Dust and smoke rose in a vortex. Dark Sky disappeared.

What's in there with him? the pearl dragon gave me a worried look.

Something terrible. I shuddered.

Down below, the bullhorn was silent. Grey haze hung over everything. Whatever had fallen from the sky was moving at the center of the roof.

"DRAGONS, ATTACK ON MY SIGNAL." Azarel sounded angry.

The Rieger flickered and smoked under a half moon. My dragon and I waited on our edge of the building where the air was clearer. Midnight scales glinted in the haze and a dragon hissed. Then a dragon laughed, harsh and grating, Dark Sky's laugh.

Something's not right. My arms tightened around my dragon's neck.

I agree.

I felt the tension in her shoulders.

Shadowy flames erupted from the smoke, billowing toward us, and she snuffed them out with a cloud of vapor.

You know Dark Sky loves that frost stuff, she said.

Clinging to her spine, each breath and heartbeat told me how nervous she was—but she was acting brave, and so did I.

We've got this, I told her.

Twisting green flame flared to our left, visible through the murk. I hoped Dandelion was taking good care of Keller and Mom. Wind swept over us and the smoke began to clear. *Finally*. I forced myself to watch, to see what waited in the center of the roof.

But I still wasn't ready for what came next.

Two enormous dragons crouched in the moonlight. Crimson scales streaked their spines and their yellow eyes were cold. Their jaws gaped like hungry sharks.

Two Dark Skies? Only my dragon's internal gravity kept me from falling off.

This isn't possible. She took quick, shallow breaths.

"TAKE THEM DOWN," Azarel roared.

But the Dark Skies were already in motion, rushing Breaker two on one. They collided like tanks, smashing him backwards. Breaker's tail whipped the air and he dug in with his claws, but he couldn't hold on. Fire flashed from Azarel's hands but it wasn't enough. I caught a glimpse of Wyatt's wide blue eyes. Then he and Azarel and Breaker were gone, thrown off the side of the Rieger. My jaw dropped open.

It couldn't be real. Just couldn't.

"Wyatt!" Mom's scream echoed over the roof.

The Darks wheeled to face *us* as the crowd shrieked below.

"Guess who's next?" one of them snarled.

My dragon stiffened under me.

Oh no oh no oh no, she said.

I'd never felt more like a coward in my life. But I couldn't move, couldn't run, caught in the glare of the hungry yellow eyes.

"Don't you like these odds?" said the Sky with dirty, smoking scales. They were both vicious, huge—and stalking closer.

"You're a pretty little thing," the new Sky said. "But not for much longer."

"No, you won't," my dragon gasped.

"THEY'RE OUTNUMBERED," roared the red dragon.

"Attack on my signal," Dad yelled in a choked voice. "Three—two—"

My dragon's muscles twitched.

No, wait, I said.

But she'd already shot forward.

The rooftop blurred under us. All I could do was hold my breath as we flew through oily fire in a cloud of frost. My dragon's claws hit something solid and blood misted my cheek.

First blood, Conley. We—

But a heavy tail hammered her down. The air rushed out of me as I hit the gravel and saw stars. Flames roared near my face and the night exploded with screams and snarls. I tried to move but couldn't.

The world rushed back into focus.

I lay on my back, one foot trapped under my dragon. She was struggling to rise but the new Dark Sky held her down. Jaws gaping, it reached for me and my dragon twisted to meet the attack. The Dark turned on my dragon—razor claws pressed her throat. They cut deeper...and deeper...

"STOP!" I screamed.

The original Dark bellowed in pain behind us.

"Be right back," his partner hissed. It lunged away, the frost dragon shuddered, and I pulled my foot free. Head pounding, I scrabbled onto her back. When I wrapped my arms around her neck, her blood was hot and sticky.

Her jade eyes met mine weakly. *Don't worry about me.*

I turned just in time to see the Darks spring into the sky, snapping their jaws.

"After them!" the red dragon howled.

"Wait!" Dad yelled from its back.

"Should we chase them?" Dandelion asked.

"THEY'RE GETTING AWAY." The crimson dragon jumped skyward as Dad pounded it with his fists. He and James soared after the Darks on the fierce red reptile.

Leaving us behind to pick up the pieces.

CHAPTER 34
NO GOOD AT ALL

You know that feeling when your life is bad, really bad, and you fall asleep, and when you wake up, you feel ok —for just a few seconds? My eyes flew open. My skin felt hot. Apparently I'd blacked out, slumped on my dragon's back. Her head drooped, almost touching the smoldering rooftop. Blood dripped from her neck into the glowing gravel, and in a second, all my bad feelings rushed back in.

We'd failed, totally failed, and nothing would ever be the same.

My brother was missing, maybe dead. Azarel was gone too, and Breaker—and Dad and James were out there somewhere in the night. My heart pumped pure pain and tears spilled down my face. The Darks had been too much for us.

"Sorry," my dragon groaned. "I didn't protect you."

"I didn't do anything to help." I couldn't meet her eyes.

When I slid off her back, my head swam. One of my ankles throbbed, and I didn't trust it to hold my weight. The longer I was conscious, the worse I felt. The frost dragon crept to the ruined railing. She felt awful—I could tell. Mom and Keller were already there, standing on the side. Dandelion crouched next to us. We looked over the edge, and hundreds, maybe thousands of people stared back at us, screaming and taking pictures.

"We need to go," Mom said, but she kept looking down.

There was no sign of Wyatt or Azarel or the blue dragon.

"We're famous," Keller said.

We were famous, all right. Famous losers.

Footsteps crunched the blackened gravel behind us.

"Guys, time to move," the green dragon whispered.

When I turned, a dozen men in uniforms were fanning out across the roof. They wore body armor and helmets and carried big guns with clips. SWAT was stenciled on their clothes and moonlight gleamed on their bulletproof shields as they fanned out. One man lifted his hand and waved the line of soldiers forward. The team stalked toward us.

"GET ON YOUR STOMACHS, HANDS BEHIND YOUR HEADS!"

I didn't have any more freak-outs left in me. I just sat there hugging my dragon's neck, wondering what would happen.

Luckily, one of us had some initiative left. Quick as thought, Dandelion breathed green fire across the roof. It hung in the air like a leafy curtain between us and the soldiers. The twining flames snapped and shimmered. At least one of us was still thinking.

Mom drew in a sharp breath. She shoved Keller onto Dandelion's back and turned to me.

"Coming." I pulled myself onto my dragon as the green sheet of flame flickered faster and faster. Dandelion was already soaring into the sky as Mom and Keller hung on.

"Conley!" Mom yelled.

I leaned into my dragon's rough, opal neck.

"Let's get out of here," I said.

She took a deep, shaky breath.

Dandelion's fire crackled into sparks and the assault team rushed us. Their bulky shadows hurtled across the burning roof. Then we shot upward into blackness, and the Rieger became a rectangle traced in fire. We got a little closer to the stars, then turned and soared away, following Dandelion's dark shape through the sky.

A few minutes later, we landed on the Brick House's roof. Glowing lights led us to a concrete landing pad I hadn't known existed—even though I should've seen it coming.

We slid off our dragons, Mom picked up Keller, and we looked back over downtown. A half mile away in the Dragon District, fire reached into the night like greedy fingers. The pearl dragon's head appeared at my shoulder. Her eyes met mine, glanced away and came back.

I was keeping my thoughts to myself and I guess she was too.

"Everything fell apart," I said.

She nodded. I remembered the deep cuts in her neck and told myself I shouldn't be angry at her. But I *was* angry—not just at her, but at Azarel, at Breaker, at the Dark Skies, and especially at myself. We'd failed. All of us, failed. But especially me—and her.

"Why'd you attack too soon?" Itchy heat washed over my neck and face. "We still had a chance, and then you flew at them–"

"I *gave* us a chance," she snapped. "We drew first blood, while the others were still scared, and it could have worked." Her eyes blazed, then her head sank to the roof wall. "But it didn't work, I know that..."

Hearing her say that took the anger out of me. Whatever else she'd done, she'd been brave. Braver than me.

I hesitated, then patted her smooth, triangular head. Her scales were cool and dry to the touch.

"Will you be ok?" I said.

"Yeah." Her head moved as she scanned the Dragon District and the sky. "I thought we were better than that. I didn't think we could lose." She took a deep breath of summer air and shivered. "The second Dark Sky had its claws in me and I couldn't shake it off. I couldn't get free..." She trailed off.

I could see her pulse beating in her neck. Blood leaked from the jagged puncture wounds. She was hurt worse than me. Feeling guilty, I lifted my hand off her head.

"Thanks for trying to protect me."

"Thanks for getting us off the roof," she said. "I might've just given up."

For a second, I wondered what the police would've done with a twenty-foot frost dragon. Then Mom took my hand and held it. Keller had her other one. Neither of us could bring ourselves to talk, I guess.

We watched the Rieger burn.

A shadow drifted across the moon. I thought about Wyatt and Dad and James, but my mind kept dancing away. Maybe it's not real, I thought. Maybe it's not as bad as you think. Even though I knew, deep down, that it was.

Something jabbed the insides of my chest at crooked angles. I knew what it was. A drinking straw, flattened and bent and dirty, still waiting for its owner. I leaned on the roof wall, trying to fight the darkness rising inside me.

A few raindrops fell, splashing the steel and concrete, dripping onto the glowing footlights. With my head down, it took me a minute to realize it wasn't raining.

My dragon was crying. Her tears were big and drippy.

I couldn't believe it. A dragon, sobbing. And I couldn't stop what happened next. More raindrops hit the roof, smaller but falling faster. We stood there in the dark, feeling awful together.

"It's the hot tub for you, then the cold tub, then anti-flame lotion." Watson was playing doctor, but he was furious. His movements were jerky, his eyes dark. A roll of gauze escaped his jaws and bounced off the bright kitchen counter.

"I should've gone with you," the beardie said.

Most of my skin was burning, unlike the bag of ice on my swollen ankle. As soon as we'd come inside, Mom had wiped rubbing alcohol over my scraped face, arms and knees.

Nothing she or Watson did could soothe the hollow ache in my chest.

"The two Darks could be related." Watson's claws clicked on the steel prep table as he assessed my scrapes. "Sky could have nephews or nieces, or it could just be a surface likeness."

"Sure," I said.

Mom and Keller's feet tromped down the stairs and the sounds made the Brick House feel huge and empty. I raised my head, trying to read the house's mood after the disaster. But the lights glowed steadily. Cool air washed my skin. Everything normal. Nothing out of place.

It made me angry. I wanted clunking appliances, fans whirring at hyper speed, jets of fire shooting from the stove—something to show everything was falling apart.

If I'd been alone, I might've started yelling at the walls right then.

Mom and Keller appeared in the kitchen. Mom looked pale, but my six-year-old brother had on his Curious George pajamas and seemed fine.

"Ice cream time." He climbed onto a stool next to me. "It'll be good after all that hotness. James and Daddy better get home fast, the chocolate's almost gone."

"What about Wyatt?" I said.

Keller shrugged. "There's lots of vanilla."

I swallowed. Vanilla was Top Ten's favorite.

Please make them all be safe, I prayed.

Keller looked from Mom to the walk-in freezer, then his eyes widened. "Do dragons like ice cream? I'll ask Dandelion." He hopped down and raced toward the stairs.

"Honey, wait," Mom looked at Watson. "Do dragons like ice cream?" But before the lizard could answer, she sank onto a stool and put her face in her hands.

Keller raced back into the kitchen, skidded to a stop and hugged her knees. I hugged her too. Watson crawled along the tabletop to pat her elbow.

"The dragons will bring them home," he said, "you'll see."

As far as Keller was concerned, that was a promise. He ran off again, heading for the roof access door we'd just discovered. Then we heard him squeal. "You're back!"

Mom jumped to her feet and we ran through the great room in time to see Dad and James arrive, followed by Azarel and Wyatt.

My knees almost melted with relief.

"James, we're having ice cream!" Keller yelped.

"Yay!" James jumped the last three steps, tumbling into a summersault.

I staggered forward and joined the happy crowd. When all the hugging was over, Dad said, "Let's have that ice cream. All we can taste is smoke."

A few minutes later, I leaned against the glazed Mediterranean tiles of the hot tub, a bowl of double fudge chocolate at my elbow. My brothers splashed in and out of the pond-sized pool, tracking water across the floor and fogging up the plate glass windows. Despite our epic failure at the Rieger, they were in a great mood. And no wonder.

"We chase bad dragons," James told us, bobbing up and down in his inflatable vest. "We play hide-and-seek."

"Dandelion flamed a green wall," Keller informed him.

"Hooray!" James said.

One seat over, Dad gave me a tired smile. "It should've ended tonight, son, but we can feel good about our chances. When they looked back and saw us, they really started flying. I think the red dragon has their number."

Wyatt did a cannonball, showering us with clear, fizzy water, and Dad didn't even get on his case.

"We chased them too," Top Ten told us when he surfaced. "Me and Breaker started flying right before we almost squished a bunch of people. Then we flew up, up, up, over the moon, to swoop down on Dark Sky like Batman. Everyone knows about us now." He spread his arms along the rim of the pool and leaned back, vanilla ice cream leaking from his smile.

"True," Dad said. "The dragons will be all over the news, but that's not our problem. Hey, there's something crazy—it's the story of a lifetime and I can't write about it."

"At least not yet, honey." Mom sat at a bistro table overlooking the chaos, sipping a drink in her fluffy pool robe. Her face was pink and happy under her freckles.

Azarel had joined her, refusing to get wet. His boots scuffed a rhythm on the guard rail, but even with his nervous energy, he looked satisfied.

Even Watson had loosened up. His dark throat lightened to rosy brown as he floated around on a life vest, using his tail as a rudder.

"They ran from us," he pointed out, eyes gleaming. "Ran like baby basilisks."

That left *me*.

I understood why everyone felt good. We hadn't won but we hadn't lost either and not losing was a big deal. The relief I felt was huge, like a bubble of hope surrounding me, lifting me and floating me along with the rest of my family despite my swollen ankle, my blisters and gashes. Dad and Wyatt and James were ok. So were Azarel and Breaker. We'd survived the ambush, and now we wouldn't be surprised by two Darks again. Like Watson said, even though they'd escaped, the Skies had flown away. We had their number.

There were lots of reasons to feel happy. The problem was, no matter how many times I tried, the reasons didn't lift my heart. The twisted plastic in there was getting thinner, sharper, tightening like a wire net—until the moment when something would snap. And when that moment came, what would happen to me? Who would I become?

I blinked as Dad put his arm across my shoulders. Wyatt patted my knee, then swam off to steal Keller's ice cream. Mom smiled down at us as my little brothers screamed in the hydro-massage seat and everyone was happy.

Except me.

CHAPTER 36
THE DREAM

"Get out of here." Watson said sounded serious. "You've got a date with the cold tub, kid." The lizard crawled off his life jacket into the shallow water on the stairs.

"Dad, do I have to—"

"Do what the beardie says, son."

Gritting my teeth, I limped out of the tub, steam rising from my skin.

Watson led the way across the puddled tiles to the cold tub on the far side of the splash room. It wasn't nearly as popular as the hot tub. And no wonder. No one likes the feeling of his organs shriveling up inside.

"Get in there," he said. "Don't think about it, just do it."

I folded my arms, balancing on my un-sprained foot. "I guess you know a lot about first aid," I said, "but it's not like you're a doctor—"

"I *am* a doctor." Watson scowled.

"Sure, you're *our* doctor, but—"

"My M.D. is on the office wall," he snapped.

Apparently I'd missed that.

Frowning back at him, I slouched down the steps into the cold current and immediately started shivering. "Now—I feel —even worse," I said through chattering teeth.

Watson looked smug. "Five minutes, minimum." As he studied me, his eyes softened. "Look, kid. You feel like you're alone, and none of this is fair, and you're in pain, and it should already be over. Well, you're right."

I hugged myself tight.

Watson put his head on one side. "Except one thing." He jabbed a claw at me. "You're not alone, hear me? Your parents, total civilians, lined up to fight for you without a second thought. Your brothers have your back, tough little kiddos. Me, I'm fond of you. Azarel, he tolerates you. And the Brick House —well, the house has always been on your side."

I nodded convulsively in the icy water.

"Good." Adagio cuffed my shoulder with his bunched-up claws, leaving a tiny blue mark. "Happy we're on the same page."

By the time I made it to my bunk bed, wrapped in a flannel bathrobe, I'd lost track of what Watson had done to me. After freezing me in the cold tub, he'd brushed on weird-smelling purple antiseptic. Then he'd patched my worst cuts with butterfly bandages. Then he'd wrapped my ribs with gauze as I'd zoned out, staring up at the locker room's teak rafters. You're not the only one hurt, I reminded myself.

"Hey Watson," I said. "After you're done helping me, can you make sure my dragon is—"

"Already did. Priorities, kid."

"Ohhh." I decided to stop talking to the annoying lizard.

Lying in bed, I realized the beardie had rubbed me with lotion at some point. My flame-singed face felt oily against my pillow, but I was too tired to care.

Watson says you're on my side, I told the Brick House. But you have an awful way of showing it. Terrible. The worst.

"You lured me in," I whispered. "Yeah, you. You're killing me and you don't have a word to say. I'll bet you like watching me suffer, don't you? Maybe you haven't noticed, but I'm taking all the worst hits. Getting knocked down over and over and you just let it happen, you silent, stuck-up–"

Feathery magic fell on me from the ceiling. Maybe it was the house taking a breath. I felt like I was shrinking in my bed, dwindling to the size of an insect as the Brick House towered above me—an immovable fortress with a mind of its own who did what it wanted all the time and was too huge, too ancient, to care about a tiny speck like me. The house rushed upward, brushing the stars—but at the same time, it was right there next to me, above and below and on all sides.

"Ok," I gasped. "Maybe you know what you're doing."

Then I was asleep.

Later I had a much worse dream.

I crouched in a hot, dark place, tearing at the floor with my claws and snarling. This wasn't the victory dance I'd planned. Those wild crowds—mine. All that blood, all that life, all that panic. The hot, salty buffet of human flavors, well, I'd still have it. Rock dust showered down as I gouged the burrow deeper. Then I moved to the entrance, stiff and hungry, scales aching.

An American flag snapped in gusts of night wind. Spotlights lit my building with an eerie green glow. Far, far below, cars rolled down roads as thin as pencils. People streamed under streetlights like lines of happy ants—but not for long.

"Come inside, Sky," a voice hissed behind me. "They'll all burn, later." I dragged myself back down the concrete tunnel, feeling its latent heat. An ideal place to hide our treasure. Then my spine prickled. An intruder! I twisted and snapped—but no one was there.

Of course.

"Get away from me, Conley Hoss. Just can't wait to die, can you?"

The human me tossed feverishly in my bunk, and a faint sound came from the window. *Scritch, scritch, scritch.* My dreams were running together. I sat up, somehow knowing, even in the dream, what came next. I glanced at Wyatt's empty bed—except it wasn't empty. He lay face down, snoring softly. That didn't make sense, but I did what I always did and climbed down from my bunk. Keller and James were in bed too.

Another change to the dream. I didn't like it.

Then hot, sour air washed my face as I looked out the window and a pair of lamp-like eyes flicked open.

No matter how many times it happened, it was still terrifying.

I yelled and jumped back as a dragon slid inside with a dry rustle of scales.

Wake up, I told myself. Wake up.

Dark Sky laughed. "You are awake."

My mouth dropped open.

"You've become an irritant," he said. "A spy. No longer useful. And I'm hungry."

Hot saliva dripped from his jaws and fizzed like acid on the floor.

I passed a hand across my eyes. "You're—not really here. You're too small."

"Ha!" He rolled his shoulders, dry scales flaking off. "I slink, I swagger, just a question of sun and shadow—but mostly a question of *what I want.* And what I want right now is your heart. So I got smaller." He picked his teeth with a claw. "How is your heart, by the way?"

I opened my mouth, shut it.

The dragon's eyes narrowed. "Someone taught you to guard your thoughts."

"Leave me alone."

His snout came closer, smelling of dirty charcoal. "Open up, and I'll let you live five minutes longer, or—your pick—kill you fast."

I shook my head no.

"A little honesty won't hurt you," Dark Sky whispered. "Not like *I* can." He extended a razor claw.

I shut my eyes, struggling to hide the contents of my head.

"Where does everyone sleep?" he hissed. "Where's Azarel? Where's your mom and dad?"

"I'm the one you hate," I gasped. "Leave them alone."

The dragon laughed. "Sure. Ok."

I wanted to grab for the door knob, but I knew that would kill me instantly like it always did. Instead I forced my hands to my sides and focused on the dark behind my eyelids. What could I do? I had an idea—but it came out as a panicked, silent scream.

"You're freezing up, little rabbit," Dark Sky said.

In my mind, I kept yelling—trying to hide my fear.

"Can't hear you," he whispered.

But I hear you, said a voice in my head.

My eyes shot open. The monster's toothy grin was inches from my face.

"Tick tock," he said. "Too bad, you could've told me some very interesting things. But now you've earned the right to die slowly." His talon traced my chin, then ran along my chest.

The claw cut into my skin.

"Wait," I gasped. "I'll talk to you."

"Hmm." Dark Sky's talon touched my ribs like a scalpel. "No, too late."

"*Not* too late," said a voice at the window.

The pearl dragon's head and shoulders shot through and she clamped down on Dark Sky's body. He howled and tore at the floor as he skidded backwards, bracing himself against the window frame. His wings flared helplessly against the bricks. For a long second, his wild eyes burned into me. Then glass and steel shattered as he hurtled into the night.

I stood in the empty room, shaking as the two dragons crashed below.

"What's going on?" Wyatt said.

"Why are we awake?" Keller asked.

Pressing my ribs, I staggered to the window. Two stories down, shapes twisted in the dark. A flash of light crackled, followed by a wet crunch, then nothing.

"What happened?" I whispered.

Nothing moved. Then–

I did it, the frost dragon told me. *Seriously, I did it. Gold and glitter, did you see that?*

Was Dark Sky trying to trick me? But he would never say, "gold and glitter."

You came, I said. *You got here.*

Of course I did. Don't tell anyone else, but I thought we'd both die.

Rising from the yard outside, her giggle was nervous and musical, the first dragon giggle I'd ever heard. It made me feel less terrified. It also made me feel like a jerk.

"I didn't think *you'd* die," I said out the window. "I just wasn't sure you'd hear me, or if you did, you'd be too busy–"

Stop talking, she told me. *You're about to ruin this.*

Wyatt bumped into me, rubbing his eyes. "Who are you talking to?"

"Uh, my dragon."

"You should be asleep," he grumped.

"I'm hungry." Keller tugged my elbow.

"Why this day have no sun?" James groaned from his bed.

Top Ten squinted down at the yard. "Is there really someone down there?"

"It is I," my dragon murmured spookily. "The ghost dragon who strikes at midnight. Woo—WOOO."

Well, at least she was feeling pretty good.

Wyatt gave me a look. "Are you sure this is a dragon we know?"

Some of the terror left my body.

As we hurried downstairs, lights flooded the house. At least, my brothers hurried while I limped along, trying not to slip with the tingly goo coating my body.

I can't believe what Dark Sky said to you, the frost dragon said.

Watch out, he might get big again.

Not possible—no sunlight, dummy. If he didn't taste like tar, I'd tear off his wings right now.

Oh, wow, that's gross—but I kind of like it.

My parents and Azarel caught up with us as we moved in a shadowy, jostling crowd down to the yard.

"What's going on?" Mom grabbed Keller and James.

"Everything is ok," I said. "There's a—a surprise in the yard, but don't worry or freak out, he's already been zapped, so—"

"Zapped is not a thing." Azarel shoved his way through.

"Hey everyone, it's me." The frost dragon slid out of the shadows, playing to the crowd. Her scales shone under the moon. "Dark Sky is over there in the tomatoes. Does lightning count as zapping? What you're about to see may shock you."

She shot me a look.

"Watch your mouth, princess." Azarel crunched through the yard and leaned over a shadowy bulk in our vegetable garden, hands on his knees. "Did you kill something and drag it home? Hell's bells, am I dreaming? Finally, a little luck!"

The frost dragon beamed.

"How did this happen?" Azarel asked. "Snatched him as he was flying past?"

"Um, not exactly," my dragon said.

I didn't know you could shoot lightning, I told her.

Neither did I—but don't tell anyone I didn't know, ok? Seriously, I just saved your life.

Ok, fine.

But I crossed my fingers, just in case.

"Conley, you're bleeding." Mom's hand tightened on my wrist.

"It's nothing. I'm ok."

"That looks like stitches, kid," Watson said.

I hadn't noticed the beardie clinging to Azarel's lapel.

"How bad did he hurt you?" The pearl dragon didn't seem bothered by all the adults examining us. "Let me take a look."

"Not bad," I said. "He didn't have enough time."

"Thank goodness," Mom said.

At that moment, I realized I liked my dragon a lot. I was lucky to have her for a partner— even if she was the snobby princess type.

Wait, what? Tell me you didn't just think that.

Uh oh, I'd been careless. She sounded mad.

"Conley, are you in shock?" Dad said.

Top Ten shoved in beside me. "What happened in our room?"

"My dragon saved my life," I said.

A questionable choice, I now see, my dragon said.

CHAPTER 37
THE DRAGON HOSTAGE

It was a good moment to stop talking to my dragon, so I told everyone else what had happened. They got quiet as we stared at mini-Dark Sky in the early dawn light, sprawled in the wreckage of our garden.

"That a baaad dragon." James was wide-eyed in his boxer shorts.

"Why'd he show up here?" Dad looked angry. "He's supposed to be on the run. And how can that be him?—he's not even pony-sized."

"Dragons can shrink fast in the dark." Azarel scowled up at my shattered window. "I never would've thought he'd try anything with all our dragons right there on the roof."

"What did Dark Sky say to you?" Watson asked.

I replayed the scene in my mind, although I would've preferred not to. Dark Sky's eyes snapped open, hot and hungry as he lunged into my room. "He said it wasn't a dream, that I was awake." I closed my eyes to remember. "He said he was tired of me, that I was irritating—a spy. He said—he was starving." I swallowed.

"Wait," Watson said. "Why did he say you were a spy?"

"You know." I gestured vaguely. "The way we're always connected, me following him around..." Then I put two and two together. "Oh wow," I said. "I think I saw something in my sleep I wasn't supposed to."

By then the other dragons had joined us, poking their snouts in for a closer look. One by one, their faces split into horrifying grins. If our neighbors had looked out their windows, they would've run away screaming.

"Get him outta here," Azarel told our gathered inferno. Our dragons looked at Sky's unconscious body reluctantly, even though they were all three times his size.

"Yessir, Azarel sir." Dandelion saluted but didn't move.

Azarel rolled his eyes.

The red dragon grabbed Dark Sky's tail in his jaws and dragged him a few feet.

"Watch the lettuce," Mom said.

The red spit the tail out. "Gross, I can never un-taste that."

Told you he tastes like tar. The white dragon glanced over.

Maybe she'd forgiven me.

Uh-uh, not this snobby princess.

"Let's roll him," the red dragon said.

Grunting and snarling, our inferno got it done. Watching the killer dragon's limp body flop through our yard like a hideous rag doll, shoved by other dragons, was the most bizarre thing I'd ever seen. I couldn't take my eyes off them as they barreled him through the gate.

Azarel disappeared to help.

"Breakfast?" Keller asked.

Thudding sounds came from the cellar as we made our way back inside, and everyone fanned out to get dressed. I was hiding in my walk-in closet, trying to pull on a t-shirt when Watson found me.

"Take that off," he snapped. "Back to the locker room."

I groaned and let him herd me down the hall. Once I'd looked at the slash from Dark Sky's claw, I'd known Watson would be after me again. If I hadn't seen it with my own eyes, I never would've believed a lizard could use a hypodermic syringe, but Watson made it look easy, stabbing my ribs with local anesthetic. As I lay under a heat lamp on the massage table, he took the opportunity to quiz me about my spying.

When I told him about Dark Sky burrowing into the top of a skyscraper, his eyes lit up. The needle sagged dangerously in his tiny claws.

"Hey, watch out," I said.

"So they have a den," he said. "A secret lair. This is big. Excuse me for being blunt, kid, but Sky should've killed you the day you met. He just had to have his inside joke, his extra edge. Using you like an energy drink. Well, now we'll turn it back on him."

Maybe Watson and I were bonding. I'd never heard him be so un-secretive before and honestly, it freaked me out.

"Does this mean it's over?" I asked. "We won?"

Watson darted his brows. "We're getting close." Then he set to work on the the sutures.

"Ouch, ouch, ouch," I groaned, but he saw through my complaining.

"For a tough kid, you're kind of a baby," he said.

I made a face. Nevertheless, I felt grateful when he smoothed a shimmering bandage over the stitches. "Waterproof *and* fireproof," he said. "Take a shower. Rinse off that green-brown goo—the burn repellant's done its work. Then you can go whine to your mother."

"Heyyy." I saw the twinkle in his eye as I stood up carefully.

"Keep me informed if Dark Sky leaks anything else. *And* the Brick House—look at the powerful entities playing tag in your mind. Keep me in the loop, kid." He pointed his needle at me until I nodded.

Back downstairs, the kitchen was total chaos. Dad was frying bacon and eggs, Azarel was making coffee, and Mom darted back and forth between the toaster and the waffle maker as James grabbed her knees chanting, "corn flakes, corn flakes." Wyatt and Keller had taken advantage of the situation by pouring huge glasses of orange juice that were dripping on the floor.

Watson must not have liked what he saw. "Turn yourself around," he said from my shoulder. "Let's come back in five minutes."

In the first floor media room, we clicked on the huge flatscreen tv, which seemed like a strange choice at that particular moment. I thought maybe Watson wanted to introduce me to a favorite show—some cool, gritty gangster series, probably—which made me feel good, special, like the two of us were getting closer.

Live-breaking blinked on the screen.

Darn it, he'd turned on the local news. Then I felt him stiffen on my shoulder and saw what he was seeing. The scene was a six-lane bridge over the Missouri River, and the bridge's huge cables were vibrating like strings. A reporter walked through honking, gridlocked cars, talking over her shoulder.

"Traffic is at a standstill on the Broadway Bridge," she said. "The mayor's office suggests military aircraft or even UFOs are causing all this craziness." She gestured at the shaking cables and drivers leaving their vehicles. "But after what happened last night, people have other ideas—and I'm with all of you. C'mon, we know what we saw! And don't tell us the flames were caused by climate change."

She paused as something crashed further down the bridge. "You've heard the chatter. You've seen the viral videos. And now, less that twenty-four hours later? We're investigating this as another case of—*dragons*." She smiled.

"AZAREL!" Watson gave a strangled yell. "Walk away," he hissed at the screen. "Turn around right now."

The reporter was still talking. "With a record number of eyeballs on this broadcast—thank you, by the way—it's obvious this city cares about its dragon heritage. As a result, we're launching our first real investigation in years. Could this be a military exercise—or have the dragons truly returned? I'm here to find the truth."

"I don't know, Lindsay," said a studio voiceover. "Our experts and fact-checkers say dragons are extinct, and there's no possible way they could appear in Kansas City."

"Time for some old-school reporting," Lindsay the reporter shot back.

"I doubt there's any *real* danger—but still, be careful."

"Don't worry, I wore my running shoes." She smiled.

Then without warning, people started screaming. I wanted to cover my eyes. The camera lurched toward the river as a car crashed through the concrete wall and plummeted toward the muddy water. A tiny figure jumped from the driver's side, spiraling away before the car splashed down.

A fist struck the table beside me as Azarel joined us.

"Oh no!" The reporter said. "What's going on?" The camera cut back to her face, which had become several shades paler. She opened her mouth, but the camera's mic was overwhelmed by an echoing bass roar. A huge silhouette filled the archway behind her.

"Not again," Watson said. "Not all over again."

Azarel clenched and released his fists.

Screams rang out as an enormous dragon towered over everyone, roaring and breathing flames. People dove from their vehicles, running for their lives. A car whooshed into a fireball.

The reporter froze like she was paralyzed, and the camera filmed the back of her head.

"Retreat," yelled the unseen news anchor. "Get out of there, Lindsay—but maybe walk backwards. Safety first, but you know, keep it rolling."

The cameraman's angry reply was drowned out by the dragon. "BRING ME DARK SKY," the monster roared. "UNTIL HE GETS HERE, A CAR GOES OFF THE BRIDGE EVERY TEN MINUTES."

I reached up and pried Watson's talons off my shoulder.

"What's it talking about?" Lindsay asked, her eyes wide.

But it was a mistake for her to take her eyes off the dragon.

With horrible speed, a rush of dark scales filled the screen, and the live stream ended with a scream and a crunch of static.

CHAPTER 38
GHOST

Azarel slammed his palms on the tabletop. Dad wordlessly gulped coffee. Mom held her mug with both hands but didn't sip. Everyone stared at the tv where the bridge footage was on endless loop.

"Let's burn him to cinders on the bridge," Azarel growled. "Our inferno can be there in minutes." When no one replied, he threw himself into an armchair.

"This dragon is no idiot," Watson said.

"We can trick him, right?" I said. "With our four dragons, we can, um, surprise him or something, and make sure everyone's ok, and then..." I trailed off, because an awful feeling came over me, like someone was pouring my gut full of concrete. "Wait," I said. "We can't—we're not going to—not Dark Sky–"

Watson's throat was almost black, his eyes glittering like chunks of coal.

Mom's fingers touched my shoulder. She tried to say something but her words got stuck.

"We don't have to let Dark Sky go, do we?" I said.

Watson closed his eyes. Dad slammed his mug down so hard it broke, and Azarel lurched to his feet, knocking his chair over backwards.

"You have my word," he growled, "Whatever happens, Sky won't lay a claw on you. I'll see to it if it's the last thing I do."

He stomped out of the media room. I glanced at Watson, but he was hunkered on the table, tail twitching. All of a sudden, I wasn't sure what to do with myself. I felt like I was floating, my life veering out of control again.

Downstairs, I stood in a corner of the loud, messy kitchen, trying to focus on little things. James eating cornflakes from a box. The bacon burning. After the frost dragon saved me, I'd felt good, almost bouncy. Dark Sky once again locked up in the basement felt like a huge black funnel cloud, churning toward our house, had disintegrated into harmless wisps of mist. The bruised, tangled feeling in my chest had started to dissolve—and now, just a couple hours later, the tornado came rushing back.

Because the second Dark Sky was just as sly and ruthless as the first.

Mom slid me a bowl across the counter. "Eat something, honey."

She looked as pale as that reporter who was probably dead now.

Granola, yogurt. I was back on the survival diet, and I wanted to throw it all against the wall. My spoon quivered in my hand, but I forced myself to take a bite, knowing I'd need the energy.

You're not alone, I told myself. *It only seems that way.*

Five minutes later, my health food breakfast was gone. I could feel my insides slowly twisting into knots, and I needed something to do—someone to talk to—even if it was complicated. In fact, complicated might be better. Anything to get my mind off what was happening.

Hey princess, I said, trying to sound brave and kind of casual. *I guess you heard the news.*

Several moments of silence.

Don't call me that, the frost dragon said.

It looks like we have to fight some more.

She didn't reply.

I'm sorry if I hurt your feelings.

Another long moment, then:

Oh, well, you know, stuff happens...

That didn't seem especially promising but I plunged ahead.

I'm feeling pretty nervous about all this. I thought it was over, mostly anyway, and I could stop being tied to Dark Sky and—having bad dreams and feeling bad, but now—now it's all back again.

She paused. *He did all that to you?*

Yeah. But I didn't want her to think I was a whiner, so I added, *Hey, guess what? I thought of a name for you.*

She shot her answer right back.

I'm sorry about all that, but still. You're a jerk. Dragons don't take names from jerks.

Ohh... I should've known things wouldn't be so easy. One more thing going badly. Beast guts. I tried to think off all the words Azarel said when he was angry. Bloody hash. Smoking beastly–

Hey Conley, the dragon said. *Bring me some toast, ok? Maybe I'll forgive you.*

Wow. I hadn't seen that coming.

This dragon doesn't want a friend, I thought. She wants a delivery boy.

I stared at the bricks in the kitchen wall, but it wasn't like I had anything better to do, so I slid a piece of toast from Wyatt's plate while he made faces at Keller. By the time I'd limped up three stories, plus the secret stairway to the roof, my ankle throbbed and my stitches tingled. I didn't see the point in bringing toast to a dragon who could eat an entire cow.

But I'd already climbed all that way, so I hit the button and the roof door shot open with a smooth hiss. On the massive landing pad, it felt like a hundred degrees even though it was barely 8am. The pearl dragon leaned against the low roof wall, tail curled around her feet. Her eyebrows shot up when I appeared, and she glanced around with a pleased look on her face.

I followed her eyes, struggling to catch my breath.

The red dragon snorted at me.

Breaker shook his head. "Sad."

"You've got him *so* well trained," Dandelion said. "I'm jealous."

I held out the toast, my face burning.

"Wait a minute," the pearl dragon said. "Where's the jam? I definitely mentioned jam—strawberry, please."

"No." Sweat trickled down my face. "You didn't say that. I can't..."

The frost dragon frowned at me. Then her snout curved in a smile and all the dragons started laughing. It sounded like a bell choir backed up by cymbals.

Holding the crumpled toast, I felt like an idiot. I threw the toast at my dragon—she easily caught it—and turned to go.

"No, don't leave," my dragon gasped, wiping her eyes. "You're such a sweetheart. I love toast, thank you so much." She took teeny bites.

I wished I could sink through the poured concrete at my feet.

"They're kind of cute when they pout," Dandelion said.

Now we're even, the frost dragon said in my head.

I tried to think of a comeback but I had nothing.

"It's ok," the red dragon said.

"Yeah, don't take it too hard," Breaker said. "You'll get back at her eventually."

"That's right." I sat down next to my dragon as she continued to take incredibly small bites of toast. "I hope you're happy now."

"Oh, I am." She smiled.

And I felt happier too.

Ten minutes after that, my whole family stood on the tree-screened back drive, watching Azarel and Dad shove a huge duffle bag into our minivan. We'd discussed our plan—and our plan was scary. Even my little brothers were quiet. Dragon snouts were visible at the edge of the Brick House's roof. The duffle twitched and shuddered in the trunk.

"Guess we're set." Dad slammed the door.

"Locked and loaded," Azarel growled.

"Wait." Watson's throat bristled on the big man's shoulder.

We watched him raise a taloned fist.

"FEAR NO FIRE," the lizard shouted. "GIVE NO QUARTER. LAUGH AT TROUBLE—AND TELL THE STORY!"

"Laugh at trouble." Azarel struck his heart with a closed hand.

"Yes," Dad said.

"Tell the story before bedtime," Mom said.

I swallowed. "One more thing," I said. "Before we go, I think my dragon has a name."

The air shimmered as the pearl dragon sprang from the roof to crouch beside me, her head on one side.

"It's fine," she said. "Go ahead."

"Ghost," I said. "Now you see her, now you don't."

"It's all right," she said.

Watson gave me an approving nod, then dropped from Azarel's shoulder and scrambled toward the Brick House.

Please tell me you're kidding and you actually like it, I told my dragon.

She closed one emerald eye and opened it as I climbed into the minivan. A dragon wink. *Actually, I love it*, she told me. *Mysterious, scary—kind of perfect.*

Then she was gone.

I swallowed again, hard, as I slid the door shut.

See you later, Ghost.

CHAPTER 39
DEATH TRAP

I'd never seen a carnival or sports stadium as crazy as the scene by the Missouri River. The first thing you noticed, driving north through downtown, was the smoke rising from the Broadway Bridge. The closer we got, the more crowded the streets became.

People were parking on curbs and surface lots and hiking in, lugging binoculars and coolers. Food trucks crammed the sidewalks and the lines for burgers and tacos, stretched around corners, showed that lots of people had skipped breakfast to get here. Hyped crowds hurried toward the river.

It gave me a weird feeling in the bottom of my stomach. At Prairie Refuge Middle School, we'd learned how the Romans used to fill coliseums with screaming fans who came to watch people fight monsters and die.

This seemed a lot like that.

We cruised around looking for a spot until Dad swerved down an alley and parked illegally by a loading dock. We climbed out and stood there in the dirty alley. Mom grabbed James and Keller, but not before she'd pulled me close.

"Be brave," she whispered as she ruffled my hair.

Her hug was the best medicine for what was happening.

Wyatt was quiet, and I knew he was trying to make sense of all this, probably deciding who he needed to fight. He looked sullen, chin down, hands jammed in his pockets.

"Stay cool, Top Ten," I said.

"I'm always cool." He gave me the tiniest smile.

Dad's jaw was hard, like he was a decade younger and the bell was about to ring in a boxing match. Mom's blue eyes were wired open, mouth tight. James looked pouty and ready for conflict, a cowlick of blond hair standing on end. Keller had a huge grin on his face, and I wished I knew what he was thinking. Azarel looked like he always did—huge and dangerous—except a hot, invisible energy crackled off him that made you want to keep your distance.

"Let's get to the starting line, Hosses," he said.

He and Dad each grabbed an end of the duffel. Watching them shift the heavy, squirming bag, I was glad I didn't have to touch it. Shoulders straining, they shuffled toward the river and the rest of us fell in line. There were some tense moments when the duffle lashed out and knocked people flat. But anyone who got up, bruised and angry, turned away when they saw Azarel.

Finally we reached the yellow police tape where the crowd was thickest. People muttered and shot us looks as they moved out of our way. Groups were staking out space with lawn chairs, drinking beer and pointing at the river. It was like a Chiefs tailgating party except no one knew who they were cheering for. Police officers patrolled the line, keeping an eye on the crowd.

"No time to waste," Azarel said. "No time to be subtle."

As I tried to picture him being subtle, Mom lifted the police tape. He and Dad ducked under, and right away, a uniformed cop came jogging over.

"This is a crime scene, folks."

"Just keep walking," Azarel told Dad.

Mom's mouth hung slightly open as we watched from the safe side of the tape.

"This thing's heavy," Azarel grunted. "Gotta keep moving."

The duffel bag squirmed wildly.

The officer put a hand on his gun. "Who are you—and who's in there? This isn't funny."

"Do you see us laughing?" Azarel said. "We're with the Dragon Agency."

Now they were twenty feet away and still moving, the cop stalking alongside but not getting too close because every few steps, the duffel lunged his way. Under different circumstances, it would've been funny. Then I realized I'd missed my cue. I was in the wrong place and I wasn't sure how to fix it. So I did the only thing I could think of.

I lifted the tape and started running.

The crowd came to life, screaming like I was climbing too high on a playground. At the same time, people were excited, cheering me on. I ran faster, away from the hot, eager eyes. For a second, I forgot I was running toward a dragon.

"Let us handle this," Azarel was saying as I caught up.

The cop saw me. "What the—"

I dodged behind Dad.

"I can't allow a child on this bridge," the officer snapped.

"He's with us," Dad snapped back.

By then we'd reached the maze of cars. I darted in, Dad and Azarel staggering after me. The officer stood in a gap between two vans looking frustrated.

"I'm coming with you," he said. "Doesn't matter if I believe you, I'm still responsible. So don't argue."

Azarel and Dad shuddered to a halt.

"You're a serious person," Azarel said. "And I respect what you do, so I'm gonna take time we don't have to tell you we're dealing with a serial killer, a flying, fire-breathing biohazard. A convicted criminal dragon who was sentenced to life. He's wanted on five continents—'Presumed deadly, do not engage'—so you're not responsible for this, believe me. Now step aside, sir, and let us do our job."

It was a polite speech, and scary. I shivered.

The officer took his hand off his gun and ran it through his silver hair.

"Want me to knock you down?" Azarel said. "To make it look good?"

"Not a chance," the officer said. "Just get moving. I'm Captain Estrada. When this is over, I'll see you at the station."

Azarel grunted. We lost sight of the cop as we moved behind a pickup.

"Good man," Dad huffed.

The duffle bag seemed to be growing heavier, and that's how I felt. Slower, darker, like I was made of rock. But Dad caught my eye. We'll be ok, his look said.

So I kept moving.

As we neared the middle of the bridge, the road became a junkyard. Blackened cars jackknifed everywhere. Smoke rose from the asphalt. Mostly the cars were empty, but here and there, people crouched behind bumpers and open doors. I wondered why they didn't run away until I took a closer look. Pupils dilated, limbs twitching, they looked like survivors of a zombie attack.

"Go on, get moving, shoo," Azarel told them.

They stirred and started to move like they'd been waiting for permission—and maybe they had. Now the heat was intense, flames licking at shiny puddles, and I got the idea the whole road could go up at any second. Then we saw the barricade.

Burned-out cars were stacked twenty feet high. Dad and Azarel shuffled to a stop, then sidestepped to the edge of the bridge.

"Three, two, one," Azarel said. The duffel bag thumped the wide concrete wall, and the two of them stepped back, shrugging their shoulders, rubbing their arms.

"Man, we're gonna be sore tomorrow," Dad said.

Behind the towering barricade, something moved.

Dad's hand fell on my shoulder.

I thought about how weirdly quiet the bridge was. Above the metal cables a jet made white lines in the sky. Get away while you still can, I thought. You're not safe, not even up there.

Azarel tugged his leather overcoat tight. He cupped his hands to his mouth. "Come out, come out, wherever you are. Time to stop hiding. What's your name—Dark Shy?"

Behind the wall of cars, a dragon hissed—and I winced.

"LEAVE YOUR CAMPFIRE CIRCLE," Azarel shouted. "WE'VE GOT YOUR TWIN."

The metal castle began to shift, cars scraping, steel screaming.

My fingernails dug into my palms as a heavy, triangular head appeared. With its body hidden, it looked like a cobra or mamba as big as a house. The dragon's smoky yellow eyes locked on the squirming duffel bag.

"Bring him here," it snarled.

"Let's be real." Azarel folded his arms. "He's sitting on the edge of the bridge for a reason. Open up your castle."

"How do I know it's him?" Smoke rose from the dragon's nostrils.

"Ha." Azarel's smile didn't reach his eyes. "You think I'd

knock out one of my own dragons, gag him and fold him in half?"

The duffel bag hissed and the huge dragon stiffened.

"CLEAR A PATH," Azarel roared, and gave the bag a kick.

The second Dark Sky roared back. It head-butted a car at the top of the barricade, and the vehicle crashed nose down, fluids splashing. If the bridge went up in flames, I wondered who would die first. Then the wall gave way, screeching like a freight train with its brakes on. The dragon stood in the gap, smoke swirling around it.

"Come on out," Azarel said. "Keep your distance."

Talons tearing the road, the huge beast stalked forward.

Its vertical pupils never left us.

"Let's get one thing straight," it snarled. "I'm not another Dark Sky. I'm Dark Queen—and we're not twins."

Uh oh, I thought.

Azarel's face was blank. "I guess every story is a love story after all." Then his eyes got hard. "I go in, assess the situation, then we make a deal. Otherwise..." He nodded at the heavy, twitching duffel. "It's a long way to the bottom."

Dark Queen stretched her jaws wide and didn't say a word.

I had the horrible idea she was smiling.

CHAPTER 40
MORE THAN 39

D ad and I stayed by the duffel as Azarel moved forward, hands raised and ready. He disappeared behind the wall of cars. Queen stared at us with dripping teeth, and Dad squeezed my shoulders. His heartbeat thumped against my back.

The dragon handler crunched back into view.

"Go open your traps." His fingers curled as his coat flapped in the river wind. "I counted thirty-nine people sealed in those cars. I need to see all thirty-nine right here."

The dragon hissed, and sparks floated from her nose—she disappeared.

Azarel bent close to us. "Listen," he whispered. "We knew it might be a she, and sure, it complicates things, but if it comes to the backup plan—and hell's bells, let's hope it doesn't—they'll be vulnerable, right? Yeah, they'll be on edge, frothing at the mouth, so don't forget—"

Metal shrieked behind the barricade and Azarel snapped back to attention. We heard screams. Then people began to appear, running for their lives. College kids and hipsters, vacationers and young professionals. Shoes missing, clothes in tatters, they barely looked at us as they stumbled and sprinted past.

"What was your count?" Azarel asked.

"I had thirty-nine," Dad said.

"Me too."

I'd forgotten to count.

Dark Queen's head and shoulders loomed in the the barricade. "Your turn," she snarled. "Put Dark Sky in the center of the road."

"And what if we don't?" Azarel asked.

The dragon showed her shark-like teeth. "Listen."

We listened. Gasoline hit the roadway, drip, drip, drip. Further down the bridge, a car whooshed into flame. When I looked back at the dragon, she was grinning. Because there was another sound. Tinny and far away. Someone screaming. It was horrible, maybe the worst sound I'd ever heard. Pure terror, death getting closer. Our plan had gone terribly wrong.

Azarel looked out over the river. "Where is she?"

Dark Queen's laugh was like knives and forks. "Poor thing's wrapped inside a trunk, wearing it like tinfoil." She licked her lips. "You can let her roast slowly—or you can save her."

"Let her go," Azarel growled.

"Step away from Dark Sky," the dragon snarled.

Azarel moved to the center of the bridge.

Dad hesitated. "My son stays out of it."

The dragon narrowed its eyes. She nodded.

Dad's eyes met mine and my chest tightened. He followed Azarel.

"After me—and stay close or else." Dad and Azarel followed her inside the metal fortress. I stood alone and waited for the next bad thing to happen.

Metal screeched. The screams got louder, then a young

woman staggered through the gateway, sobbing. It was the reporter from the news.

I bit my lip.

Dad and Azarel ran from the wreckage, and I thought we all might have a chance to get away, but Dark Queen's tail shot out and lashed the reporter to her knees.

"Not so fast." The dragon sprang to crouch over her.

I couldn't see Azarel. On my side of the bridge, Dad dodged as Queen took a swipe at him.

"You tried so hard," she sneered. "Now I've got the girl, and I've got you, and in a hot minute, I'll even have the little Hoss. Sky will be so pleased."

She raised a claw to the reporter's throat.

The girl twisted away.

"Noo!" I shouted. "Stop!"

The dragon brought up a second talon, flexing it by the first like a pair of scissors. The scissors began to close.

I couldn't stand it.

So instead of watching, I charged the duffel bag with a battlecry. No more devouring and taking. Time for Dark Sky to die. As I skidded over the asphalt, I felt Queen's eyes stab toward me. Her howl thundered in my ears, and I looked over my shoulder.

It was a mistake—instead of getting the bag, my flying tackle hit the concrete wall. Stone slammed my stomach. Wind tore at my face as I dangled over the edge. Then one of my flailing legs caught the duffel. As I jerked myself back to safety, heat exploded behind me like my ankles were in a campfire.

"BURN, LITLE WORM," Dark Queen screamed.

Falling to the roadway, I held my hands up against the flames.

But a shield of golden fire surrounded me, eating the dark fire back.

My heartbeat pounded in my ears. I wasn't dead, so I pulled myself to my feet. Gasping, I shoved the snarling duffel —once, twice. It wobbled on the edge. I brought up one leg and kicked it. With a terrified hiss, the bag plunged off the bridge.

CHAPTER 41
BURN YOUR BRIDGES

The bag dropped like it was stuffed with cinder blocks as a huge shadow rushed overhead. I fell to my knees, taking ragged breaths. When I looked up, the golden shield of fire was crumbling to nothing. Azarel's hands were still glowing as he knuckled my shoulder. Smoke rose from his clothes.

"Good moves, Hoss."

Dad grabbed me in a bear hug and we looked over the edge as Dark Queen plowed into the slow brown water of the Missouri River. Huge plumes of spray shot up.

"Maybe she'll drown too," I whispered. Dark Sky had ended up in the river. That had been our goal, even though it hadn't happened the way we'd planned.

"DRAGONS DOWN," Azarel shouted. Shimmering reptile shapes broke from the clouds high overhead and swooped toward us. The crowds on each end of the bridge went crazy. Their screams sounded like high-pitched static as Breaker, Dandelion and Ghost landed on the bridge. As planned, the red dragon was missing, and I hoped we could afford his absence.

The frost dragon's eyes widened when she saw me. *Yikes, you okay?*

I sucked in a deep breath. *Yeah.*

She drew her eyebrows up. *I knew we should've flown down sooner.*

Behind us, Azarel helped the young reporter to her feet. She stood there shaking and staring at our dragons, wiping her eyes.

"We're on your side," Azarel said. "Just get off the bridge."

"I thought it would be different, investigating dragons..."

"Things *will* be different," Azarel said. "We're the Dragon Agency, and we're back."

"The Dragon Agency." She stumbled away, glancing over her shoulder.

Azarel turned. "Dandelion, go pick up the crew."

The green dragon flashed away as the rest of us scanned the river far below. A froth of bubbles appeared, then a dragon's head broke the surface. Something scaly twitched in its jaws.

"Hell's bells," Azarel snarled.

Dad slammed his fist on a car hood and I bit the side of my cheek.

That's just not right, my dragon said.

Dark Queen thrashed the river to foam and cleared the waves. Wings flailing, she lifted away, flying over the river. Behind us, Dandelion bounded up the car-strewn roadway, clearing the ruins like they were broken glass. Mom and my brothers were on her back.

The huge dragon circled below, its eyes evil slashes. Then the Darks were gone, under the bridge and out of sight.

I couldn't believe they were both alive.

"Get on your dragons," Azarel said. "We've got to keep this fight over the river."

He vaulted up behind me on Ghost. Dad and Wyatt doubled up on Breaker, and Keller and James stayed with Mom on Dandelion. As my family crawled into place, Dark Queen swept out from under the bridge, climbing to soar above the archway. Her hide gleamed in the summer sun, and smoke streamed from her open mouth.

"GET OFF THE BRIDGE," Azarel yelled.

Leaning into Ghost's neck, I closed my eyes.

Rock music played from speakers on the shore. Smells of charcoal, gasoline and burning rubber hit my nose. If I kept my eyes shut and took deep breaths, I could almost pretend I was here to watch an air show. Almost.

I imagined a fighter plane roaring overhead.

Here we go, Ghost.

Here we go.

The white rocket I was riding launched skyward to intercept it.

CHAPTER 42
THE FIGHT AT THE RIVER

A wave of fire crashed over the Broadway Bridge, eating gasoline. Cars exploded, one after another. The chain of explosions went on and on. As the bridge became a firestorm, crowds screamed on the riverbanks.

Ghost climbed through the summer sky, flanked by Breaker and Dandelion. Looking down was like watching a movie disaster in person. Dark Queen hovered over the bridge, enjoying her handiwork.

"Dark Sky is hiding," I shouted at Azarel.

"Watch out for his tricks," he yelled back.

Our trio of dragons soared in a tight formation over the river.

Azarel bellowed so everyone could hear: "GHOST WILL RELAY MY DIRECTIONS TO YOUR DRAGONS, WHO WILL PASS THEM ON TO YOU."

Go get Dark Queen while she's still alone, Ghost said, and I realized she was speaking for Azarel. Just like that, the fight started. We plunged down, sunlight glinting on a million scales.

First blood, I said.

Will be ours, said Ghost.

Dark Queen swept her wings, rising over the burning bridge like an enormous bat. My heart thumped wildly—once, twice—"Now!" I shouted—and Ghost twisted onto her side, dodging the wicked talons, reaching and slashing as we tore past.

Yeah! I told Ghost. *You're too fast for her.*

She arched her neck so I could see her smirk.

We flew in a tight circle just as Breaker took his turn, diving from the clouds. Queen's wings became a blur, rising to meet him, but Breaker tucked and rolled like a tumbling acrobat—or maybe a tumbling river. As he left the summersault, his talons shot out like knives.

The killer dragon floundered, streaming blood. She spiraled toward the muddy water. *Let's get her*, Ghost and I said at the same time. We came in like a guided missile in a haze of mist. I clung to my dragon's neck as she punched the disoriented Queen with all four feet and swerved away, tail skimming the river.

"WELL DONE!" Azarel roared.

"*Very* well done," I whispered.

For a second, as the wind roared past, I felt wild and strong, armored and invincible, a knight on horseback with colors streaming—yeah, I really felt that—me, Conley Hoss, on the back of my smart, brave dragon. The wind brought tears to my eyes and a wild yell escaped my throat. For a second—one split second of scary joy—I didn't see how we could possibly lose.

From the corner of my eye, I saw Dandelion soar along the bridge, breathing a long sheet of fire that hung from the burning road.

Now bury Queen in the waves, Ghost said. *Pound her under, but keep an eye on the fire curtain—Azarel's orders.*

Ghost and Dandelion soaked Dark Queen in flame as Breaker climbed for another dive. The killer dragon screamed, breathing bursts of oily fire, but the effort was taking its toll.

Here comes Breaker, Ghost told us. *Get ready to get out of the way.*

High above us, the blue dragon pointed his nose down. Tail streaming behind him, he hurtled closer and I braced for impact—but at the last moment, Ghost and Dandelion swept aside like elevator doors. Breaker shot through the gap, and Dark Queen's eyes widened as he thundered down. She crashed into the river with a strangled howl. But Breaker had miscalculated. His wings flared wildly as he and Dad and Wyatt disappeared in an explosion of brown spray.

I stared. Mom screamed.

Bubbles swirled where they had disappeared.

No, I thought. Not possible.

Azarel is going after them. Ghost sounded panicky.

Behind me, the dragon handler flung off his overcoat. Ghost skimmed the lapping waves and Azarel gathered himself. As he dove into the churning water, green fire crackled at the bridge.

A huge shadow fell on me and Ghost.

Dark Sky was attacking.

CHAPTER 43
BOILING CURRENTS

Dark Sky barreled through the green fire, snarling as it burnt his scales. His eyes skipped over Dandelion and locked on me and Ghost. Sunlight flashed off his teeth.

Ghost, roll! I told her—and she did, claws out like daggers.

Then he rammed us.

Clinging to Ghost's spine, I heard Sky's roar and her scream, felt the shuddering impact—then water rushed us like a muddy wall. *Hold on hold on hold on.*

The river hit me.

The world turned wet and dark.

I clung to Ghost's neck as she thrashed from side to side. When I opened my eyes, silt rubbed my pupils. There was no up, no down and no Azarel, just currents slamming into me. I pressed close to Ghost as her whole body shook with a heavy blow, and heard her gurgling wail.

You can do it, Ghost.

Bubbles escaped my mouth. Brackish water leaked in.

Another violent impact shook my dragon and the river yanked me free.

My chest burned. I clawed desperately at the thick water. Dark, boiling currents surged past. Gold light flashed through my closed eyelids, but it was too late. The river washed me away, sloshing and burning down my throat. My lungs blazed with pain.

An arm like a steel cable grabbed me.

When my eyes opened, all I saw was white sand. A minute later, I realized the gleaming beach was dragon scales. My face rested on Ghost's gritty skin, my arms and legs draped over her back. I thought we'd both died and gone to Heaven.

But there wouldn't be blood in Heaven.

Ghost was leaking crimson, blood trickling down her ribs. As soon as I turned my head, I puked brown water. Shaking all over, I got to my knees, wiping dirt from my eyes. The waves below were getting smaller fast.

We were flying.

"Conley," Mom wailed.

Far below, Dandelion circled the churning water like a green gunship. My parents and all my brothers were on her back, dripping wet. Somehow, Azarel had saved us all, but there was no sign of the dragon handler. No Breaker either.

I raised a shaky arm and waved as we gained height.

Ghost beat her wings desperately, wincing as she cleared the bridge.

"They're after us," she gasped. "They want us more than anyone. We have to run."

I wrapped my arms around her neck, my throat raw.

Ok, I told her. *Ok*.

Our first plan had failed. Now we only had one chance left. Plan B was our last shot.

My family didn't take their eyes off us as Ghost soared away.

She wasn't a fast flyer now.

I put an arm around her neck and squeezed. She tried to laugh and winced.

As we flew shakily across the sky, I added Ghost to the list of people I'd promised to protect. Dad and Mom, Wyatt and Keller and James—and Ghost.

That made me think of Azarel, and I hung my head. He'd promised to keep me safe and that's exactly what he'd tried to do. But no one had looked out for him. I felt sadness bubbling up behind my eyes.

I won't let them get you, I told Ghost.

That's sweet, she said.

I waited for the snort or eye roll, but it didn't come.

I didn't let myself look back, not yet, but I knew the Darks were getting closer.

CHAPTER 44
TEARS OF GLASS

The sun baked my clothes to bloody crusts. When we flew past skyscrapers, their windows reflected a reddish blur. Far below, cars pulled off roads and stick-figure people waved and yelled, their voices distant squeaks.

My wing isn't working, Ghost told me.

Her left one made a raspy, grating sound. When I looked back, I saw the Darks, both of them. They'd risen from the river and they were gaining on us like nothing could stop them. Not fire, not water, not a whole inferno of good dragons.

They see us, I said.

Ghost tucked her wings and dove below the rooftops, flying along Main Street in the heart of downtown. People on the sidewalks screamed and dove for cover as she dropped ten feet.

Watch out, Ghost, you're about to—

Her tail sheared off a traffic light, and metal crashed into an intersection. I felt her shoulders bunch and strain as she ground her teeth, fighting to climb higher.

Cars swerved and collided as she turned a corner. Ghost let out a groan and I wrapped my arms around her neck. Then, as she slowly gained altitude, we both stiffened.

A chorus of screams came from the intersection behind us.

They're here, she said.

Ghost, can't you get any higher?

Instead of answering, she flung her wings around me, tucked her shoulder and dove. I felt her body shake and heard glass shattering. When she unfolded her wings, the light was dim, glowing from a low ceiling. We'd crash landed in a maze of cubicles. The empty skyscraper was like another world, dull, musty and safe—but only for a second.

Run, Conley, she told me. *We have to make this hard for them.*

I'm not leaving you.

Oh yes you are.

Ghost pulled me off her back, teeth pressing my shoulder. Her shove sent me spinning.

Find the stairs and run, Conley. Her voice was a half-sob.

The Darks roared outside.

Get out! Ghost screamed in my head.

I staggered into a hallway lined with ugly paintings. White light flashed behind me. An explosion threw me against the wall. Broken glass from picture frames rained down, and smoke rolled toward me. Crashes and snarls rocked the cubicle room, louder than a heavy metal concert. Flames flickered toward me over the carpet.

This wasn't right. Ghost shouldn't be fighting the Darks alone. I turned to go back—at least I could distract them—but heat singed my face. Fire was turning the hallway into a furnace. My hair smoked and I sprinted toward the stairwell.

Please, please, let Ghost be ok.

I staggered up two flights of echoing stairs with the dragon-fire crackling behind me. Smoke crept into my lungs. I hit a crash-bar and collapsed, gulping cool oxygen as flames crawled along the ceiling like hungry worms.

I'm sorry, Ghost. I said I'd protect you but I lied.

As I ran through the burning building, its windows started to weep. Glass tears streaked the walls as blinding light shone in. Why were the windows crying? Did they feel sorry for me? My head felt fuzzy and my lungs felt worn out.

Then I started getting weird. I tried to resist, but I was too beat up.

And anyway, the change felt good.

I felt bitey, then ravenous, and I stopped caring about the heat. I stopped caring about everything, really. Everything but me. Conley Hoss would be gone in just a minute now—gone in a flash, gone in a snap. The human me slowed to a walk. It stood at a giant, melted window, staring at the serrated skyscrapers, the spiky towers, the cold and beautiful castles. I'd take them one by one. Some I'd burn. Others I'd keep forever.

Then the strangest thing happened.

The skyline dissolved in a swirl of glass and steel. One building towered over the rest, warm red stone and hard timber, full of resting power. A building I hated—no, wait. A building I...loved?

My human self put a hand to its head. Stop that, I said. But he wouldn't listen. The human boy was pushing at me, breaking away. NO–

Suddenly I, Conley Hoss, was alone and I was me and I was in pain—but the Brick House rushed toward me. Light shone from its gutters and windows, clearing my smoky mind. Shade fell from its mighty columns and wrapped me in calm like a magical cloak. Something inside me came back to life.

I remembered I had a family and at least two friends and a dragon I'd promised to protect.

"I'll keep fighting," I said.

Behind me, Dark Sky laughed.

"Too late." He ground his teeth. "Now hold still."

"No," I said.

A summer breeze ruffled my hair like my mother's hands. The dragon roared. A thousand tongues of greedy fire surged toward me.

I jumped.

CHAPTER 45
THE LAST DEPARTING FLIGHT

I was a toddler, a baby like James, closing my eyes to hop into a sea of blue.

But the ocean wasn't splashy. It was Breaker's back. As I crashed into his spine, air left my body in a choking gasp. Sky bloomed around me.

Small, strong fingers grabbed my wrist.

"Got you," Top Ten said. "I told you I'd keep you safe."

If my throat hadn't felt so weird, I would've laughed.

"You look awful." Breaker's wings took us away from the window and up. "Almost as bad as Ghost."

"Ghost did her best." My voice tasted like ash.

Wind jostled us as the blue dragon rose over the skyscraper. He drew a huge breath, ribs bulging, and dove toward the ruined building. Far below, Dark Sky looked like a scaly cat leaning from the the window. As we shot past, the killer dragon jumped back—too slow. Raging fire blasted him into the office building.

"Right up the nose," Breaker growled. "That'll buy us time,

but I'm tired of running. Time to burn those rotting bloodworms."

"I broke my promise," I croaked. "I didn't protect Ghost."

"Well," Breaker said, "that's not much of a promise, you being a human and her being a dragon, but hey, I guess you kind of kept it, acting like bait and running all over the skyscraper."

"I didn't keep it," I groaned. "She's dead."

"Dead?" Breaker frowned. "I don't think so. She's not looking great, but still breathing— so technically not dead. You didn't think we'd let the Darks finish her off, did you?" He pointed with a talon. "There's your girl."

I shaded my eyes and followed Breaker's claw. Fifty feet above us, sun gleamed on pinkish scales. Two reptiles flew in upward spirals. Dandelion was circling Ghost, her scales blood-washed as she struggled through the sky like a plane with an engine out.

Tears came to my eyes and Wyatt patted my shoulder.

Breaker looked back at us, his face stormy. "She doesn't look so good, does she? Not her usual pretty self. You can be sure the Darks will pay for that."

"Pretty?" I choked. "Who ever heard of a pretty dragon."

Breaker snorted. "Have I mentioned how ugly humans are?"

I had a comeback ready but instead I had a coughing fit.

"Yeah, Ghost was a looker," Breaker said. "Hope the scars don't hurt her pretty face."

I didn't have an answer for that.

Please, I prayed, just let her live out the day.

But I wondered who could hear me.

A minute later, we caught up. My family waved and cried when they saw me. Ghost was dripping blood and soot. Each wing-stroke made her groan and we could hear every breath she took, rattling in her chest.

Oh Ghost, I said.

She didn't answer.

The crest of a gothic tower rose above us—a tower I'd seen up close before. If it had been night, the stone would've been washed with ominous green light. An American flag flapped on a silver pole. Another second and we'd top the roofline. This was the end. The last move in our game of death-chess.

Ghost's wings grated like chalk on a board. She started sinking.

"I'm sorry," she sobbed. "So sorry, I just can't."

Goodbye, Conley.

Her wings swept the air like torn paper fans as she fell.

CHAPTER 46
THE LAST FIGHT

"Jump off!" Breaker shrugged, giving me and Wyatt extra lift as we flung ourselves onto Dandelion's crowded back.

The blue dragon's wings *whoosh-whooshed* in a blur, then he soared under Ghost and kept rising—but only for a second. They hit the top of the skyscraper with a sickening crash. Ghost lurched onto the roof and lay there, dazed, as Breaker spun away in a cloud of dust.

The rest of us poured off Dandelion's back and rushed across the rooftop. When Breaker touched down, I was coaxing Ghost toward a hole in the molded concrete tower. Thanks to my dreams, we'd known it would be there. Her slow, painful crawl was hard to watch. Dandelion took her place next to Breaker, guarding our retreat. My family had barely reached the shadowy opening when the Darks thundered down from the sky.

"You picked the wrong place to run," Dark Sky snarled.

"Now you'll die," hissed Dark Queen.

We ran into the tunnel as the Darks stalked forward. Ghost

dragged herself a little way inside, then she coiled her tail and closed her eyes. *Please, keep moving*, I begged her, but she wouldn't. The burrow curved away into the concrete block, and my family ran for cover. We were a thousand feet off the ground, but it felt like rushing down a twisting, underground tunnel. The further we went, the darker it got. That's when I had a crazy idea. It was something Azarel had said without spelling out, in that offhand way of his.

"They'll be vulnerable, right?" he'd told us on the bridge. "Yeah, they'll be on edge, frothing at the mouth, so don't forget–"

Don't forget what? I couldn't be sure but I thought I knew.

If only he was here.

We reached a dead end, and the burrow widened into a rocky cave. Hardly any light now. We all had to feel our way and the smell was awful. Off on one side, a huge, spiky bulk took up half the cavity, like the Darks hadn't finished construction. While the rest of my family headed toward it, I kept searching, probing the darkest corners of the den. And then I found what I was looking for. I could hardly believe it, but after that, I knew what I had to do.

My parents were shushing Keller and James. Wyatt was leaning against the wall, catching his breath. At just the wrong moment, he looked up—and saw me moving back up the tunnel. *No, Wyatt.* I put a finger to my lips. *Don't follow me, not this time. Please don't follow me.* But I knew he would. They all would—which meant I had only seconds.

I stumbled up the tunnel, turned a corner, and staggered into light and heat. Dandelion and Breaker didn't see me. They were shoulder to shoulder at the opening, snarling and breathing fire. I made it over to Ghost and dropped to my knees behind her. When I touched her neck, I could barely feel her pulse.

"GET OUT OF OUR HOUSE," Dark Sky roared on the roof.

"Fly away dragonsss." Dark Queen's hiss was crazy.

And I knew Azarel had been right. Everything we'd known about the Darks had changed. Their cruelty had lost its cool edge—but that wasn't all good, because they were about to go insane. Writhing green flames filled the entry as the Darks screamed outside.

"They're about to come through," I heard Dandelion whisper.

"I'm ready," Breaker growled.

I hunched down behind Ghost's body. I had to be ready too.

The green flames crackled, and Dandelion's sticky fire clung to the Darks as they plunged inside, but they barely noticed. Eyes flaming, jaws frothing, their heads snaked back and forth.

This was it. Now or never.

I stood up slowly. Four sets of dragon eyes flamed toward me.

"Conley, no." Dandelion looked horrified.

"Run for it," Breaker ordered.

The Darks looked stunned—but pleased.

Then I lifted the gleaming orb in my arms. Football-sized and heavy. "We've got your eggs," I said. "Surrender."

"Aaashhh," the egg said.

It was like throwing a match in gasoline.

The Darks hurtled forward and the egg fell with a clunk as I dropped behind Ghost and covered my head. The noise was like dinosaurs in a burning junkyard. I tried not to breathe. And then, even though I knew I shouldn't, I inched my head up— and found myself looking into Dark Queen's crazy eyes.

Oh no, I thought. Oh no.

She swept the egg away and then Dark Sky was there. The

egg had unbalanced them and made them crazy, but it was working too well. They were too much for Breaker and Dandelion. Everything was happening too fast. Dark Sky reached for Ghost's neck, jaws gaping.

Then he saw me too.

I got to my feet.

"I guess you'll never kn-kn-know"—I did my best to stop shaking—"where we hid the other eggs."

For a long second, he stared at me.

I hid my thoughts so he couldn't see the lie.

When he turned to Dark Queen, she looked dazed.

For once in his life, Dark Sky wasn't sure what to do.

I saw it in his eyes when he decided to kill me anyway.

This is it, I thought. But he'd missed his chance.

A roar echoed up the tunnel. Shock stretched Dark Sky's eyes and a blur of scales smashed into him—our red dragon. It was like colliding trains.

The impact threw me to the floor. Red and blue and green fire hit the walls—Breaker and Dandelion back in the fight. Roars and shrieking pounded my ears, except when the dragons took huge, gulping breaths, and then I could hear more horrible sounds. *Creeaak. Cra-crack, cra-crack.* Bones were bending and snapping—but whose? A barbed tail crushed a hole in the stone behind me, and rock dust showered down. Ghost's body shuddered toward me as something crashed into her.

When I had to breathe, the air scorched me. My vision blurred, and I staggered up, hands on my knees—and saw the most amazing thing.

Our dragons had the Darks pinned to the floor. They were crushing the air from the killer dragons' lungs and pounding them with flames. Burning them to ash. Hateful yellow eyes flashed at me like dying stars. Midnight hide glowed and crumbled. Their shapes blurred and fell apart, shattering—teeth and claws and snouts.

All ash.

I'll tear you to pieces...

Dark Sky's voice hung in the air.

Then he was gone, and my head hit the floor.

CHAPTER 47
PICKING UP THE PIECES

Blue sky. Blue with white puffs. White puffs and little swirls. It felt so good to lie there.

"Do you think he can hear us?" someone said.

The sky pressed down on me gently. No, it wasn't the sky, it was something else, something closer. I felt disappointed.

"Well, his eyes are open." Was that Mom's voice?

"We won," Dad said. "Conley. We won." His voice was ragged. "It's over."

"I'm not sure he's with us," Mom said.

"It's ok, don't cry," I said—and everyone yelled and did the opposite, even Top Ten—as I said goodbye to the deep blue sky and made myself sit up.

"I thought I was too late," my brother said, scrubbing his eyes. "We're a team, so don't you ever, ever try to fight dragons without me again."

"I promise," I told him.

My skin was so hot and painful, there was no point in itching. At the same time, I felt good. It didn't make sense until I realized my heart had stopped aching. I'd grown so used to the razor wire pricking me, the dirty twisted plastic, stuck in my soul, I could hardly believe it was gone.

"How do you feel, honey?" Mom said.

"Better." A cool breeze found my burning skin. "I feel...like me again."

As they tugged me toward Breaker, I said, "Wait. Where's my dragon?" When no one answered, I said, "I'm not leaving without her."

But they kept on moving me. When I dug in with my heels, we barely slowed down. Dad picked me up and put me on Breaker's back.

"Ghost is resting." Mom didn't look at me. "She doesn't want to move right now."

"That's not like her," I said.

Ghost, where are you?

She didn't make a sound.

I think there was lots of excitement on the flight home. Cheers, the whop-whop of a helicopter, our dragons banking and swooping, flicking their tails. I missed most of it, resting my eyes.

"Hiding in dark not fun," I heard James tell the red dragon. "I bring you lollipop."

"Gimme that," the dragon growled.

I looked up to see James toss a lollipop in the air. The dragon twisted and dove to catch it as Dad and James whooped on his back. I closed my eyes again.

Somehow I remember the Brick House glowing as we came in for a landing. It shone orange-red, shimmering with confidence—and, I think, pride. *Knew you could do it, kid. Knew you had it in you.* At least, I think that's what it said.

By then I was delirious.

A small, blurry lizard waited on the roof. It took one look at me and said, "Let's go, pal. If you fall asleep, don't worry, I'll just keep working."

In my dreams, I floated off the roof and into the locker room. Later, the fuzzy lizard filled a tub with foul green liquid and told me to get in. When I wouldn't, he kicked me in the back of the knee so I toppled in headfirst. It was an awful nightmare. When I woke up in the great room, wrapped in bandages, tattooed with sutures, I wasn't sure what day it was.

And I didn't care.

If any of our neighbors had looked in the window, they would've seen my whole family sprawled around the room like mannequins. If we'd been in a store window, we would've been advertising Adventure—or more likely, Exhaustion. Air conditioning massaged us, shushing our burns and bruises. The house knew we needed help.

Mom sat in a rocking chair with her eyes closed, wearing a pretty black dress. Every five minutes she gave her chair a little sway. Dad lay on a couch wearing slacks and a nice shirt and vest. He didn't move at all. It was like they'd dressed up for a party and then collapsed. My brothers hadn't bothered to dress up. They lay under tables in their clean underwear, snoring gently. Or in Wyatt's case, snoring loudly under a Batman cape.

Hopefully the dragons were resting too.

I wondered where Watson was, and Azarel.

Azarel. My stomach twisted, and I was about to remember why, but instead I fell asleep again. When I woke, the windows were dark, the shadows long. The great room's glowing chandeliers were on. I wasn't sure why I was awake. Then I heard the front door creak open.

"Who's there?" I sat up painfully. "Hello."

No one answered. When a dark snout appeared near the floor, I froze. But it was only Watson. He'd stopped looking blurry.

"Oh good," he said. "You're awake. I thought about keeping you up, concussion protocol and all, but it would've been pointless. Do you have any brain damage?"

"Umm..." I said.

"Just kidding, kid. You're a total mess, but I pulled out the stops this time. Gave you my own personal burn-salve made from phoenix tears, not widely available—patent pending. Go back to sleep." Watson crawled over to Dad's couch and pricked his elbow with a claw. "Mind giving me a hand, boss?"

Dad groaned. "Fine." He sounded like he'd been chewing a gasoline-soaked rag. "But only because you said 'boss.'" He got up and followed Watson out.

"Hey, where are you going?" I croaked.

The door swung shut. I've never liked being left behind. If I'd had the energy, I would've chased them, but instead I dragged myself to the kitchen. I draped my sheet around my shoulders, the only clothing Watson had seen fit to give me aside from boxers. As I winced my way to the double fridge, I realized why. The lightweight cotton brushed my tortured skin like steel wool.

You are messed up, I thought.

When I pulled out the orange juice, I found myself drooling. Watson had given me meds for sure. Lifting my sheet, I counted the stitches in my arms and legs and torso and lost count around forty-five. Then there was my skin, mottled like gross pink camo. No wonder he'd given me painkillers. I drank a huge glass of orange juice, then another, and my throat felt less burnt.

In the great-room-turned-nap-room, the rest of my family

was starting to stir, and I knew what that meant. Dinner. Excitement. Chaos.

Before that could happen, I staggered up the stairs. Leaning on the wall, I made it to my room, and stood in the doorway, staring at the ladder to my bunk. It was just too much. I fell onto James' bed and was instantly asleep.

CHAPTER 48
THE LAST DREAM

When my eyes opened, the Brick House was silent and dark, but not sleeping. I don't think that house ever slept. I lay in James' bed, sheet tucked under my chin, and sighed, thinking how good it was not to move. All I needed to do was lie there and do absolutely nothing. Except...the dry, ticklish feeling in my throat had returned, like a sliver of rust against my windpipe. I ignored it for as long as I could.

Then I gave up.

The clock on my dresser said 2:18am. The moon shone through the window and my brothers breathed softly in their bunks.

I stood still and listened, out of habit. Not a sound came from anywhere in the house. More important, the broken window was sealed with cardboard and duct tape. I hobbled to the door and down the hall. The door to a spare room stood ajar, moonlight spilling out and pooling on the old oak floor. Everything was quiet, as if the house was holding perfectly still on purpose. No hum of air conditioning, no creaking floorboards.

Like it was about to jump out at me.

Stop making this weird, I told the Brick House. All I want is a glass of water.

Walking was harder than I'd expected. My injuries had stiffened as I slept, and my body complained about each step. In the bathroom, I looked at my shirtless chest in the mirror. My skin was black and blue and pink but the gash from Dark Sky's claw was no longer veined and nasty. He was really gone.

Hallelujah.

I sighed and drank my water.

On the way back to bed, I looked into the empty bedroom where moonlight was spending the night. Something seemed out of place. The hardwood planks were softened with a rug. Two wooden chairs stood by the door. The curtains were drawn back so the moon could touch the puffy comforter, and the bed—thebedthebedthebed!

Someone was there.

My heart gave a sideways leap, but I was too exhausted to be scared. It was probably James. I'd taken his spot, after all. I was moving away when someone gave a muffled groan. Sad and soft. Definitely not James.

I crept through the moonlight and stood by the brass four-poster, looking down. The sleeper clutched the covers desperately. The face was turned to the window, but the blankets didn't hide everything. Long brown hair swirled on the pillow.

Umm, I thought. What the heck?

Then the bedroom door swung shut behind me, and I remembered...

My other dream. The one I hadn't shared with anyone, not even Watson, because it was too weird and awful and had nothing to do with Dark Sky, nothing to do with anything. Just a horrible, sad nightmare where this girl died over and over and I never could help her. So what was going on? I couldn't handle more death and dying. I wanted to be asleep unless— what if I was asleep already?

I pinched my burned skin and winced.

No, I wasn't. But I didn't want to be there. I wanted a way out.

The girl groaned again. Slowly, she rolled to face me.

And it happened like it always did.

She was about my age and something about her nagged me. Her eyes were closed, face bruised and pale. She'd pulled her knees up to her chest, and her breathing sounded bad. A deep red cut went across one cheekbone. Her bottom lip was split, like she'd survived an awful fight. All together, her wounds were hard to look at and I got the panicky feeling that comes over you when you see someone badly hurt, someone you don't know how to help. Her eyelashes quivered but she didn't wake.

I wanted to look away. But I didn't.

For a long time, I thought about who the girl could possibly be and why she was here, in the Brick House, and if I could escape before she died in front of me. But the moonlight kept gliding over the sheets and blankets—the moon was her only friend—and I couldn't bring myself to leave. As I watched, she became more still. The tiny quiver of her pulse weakened.

I couldn't stand it. Not again.

"It's Conley," I said. "Please don't die."

When I reached out to touch her forehead, her skin was so hot it burned me.

Her eyes slid open. They were emeralds drained of light. "You're not scared anymore," she said. "That's good, but you don't know me. No one does." Her voice was like cobwebs or dead leaves.

Right away, I knew she was wrong—and something about her told me I did know her, even though I didn't have any friends. No friends who were boys, no friends who were girls, no friends at all unless you counted brothers—which you really should. Or unless you counted...dragons.

"You're my dragon." I swallowed. "You're Ghost."

She shivered under the blankets. "I can't believe it. Watson said, he promised me—" Her words caught in her throat and she twisted in pain.

"Shhh," I said. "Just rest."

She sank into the pillow and I smoothed the comforter.

"I didn't believe him." Her whisper was so weak I could barely hear. "Watson promised, if I didn't give up, I wouldn't be alone."

I took one of her hands and pressed it.

For a long moment, I thought the dream had ended like it always did. But she kept breathing. Her skin stayed pinkish. She was asleep. Standing by the bed, I wondered what to do. How could this possibly be Ghost?

When my feet started hurting, I dragged a chair over and sat. The girl's breathing had become deep and slow. I kept watch by the bed for as long as I could, until I fell asleep.

Or maybe I'd never been awake at all.

When I opened my eyes, I was slumped in the chair at a painful angle. Morning light streamed through the spare room's window, and I glanced right and left. The bed was empty. I felt stiff and tired.

"Good morning," someone said behind me.

CHAPTER 49
THINGS GET WEIRD

The girl sat in a chair by the door, wearing a pair of Mom's sweatpants and a hoody that bunched a little at her arms and waist. One eye was mostly swollen shut. The ugly slash on her cheek looked a little less red. She smiled at me, careful with her split lip.

Over the last several days I'd seen a lot of wild, crazy things, but this—to be ambushed in a quiet spare room in my own Brick House without any snarling or threats of bloody violence—it almost gave me a heart attack.

"I felt weird, just lying there," she said. "But now I wish I'd stayed in bed."

I gave a little jerk.

"It's ok, you don't have to say anything." The girl looked at me hugging myself. "It's nice that you care. Except"—she put her head on one side—"how did you know it was me?" When I didn't answer right away, her un-swollen eye looked worried.

"I, well, I just knew." I tugged my billowy sheet around me. "I dreamed about you over and over. I always knew you were someone important, then last night I finally got it right. I could see you were someone brave. I could tell you'd been in a fight. And then, when you said no one knew you, I knew instantly I did. Of course it was you."

She nodded slowly. "Ok."

I sighed in relief, because if she wanted a better explanation, I didn't have one. One thing I knew for sure, though. Watson and I were going to have a long talk about how Ghost could change into a girl.

"But what about you?" My words came rushing back. "How long are you gonna?—I mean, how did you?—are you going to turn back into–"

"Shhh." She held up an index finger. "Thank you for dreaming about me and saving my life. I was ready to slip away and turn to ash and sleep for years until I was reborn, if it ever happened at all, but then you knew me, so I still had a place in this world, and my life wasn't over after all."

I tried to make sense of what she'd said and totally failed. It must have been obvious on my face.

Ghost looked down. "I know it's very weird, me looking like this—and you wouldn't believe how ugly and out of place and strange I feel–"

"Wait." What I wanted to say was, Welcome to human existence, Ghost—but I realized that wouldn't be very helpful. Instead I said, "You're not ugly. You'll look fine, once those cuts heal. And you'll figure this out as you go." If she'd asked me what exactly I meant by *that*, I would've been in trouble.

Adventures are fun, I might've said. As long as you don't die.

Luckily, she got to her feet, looking small in Mom's clothes, and held out her arms for balance. "I miss having wings." She shrugged, watching her shoulders. "Things will be strange for awhile."

"That's for—I mean, yeah, maybe so," I said.

Ghost took two careful steps and stood in front of me. "Dragons don't hug much," she said.

I nodded, thinking it would be awkward when you were coated in armor and spikes. Then I saw she was still holding out her arms, and they were drooping.

"Oh," I said.

When I shuffled closer, she folded her hands around my battered shoulders and gave me a formal hug, which I returned.

"Ouch," we both said.

Behind us, the spare room door flew open.

"SHE NOT DEAD!" James yelled.

Watson stood behind him in the doorway...on the shoulder of a tall, grinning, dangerous-looking man dressed in black.

"What?" I said stupidly. "What?"

"The reports of my death have been greatly exaggerated," Azarel said.

"Mark Twain said that," Watson said.

"Twain stole it from me," Azarel snapped.

Ghost and I stood there staring. Smiles spread across our poor, beat-up faces.

"Conley, Ghost, I don't do this often, but if you don't mind..." Ignoring the beardie on his shoulder, Azarel got down on one knee to wrap his arms around us both. His hug was like being wrapped in steel cables, and we groaned.

"I'm incredibly proud of you, kid," Watson said, three inches from my face.

His beady eyes looked wet, and I decided the bearded dragon meant it. You may not believe this, but it meant a lot to me that he did. Then LouAnne Jordan, the tall, pretty waitress from Chubby's, the one Azarel owed money to, appeared at the dragon handler's elbow.

"What the heck is going on?" I said.

Ghost looked confused too.

LouAnne ignored my outburst. Her lips tightened as she took in the bruises and burns covering me and Ghost—and those were just the visible ones.

"They said you two were heroes and I agree, but this dragon-fighting business is asking an awful lot from a coupla' kids."

"I'm not..." Ghost whispered. "I wasn't..."

"Not all the bad guys were dragons," Azarel pointed out. "There are good dragons too."

"Oh well, guess it's over now." LouAnne's eyes brightened. "Breakfast is served, young knuckleheads. After what you've been through, it's dinner for breakfast. Azarel told me breakfast for breakfast isn't good enough."

The big man nodded.

"Come and get it." LouAnne swished out of the room.

"I don't understand," I said. "Why's she here? I thought you hated her—and she hates you—and I thought you were dead, and we were all sad—so why–"

Azarel snorted. "Things are moving fast now, kiddo. We can't all snooze around the clock like you. In the last two days, the lines have been drawn. We've collected friends and labeled enemies. We've made plans and calculated costs. Watson brought the database back online–"

"Two days?" I said. "I slept for two days?"

"Now that lady knows about our den." Ghost was still watching the door where LouAnne had disappeared. "Are you sure you trust her?"

Azarel huffed. "She's not so bad."

"The only number on his cell phone!" Watson cackled. "Can you believe it? Washed up on the riverbank half-dead, and who does he call? A lady he owes money too. It's beautiful."

"Shut up, Adagio." Azarel tried not to smile.

Ghost and I looked at each other and shrugged. She shrugged again, watching her shoulders move under Mom's sweatshirt.

"I guess we should try to eat something," I said.

"This is going to be weird," she said.

And it was.

CHAPTER 50

DRAGONS OVER KANSAS CITY

My little brothers were already tucking in when we arrived, stuffing their faces and talking with their mouths full. A cheer rose when Ghost and I appeared. I guess I really had been sleeping for two days.

LouAnne's breakfast covered the entire eight-burner stove, and I understood why Azarel liked her. Even though she acted all cool and tough, it would take a special kind of person to cook a feast like this.

I made sure Ghost put plenty of food on her plate and watched her sniff it. It was obvious she wasn't sure where to start, so I handed her a piece of toast.

"Your favorite. Easy on the stomach and you don't need a fork."

She smiled at me.

"But you will need a fork for the other stuff."

She frowned.

I helped myself to mashed potatoes and gravy and some kind of spicy ham stew and green beans and bacon. Then, when I felt less like a walking skeleton, I tried the collard greens and pan-fried chicken and blackened catfish and fried green tomatoes and okra. It was so good I never wanted to stop eating.

Since Ghost was figuring things out, I tried not to watch her eat, but that was hard. She had trouble with her fork, took enormous bites and chewed too fast. Luckily, her manners improved as breakfast went on. When she caught me watching her, she raised her eyebrows.

"Do you want to say something?"

"No," I said.

After breakfast, everyone moved to the media room like it was something they'd discussed. There waiting for us was more proof that Ghost and I had missed a lot. Three tiger-sized dragons basked in the morning sun. Breaker and Dandelion had each claimed a patch of carpet. The red dragon stretched on a couch.

"Get off that leather!" Dad yelled, and everyone laughed except Mom, who put a hand to her forehead. The red dragon slithered to the floor. The rest of us sprawled on sofas or lay on the rug, recovering from breakfast. Within minutes, James was napping on the red dragon's belly.

Ghost and I sat stiffly on a couch.

Dragons are subtle, but I noticed the lounging reptiles slide their eyes at Ghost, sizing her up before they looked away. They nodded at her but none of them spoke. She picked up a pillow and clutched it to her chest.

"Welcome to our daily media briefing." Dad reached out to squeeze my shoulder but caught himself in time. "Good to have you up, but don't overdo it, ok?" He turned to Ghost. "You too, sweetheart. Just let us know if you need anything."

She nodded.

We watched a national news special, *Dragons Over Kansas City*. "Dragons used to be as common in Kansas City as barbecue and jazz," the narrator said. "But the infamous Dragon Uprising of the 1940s crippled the industry and led to a nationwide dragon ban. This week, a mysterious entity, claiming to serve the public interest, has moved decisively to bring the ferocious reptiles back."

There were on-the-street interviews with people who'd seen our battle with the Darks. Some of them were angry. Others were thrilled.

"Normal life is sometimes missing that little something extra, you know—magic?" said a twenty-something with glittery make-up. "You just want to feel like, um, adventure is out there?"

"What are we celebrating, death?" The sour woman looked like a resident of Prairie Refuge. "If anyone needs me, I'll be working remotely from my fireproof basement."

"We're moving downtown," an older couple said. "Closer to the excitement."

"Is there such a thing as a good dragon?" The guy wore an expensive suit and a lot of product in his hair. "I fact-checked that, and the answer is no—definitely no."

"Downtown KC is hot, hot, hot," said a real estate agent.

"In my opinion, the Dragon Agency has a lot to offer," said Lindsay the reporter we'd rescued on the bridge. "We don't know much about them—at least not until they respond to my interview request, hint, hint—but they are definitely a force for good in this crazy world."

"Being a dragon—is too much power—for any one, um, dragon—to possess," said a professor who looked confused by the time he finished his sentence.

"Members of the Dragon Agency have agreed to a meeting," Captain Estrada said, "and in the meantime, Kansas City owes them a debt of gratitude."

Politicians made public statements that didn't say much of

anything. As far as I could tell, they didn't want to be blamed for the economic impact of having a no-dragon policy. And they didn't want to be blamed for dragon damage.

Ghost's eyes were half-shut at this point.

However, the show featured lots of footage from our battle, and she definitely watched that. We saw the Broadway Bridge go up in flames. Blue, green and pearl-colored shapes shot away over the river. We watched the two of us hurtle down Main Street and crash into the skyscraper, the Darks right behind. I was glad no one had filmed what happened inside.

"This part is the best." Wyatt pumped his fist. "Breaker hovers under the window and you come flying out. There you are, look at that crazy jump!"

"Wait," I said. "You've already seen this."

He smiled guiltily. "Watson DVRed it. You were asleep."

"It's ok," Dad said. "We all wanted to watch it again."

I gave Ghost a look, wondering what else we had missed.

When the news special was over, I understood why Azarel had said things were moving fast. Kansas City was freaking out. The dragons were a huge story. Tourists were flooding downtown and leaders around the world—like the pro-dragon island of Cyprus and the pro-monster region of Transylvania—were weighing in. People were arguing about when the use of dragon force was appropriate and whether Kansas City could be allowed to revive a disastrous but glorious past.

Everyone had very strong opinions.

One thing's for sure, I thought as the screen went dark. KC will never be the same.

I was glad I didn't have to figure it all out.

"You'd better believe they're trying to track us down," Azarel got to his feet. "Media, FBI, everybody." He grinned.

"Just a matter of time until they find us," Watson said with a meaningful look at my parents—but his hidden message was lost on me.

Ghost slumped over on the couch.

Mom took one look at us and came over. "You're tired, honey. Let's get you back to bed."

"No," Ghost said. "I mean, no thanks."

Mom put a hand on her hip. "The solarium then, with blankets and hot tea."

"Ok. Thanks, Mrs. Hoss." Ghost managed a smile. Her shoulder brushed mine as she eased to her feet. "Conley, I need to talk to you."

So I followed when Mom bundled Ghost into a chair in the tropical plant room and wrapped her in blankets so only her face showed.

"Be right back with tea," Mom said.

"What?" Ghost narrowed her eyes when she caught me staring.

"Nothing," I said. "You just look kind of, um..."

Like a girl's head stuck on a fat, fuzzy snowman, I thought.

"You look like some color is coming back to your eyes," I said. "Hey, that's great."

"Ahh." She closed them, soaking in the sun that beamed through the glass walls and ceiling. The greenhouse was a little toasty for me, but she seemed to love it. Orchids, hibiscus, and other plants surrounded us like a flowering jungle. Water splashed in a stone fountain. It was a nice spot if you didn't mind melting.

Mom appeared, set down a mug of steaming tea by Ghost, and handed me a glass of cold green juice. I accepted it gratefully, sinking onto a bench.

"I'll check on you invalids in a bit," Mom said. "Call if you need anything."

"Thanks, Mom." As soon as she'd left, I wished I'd asked

her for a bag of ice to dump over my head. I was wondering how Ghost would drink her tea with no arms when her eyes slid open.

"I need two things from you, Conley Hoss."

Green juice splashed my t-shirt. "What?"

"Well, first of all, I'm glad I'm not dead, glad I survived and advanced, even though not many dragons ever even *consider* transforming like this, and no wonder. Being a human feels so strange, Conley. So *creepy,* like you're exposed to all the danger in the world. And so ugly too."

It was the second time she'd said that, and I didn't appreciate it.

"The ugliness is really hard to handle," she said. "Maybe the worst part. But there must be hope." She lifted her chin. "After all, *you* live with it somehow." She touched her face. "Better to be ugly and alive than pretty and dead, right? Better a live girl than a dead dragon."

I was getting irritated by then. "Go ahead and change back if it's so horrible!"

She gave me a disappointed look. "Don't you think I would in a second? It's not that easy. But anyway, I guess I can get used to being soft and slow and not flying. I guess I'll have to. But there's something I need that I don't have. Something I can't do without. That maybe you can help me with."

She gave me a meaningful look.

A shiny tiara, I thought. A swift kick in the rear?

"Clothing that fits better?" I suggested.

She frowned. "No, but that would be nice."

"A better attitude?" It slipped out.

Her green eyes blazed. They were regaining color fast.

"A human name," she snapped.

"Oh."

"Ghost was a wonderful name," she said, trying to sound

polite, even though I could tell she was mad. "And I'd like to keep it, but not for everyday. Ghost can be my secret name. But I need another one to use around humans. It's awkward otherwise. I mean, not even your mom knows what to call me."

Good point. My parents couldn't go on calling her "sweetheart" and "honey" forever. It would make the rest of us jealous. And she'd get in trouble eventually, and then what would they call her? Hey, lazy, hey, snot-nose? And how long was this going to go on, anyway?

I realized I had no idea.

"Maybe my human name could start with G," Ghost was saying with a funny look on her face. "For old time's sake, I guess. I'd like a name that's tough, but also...pretty. To—you know, make up for how I look now."

I gritted my teeth. But I'd already told her she needed a better attitude—and for crying out loud, she'd just transformed from one kind of being to another, so I decided I should cut her a little slack. But still, it wasn't easy.

"Let's see," I said thoughtfully.

Obviously, I didn't have sisters and no friends who were girls up until this moment. Flannery was Mom's name, so that was out, but that left thousands that were fair game. Names like...hmm. How hard could this be?

I closed my eyes and pulled up the names of aunts. Meredith, Olga, Matilda. Yikes. Well, there were my cousins who I saw every few years: Shandler, Elizabreth, MacKinty. Wow. What a horrible track record and not a single G. Then it came to me.

"I met my grandmother only a few times," I said. "We got along great. And you'll love this—she loved dragons. She missed the days when the skies were full of gems. Rubies, sapphires, pearls—full of dragons."

Ghost blinked and bit her lip.

"Her name was Gwendolyn," I said. "Gwen for short."

Ghost closed her eyes. A slow smile spread across her face, prettifying her busted lip.

"It's perfect," she said. "You've done it twice now, Conley. You're officially good with names."

I smiled back at her.

And I heard every thought, how I look fat and fuzzy, how you want to kick my rear.

Oh no. My mouth dropped open, and then I started laughing. A second later, she lost her cool and joined in, laughing even harder than me.

"Humans aren't actually ugly," she choked out. "At least, not any more than other non-dragon species. Ahahaha, yes!" She doubled over. "Wow, haha, you should've seen your face." Her laughter was a girl's laughter, not a dragon's. After what we'd been through, it was pretty wonderful to hear.

"Oh, great," I said. "So we're like, I don't know, handsome cows or good-looking dogs or something."

She nodded.

"You're a jerk," I said. "And that trick won't work again, now that I know you can still hear my thoughts."

She smiled. "You'll forget eventually."

"So will you."

I didn't think the conversation was over. After all, she'd said some pretty insulting things. But the glass door shot open behind us and Top Ten barreled in, skidding over the paved floor. We eyed him suspiciously, but he didn't throw bat-boomerangs at us or squirt us with a water gun.

"Come quick," he yelled. "It's the Dragon Agency!"

CHAPTER 51
WATSON CUTS A DEAL

Gwendolyn aka Ghost and I chased Wyatt into the great room. We tried to run but it was more like high-speed limping. Azarel stood on a Persian carpet, holding his cell phone to his ear.

"...and I don't appreciate you stealing my unlisted number," he was saying. "What's that, seriously? This is *my* phone." He turned to Watson who was basking on the window sill. "They want to deal with *you*."

"Good." The lizard held out his claws for the phone. "You're too emotional to be a good negotiator."

"Beast-guts," Azarel muttered.

The beardie pressed his snout to the phone. "This is Watson Adagio—oh, hello, sir. I don't blame you, sir—it's a surprise to talk to you too. Didn't know if you were still out there." He listened. "You're correct. But Dark Sky's ashes are back where they belong. And while we could have called for international assistance in accordance with section one-four-eight-dot-one-seven of the Dragon Code, we dealt with the problem ourselves in an efficient and quiet manner—saving you the expense." He looked us and winked. "Oh, you saw the news?" He coughed. "Extreme force became necessary in the end."

Azarel grunted and paced, hands shoved in the pockets of his overcoat.

The rest of us leaned in, trying to catch every word.

"If I could cut to the chase, sir—what's our endgame?" Watson frowned. "Are we tallying up small infractions or are you willing to consider the bigger picture?"

In the silence that followed, James snored softly in a twist of the red dragon's tail.

"Happy to hear it." Watson let out a long, silent breath. "In that case, let's get to brass tacks." As he listened, his eyes grew hard. "Please wait while I relay those terms to my team." He covered the phone's mic with one foot and glared around the room.

We waited for him to explain, but he didn't say a word. Instead, he uncovered the mic and spit into the phone. "Not a chance! Those terms are gryphon scat."

The dragons huffed happily as Azarel nodded, Dad smiled and Mom shook her head. Next to me, Gwendolyn whispered, "Wow, Watson."

"I'll hang up in ten, nine, eight," the lizard snapped. "Seven, six—what's that? Now we're living in reality, and about time. One moment please." He set the phone down and sat on it as we all stared. "Unlimited licensure in North America. Other countries on a contract basis."

Azarel rubbed his chin.

"A million a year in dues, flat fee." Watson looked smug.

"Holy bloodworms." Azarel whistled. "They really want us back in the game."

"Slow down," Dad said. "You said the Agency would be calling to check in, but you didn't say they had the power to fine us."

"Not a fine." Watson beamed. "An operating fee. We'd have a virtual monopoly on our continent. It's unheard of."

Dad and Mom stared at him.

"I'm not sure we're communicating," Mom said.

"Working with the KCMO code department is like punching yourself in the face," Dad said. "I've already filed for a couple permits, and I should've just lit my money on fire."

Watson's grin widened. "That's the beauty of this contract," he said. "The Dragon Agency is a branch of the Unified Wilderness Alliance, with international treaties. The money-grubbers and buck-passers at city hall don't get a say."

Dad blinked. Mom looked stunned.

I cleared my throat. "Does that mean—we'd get paid for flying dragons?"

The beardie nodded.

Ghost-Gwen and I looked at each other. Her eyes had really come to life.

"I will be Dandelion's boss," Keller said.

Dandelion swatted him with her tail.

"Would it be...a good job?" Mom asked.

"Better than being a journalist?" Dad asked.

Azarel guffawed and Watson chuckled.

"What I think I'm hearing," the lizard said, "is that we're in. Someone tell me I'm wrong."

"We're still not even sure what's being discussed," Mom said with a panicky note in her voice.

Dad was on his feet, pacing like Azarel. "This is my family we're talking about. I need to know about the pay structure, the exact nature of the work, what kind of hours–"

"The best," Azarel said. "The best, and the best. That's what you need to know."

"What about education?" Mom said.

"I'd recommend home school," Watson said. "Even if has to be not-at-home school some of the time. You're both highly competent, and I'd be happy to teach a subject or two. If you're more traditional, I can recommend a good monster control academy."

"What about health insurance?" Dad said after a pause.

"Irrelevant." Azarel scoffed. "We have a shortlist of trusted doctors."

"The clock is ticking." Watson said. "This is a serious offer."

"So you're saying it's better than what we're doing now," Dad said.

"Yes." The lizard gave him a level look. "Do you trust me?"

"Well, of course I do."

Mom put a hand on Dad's arm. The wild look had left her face and she looked weirdly calm. They did that thing where they talk with their eyes. The whole room held its breath as we tried to decipher their secret language, but we couldn't. If the Brick House knew, it didn't give a thing away. Not a light bulb flickered. The AC didn't even hum.

Azarel and Watson were starting to look worried as Dad and Mom turned to face us. Their faces were a mix of frustration and sorrow.

Then...the fakers smiled.

"We're in!" they yelled—and the room went crazy. James woke up and started clapping. The dragons bounded around, dodging the furniture. Mom laughed out loud and Ghost-Gwen squeezed my arm so hard it hurt.

"We're in," Watson said firmly into the phone. "Provided you defer our annual dues for one year, interest free. Yes, I'm dead serious. Send the paperwork over, care of the Brick House. That's right, sir. It's time to put the Dragon Agency back on the map. Bye, now."

Then he threw the phone in the air, stood up on his hind legs and let out a raspy shriek of joy.

CHAPTER 52
THE SOLUTION

No one except Watson and Azarel knew what our Dragon Agency contract actually meant. We didn't let a little thing like that slow down our party.

After Watson got off the phone, the dragons went crazy, jumping around like scaly dogs, putting their feet on our shoulders and licking our faces. It was pretty gross, and my family had to endure it as the dragons danced around. Luckily, when a couple of them came prancing toward us, Gwen told them to keep their distance.

"Don't you dare," she said. "It would be just too weird."

Music blared from hidden speakers. "WEEEE ARE THE CHAMPIONS," the band sang, and I tried a dance with very cautious moves, staying close to the couch in case my legs gave out. Gwen stood there awkwardly until Dandelion came over, put her front legs up and licked her face, even though Gwen tried to fight her off.

"Nooo, no kisses!" she screamed.

But Dandelion didn't stop, and I had to look away before Gwen saw my smirk.

"We'll never stop caring about you," I heard the green dragon whisper.

Gwendolyn seemed happier after that. She tried a very basic dance—scooting her shoulders back and forth—and eventually she figured out high fives. Best of all, she smiled more often as the party raged on, expanding into a dragon-human conga line that marched up and down the Brick House's four stories. We sang, we laughed, we joked. We stuck our fingers in paint and added our handprints to the ancient family crest.

"Blue for grit, green for luck, white for wits, red for blood," I read out loud.

It had pretty much worked out that way.

Later that night, Dad and James named the red dragon.

"Hey James," Dad said. "Want to take a ride on Fluffy?"

"Fluffy is your brains after I scramble them," the red dragon said.

"Oh yeah?" James jumped on him. When the wrestling match was over, Dad and James revealed the name they'd actually chosen.

"Lollipop!" James said.

"*Cerberus* Lollipop," Dad corrected.

The red dragon hid his face in his claws and groaned. He couldn't hide the grin that split his snout.

"Hey, nice to meet ya, Cerberus Lollipop." Breaker punched his shoulder. "You candy-loving dog from hell."

"Deadly to his foes—but to his friends, kind and sweet." Dandelion giggled.

The second thing I remember from that night is Gwen playing with my brothers.

James and Keller jumped over her ankles as she slouched on the couch, wrapped in a blanket. Things escalated when they started to tap her knees and run away. She tried to grab them but those kids are quick. James threw his stuffed fox at her. Gwen showed him her teeth. Since she wasn't a dragon, it wasn't scary at all.

Finally, Keller whacked her with a pillow and dove for cover. Gwen spun sideways on the couch and wriggled her bottom half, trying to whack him with her tail—but she didn't have one. Her eyes widened as she glanced around the room.

It was possibly the funniest thing I'd ever seen.

But I didn't laugh.

Not for at least five seconds.

"I'll get you for that, Conley Hoss!" Her face got rosy and she hid under a pillow. I think she was planning her revenge but instead she fell asleep, slumping sideways until her head leaned on my shoulder.

The last thing I remember happened after dinner, during our toasts. In the gleaming third story bar, us kids had sparkling grape juice. Watson and the grown-ups sipped wine from tulip glasses. The dragons slurped bone broth from shatter-proof bowls.

"Here's to Conley getting healthy." Mom raised her glass.

"CHEERS," we all shouted.

Glasses clinked and juice splashed on the floor.

"To unforeseen adventures," Dad said. "That stem from dubious beginnings."

Mom rolled her eyes in the silence.

"To good endings after horrible starts," Dad said.

"HOORAY!" we all yelled.

"Here's to old and new friends." Azarel glanced around the room, his eyes landing on LouAnne Jordan, who had joined us after work.

"CHEERS!"

"Here's to having dragons and winning," Wyatt said.

"THAT'S RIGHT!"

Breaker's head appeared at the bar. "Here's to having humans and winning anyway."

"HERE—HEY, whoah, watch it!" we yelled as the blue dragon grinned.

"Here's to Gwendolyn Ghost," I said. "We like you!"

"HEAR, HEAR!"

She smiled down at the marble counter.

"Here's to the the return of the Brick House." Watson crouched on a stool, claws wrapped around his wine glass.

"OH YEAH, THAT'S RIGHT!"

There were quite a few more toasts after that, involving dragon names and fighting moves and driving a hard bargain, but my eyelids started to get heavy.

My mind wandered, and I remembered the moment I'd first met the Brick House, when it lured us in with its amenities, its secret rooms, its mystery. I thought about the way it had almost killed me, sent me into a cellar where a killer dragon waited for the root beer that would wake it after a hundred years.

And I wondered for the thousandth time who had unsealed the secret door, freeing Dark Sky's mind to manipulate Watson, to attract small, stupid boys...to liberate a vicious killer. It hadn't happened by accident. No, someone had done it.

And for the first time, as Edison bulbs glowed overhead and ceiling fans spun gently and Azarel uncorked another bottle of wine, preserved at precisely the right temperature for decades—I realized I had the answer.

Just then Wyatt bumped my shoulder and Gwen nudged my ribs, causing me to wince and fall off my stool. Wyatt grabbed my arm to help me without even snickering—it seemed like we were really friends now—and when he'd pulled me upright and gently patted my back, Azarel was looking right at me, his fiery eyes burning into my soul.

He raised his glass. "And now, my final toast. At first I didn't think he had it in him, but he proved me wrong. A tough little toothpick who turned out to be a hero. Here's to Conley Hoss."

"HEAR, HEAR!"

Laughter bounced off the walls.

"Thanks, Azarel." I leaned back, smiling. I couldn't help it.

But just the same, now that I knew the truth, I had to let the perpetrator know. And while I felt happy and relaxed, probably more so than ever before, looking down the messy bar at Wyatt and my hyper little brothers, at my laughing parents, at Gwen, who smiled back at me...

I felt scared, too.

Watson gave me a crooked grin, raising his glass.

Darn it, Watson, I thought. You could fill whole books with what you know about this place, secrets you haven't told me. All the hats you wear, all your advanced degrees—you're always a step ahead. Always ready with a scheme. And now you're back in business, calling the shots again after a hundred years.

It all made sense.

"Why are you shaking your head and looking crazy?" Gwen asked me.

"Because it's all coming together," I said. "I see it all. Everything."

Rolling her eyes, she turned away.

I slammed my cup down on the bar.

"More green juice, please!" I shouted.

It was time. Time for me to tell the culprit what I thought of him. But it still took me a minute to put my words together. And it took more courage than I'd expected, because this guy was dangerous. And I couldn't bring myself to say the words out loud. But I knew he was listening as I thought:

You're pretty sure of yourself, aren't you? I mean, yeah, you are mighty, and always a step ahead and even sort of glorious, but has anyone ever told you—ever told you you're kind of a jerk?

Gwen turned to me, eyes wide. *Wow, Conley. Is that an appropriate way to talk to the Brick House?*

I didn't say it out loud, I pointed out. *And the Brick House totally deserves it.*

She gave me a tight smile and slid my juice glass away from me.

But I was right.

In the middle of our party, under us and above us and on all sides, I sensed happiness. Tough, untouchable happiness. The Brick House was back, just like it had planned. Back like black and hope and home and other things that never really go away.

Of course, it had risked us all to get here.

When our party broke up, and we all hugged and high-fived and said goodnight, I staggered to my bunk and collapsed, but I didn't fall asleep. Not right away.

Goodnight, Gwen.

From the spare room—*Goodnight, Conley.*

Then, guarding my thoughts for a little privacy:

You think you can play with people's lives, I told the Brick House. You think you can write these crazy stories and then we have to live them, just because you're huge, and you know everything, and you've been around forever. Just because you're indestructible and not afraid of dragon fire.

Well, I've had enough of it.

I'm going to sleep.

So goodnight, Brick House.

And thank you.

THANKS FOR READING DARK SKY'S ASHES.

For all the inside stuff on the Casey Grimes universe—
including a free story, book news, and tips on fighting
monsters—sign up for *The Sylvan Spy* at
ajvanderhorst.com/invisible.

If you're wondering what to read next,
keep an eye out for *Casey Grimes #4*...coming soon.

A NOTE FROM ME TO YOU - DECEMBER, 2022

Hey, I still think it makes more sense to use this part as a letter.

Firstly, you ought to know the dream team at Lion & Co is still getting it done: Gwendolyn and Flannery, Miles and Ezra, Asher and Aidan and my top-shelf editor, Linds. They've been stretched over the last several months as demand for the Casey Grimes books keeps rising. We may have to expand our crew.

But for now we've accepted the challenge, and I have no plans to let these guys get hired away. They're all getting a Christmas bonus.

About this book, *Dark Sky's Ashes*. It's the fifth full-length novel I've published, and here's where things get weird.

DSA was the first book I ever wrote.

Back in 2013 my family was in the middle of a very rough stretch, and one of the best things I did on any given day was go upstairs at night and tell my little kiddos a bedtime story. In the middle of numerous things going wrong, it was our way of saying, Hey, we're still here, and we aren't going away, and we'll keep carving out space to breathe and have adventures— even if things are falling apart and we seem to be all alone.

Good stories have hope.

Well, things escalated as they do when you have a bunch of cute, squeaky-voiced kids who love stories. I'd been writing professionally in different mediums for years, and I decided, Hey, why don't I write a children's novel?

So I did. It contained bedtime-tested elements and story-lines I knew my kids would love. And our house was a character—with a lot of crazy enhancements, obviously.

However, my approach was similar to a good basketball player (which I am, by the way) thinking, Hey, why don't I take up baseball? After all, they're both sports.

The first draft of *Dark Sky's Ashes* was roouugh. My writing was breezy, my fiction voice underdeveloped. Of course I didn't know that at the time, so I went ahead and sent the manuscript to numerous literary agents and entered it in contests.

It got a crazy amount of attention. People loved the concept—but the writing kept letting the story down. So after some big contest wins and attention from dozens of agents, I ultimately ended up with nothing.

It was a let down. A couple years went by. Then I started writing my next kids' book, *The Mostly Invisible Boy*.

By the time I got that one done, my writing had come a long way. *Mostly Invisible* is of course not perfect, and if I ever do a revised edition, there are things I'll polish. But it was way better than *Dark Sky's Ashes* in terms of writing—and the concept was good too. At least that's what I've been told.

So I was surprised when *Mostly* earned a *Mostly Meh* in agent world. Fast forward another year, and *Trickery School* was the same way. And so was *Crooked Castle*. And so was a heavily-revised, much-improved version of *Dark Sky's Ashes* when I sent it out again.

Around that time, 2018-2019, I realized the kidlit industry

had changed. There were new agendas. New requirements that didn't get spelled out. No matter how good my concepts and writing got, no one was going to give the stories a chance.

After a lot of kicking and groaning, I decided if I had to do everything myself, that's what I'd do. Man, it was a lot of work. A whole, whole lot. But we won't go into how I learned graphic design and marketing and tested dozens of internet platforms, all while writing new manuscripts and building the Lion & Co flow. No, we won't go into that now.

When the Casey Grimes books began appearing, awards and glowing reviews started stacking up. All the agents I'd queried had told me my stories weren't extra-special-dazzly-frumptious and didn't make their hearts sing. For reasons they could not explain, the stories were not right, not good enough.

But a bunch of people liked the stories anyway. People like you. So weird. So strange. So inexplicable. If you're reading this, you're part of the problem. You weren't supposed to like these stories. Didn't you get the memo?

But here we are.

As a result, the Casey Grimes corner of the kidlit world is rapidly getting bigger, growing into a slice or even a chunk.

I may as well come out and say it.

At Lion & Co, we don't ask permission from Big Kidlit. We write what we beast-gutsing want. We tell the stories we shrieking well please—and they're stories with adventure and courage and friendship and no hidden agendas. Then we send them to you. And for whatever reason, you seem to enjoy them.

The book in your hands is the one that started it all. Full circle, it's tied seamlessly into the Casey Grimes universe.

I won't lie.

It feels great.

AJ

ABOUT THE AUTHOR

 AJ Vanderhorst lives in tornado country with his wife, kids, and several small dragons skilled at making coffee. He especially likes hot sauce. His daughters think he is good enough at basketball to play in the NBA, so he may give that a try in between writing books. To learn more about how to survive a monster attack, visit AJ online at **ajvanderhorst.com**

THE END

READY TO READ A FREE STORY, PICK A NEW T-SHIRT, OR JOIN A SECRET MESSAGE RING?

HEAD OVER TO AJVANDERHORST.COM